Praise

A _Times_ Non-Fiction Bestseller
Shortlisted for Waterstones Book of the Year 2021

'A beautiful retelling of British myths and
exquisitely illustrated too'
James Holland, _Daily Express_ (BOOK OF THE YEAR)

'Reading _Storyland_ feels like listening to a bard orate
mystical stories of the world that was. Erudite and lyrical,
Jeffs takes readers by the hand and encourages us to join
her as she guides us through the mystical landscape that is
indelibly woven into the fabric of our everyday lives'
BBC History Magazine (BOOK OF THE YEAR)

'_Storyland_ is a joyous read celebrating the power of collective
myths and the landscapes which inspired them'
All About History

'Jeffs writes beautifully, erring just on the right side
of florid, and her linocut prints make for attractive
illustrations. The stories come with explanations of sources
and legacies, and she has a lovely knack of rooting each one
in the landscape that birthed it. This gorgeous book should
live on the bookshelves in every house that cares about the
idea of Britain, what is was and where it came from'
The Times

'*Storyland* is a thing of beauty. It's filled with exquisite, minimalist black-and-white artworks of giants and devils, heroes and heroines, kings and creatures'

Herald

'*Storyland* is a spellbinding illustrated mythology of Britain . . . With Jeffs at the helm we travel through a powerful medieval mythscape'

Scottish Field Magazine

'Rich in myth and legend . . . Beautifully illustrated . . . this is an engaging book, meticulously researched and filled with drama, emotion, action and experience'

The Simple Things

'An elegant book'

Sunday Express

'I have fallen so completely in love with this book; *Storyland*, by Amy Jeffs, just one of the finest, most covetable things around. It's a mythology of Britain; Brutus, Arthur, Scotus, Bladud, a mix of new telling and ancient, with original woodcuts by the author which are so beautiful you want to eat them. The stories are about strangeness and wonder and brutality, a story of Britain from the top of Orkney to the bottom of Cornwall. It's hugely original, and starkly lovely: I've never come across anything quite like it'

Katherine Rundell

STORYLAND

AMY JEFFS

STORYLAND

A NEW MYTHOLOGY OF BRITAIN

riverrun

First published in Great Britain in 2021
This paperback edition published in 2022 by

riverrun

An imprint of

Quercus Editions Ltd
Carmelite House
50 Victoria Embankment
London EC4Y 0DZ

An Hachette UK company

Copyright © 2021 Amy Jeffs
Map and illustrations copyright © 2021 Amy Jeffs

The moral right of Amy Jeffs to be
identified as the author of this work has been
asserted in accordance with the Copyright,
Designs and Patents Act, 1988.

All rights reserved. No part of this publication
may be reproduced or transmitted in any form
or by any means, electronic or mechanical,
including photocopy, recording, or any
information storage and retrieval system,
without permission in writing from the publisher.

A CIP catalogue record for this book is available
from the British Library

Paperback ISBN 978 1 52940 800 3
Ebook ISBN 978 1 52940 798 3

This book is a work of fiction. Names, characters,
businesses, organizations, places and events are
either the product of the author's imagination
or used fictitiously. Any resemblance to
actual persons, living or dead, events or
locales is entirely coincidental.

10 9 8 7 6

Designed and typeset by EM&EN
Printed in Great Britain by Clays Ltd, Elcograf S.p.A.

Papers used by Quercus are from well-managed forests
and other responsible sources.

For my Grandmother,

Olive Crompton,

who taught me to love words.

Contents

Part Three: Antiquity

Part Four: The Middle Ages

Prologue

The tales to come are gilded by the rays of the setting sun. Written down and recited in a territory once believed to be at the westernmost edge of the world, their audiences also held themselves to be the last to witness the end of each day. To live in Britain then was to possess an edginess, a brinkhood, unknown to the great eastern citizens whose homes occupied the centre of the map. Yet myths drew threads across the globe and across time. The idea of Britain, what it was and where it came from, its connection to distant lands, and its own native qualities, fascinated its inhabitants then as it does now. Accounting for the mysteries of its coincidence of place and people produced the wondrous myths and legends that you are about to read: from stories of warlike giants and necromancers to the familiar adventures of Arthur, Merlin and King Lear. For centuries these tales moulded perceptions of Britishness. They still do, even if many have been forgotten.

Storyland began with pictures. As an academic, I had been studying medieval illustrations of the *Brut* chronicle (the origin myth of Britain) in illuminated manuscripts and wanted to try my hand. In 2018, I encountered the perfect medium: linocut. Linocut is a form of relief printmaking, as are wood-engraving and woodcut. Relief printmaking can teach you to draw in light, in the golden hour of low sun when shadows are long. You carve away your design and roll ink onto the raised surface, finally pressing the block onto paper. Print technology – most notably movable type – arrived at the end of the European Middle Ages and marks the close of the heyday of the manuscript or handwritten book. While it might seem counter-intuitive to illustrate medieval stories in print, which was alien to most of the period, the medium simultaneously evokes the medieval and the modern. It can evoke the pages of Wynkyn de Worde's late medieval edition of *Le Morte d'Arthur* and the Modernism of the early twentieth century.

I started with a series of three illustrations: *The Death of Gogmagog, Diana Sends Brutus to Albion* and *Merlin Guiding the Building of Stonehenge*. Three grew to seven and then twenty-four, as I was given the opportunity to publish them in *Country Life* magazine as a trio of articles about the myths and legends of Britain. Designing the prints and conducting the research gave rise to the book you now hold in your hands.

The way we imagine the Middle Ages is often affected by the Victorian aesthetic influence: this is something I wanted to undermine. The late medieval armour, pointed shoes and flowing sleeves of so many Pre-Raphaelite paintings of Arthur and his court represents a period of dress that considerably post-dates the writing down of the earliest Arthurian myths, which themselves were written down long after the time in which they are set (around the fifth century AD).

So how should one go about representing the characters of a mythic age? When medieval artists of, say, the fourteenth century illustrated these legends, they updated the costume and technologies according to their own setting. When it came to imagining the past, the Middle Ages was a time of unconcerned anachronism. There wasn't such a sense of the 'look' of the past, of costume evolving over time. The stories were personal and morally instructive. Readers were meant to identify with them. And while I didn't like the idea of illustrating these stories with people in twenty-first-century dress, I did like the idea of avoiding historic specificity: the idea of transforming the characters into timeless archetypes. For this reason I have shown figures as silhouettes or nude, or in the most generic, bland costume I could imagine, while capitalising on all the drama and emotion of their actions and experiences. I hope this brings the images into a world that feels at once contemporary, human and natural. I hope also that it places more emphasis on setting and experience, rather than time. The landscape is the one consistent presence, after all.

Prologue

Here I offer you a story of an empty land filling with tribes from Syria, Troy, Egypt and Scythia, until it becomes a Britain you will recognise. You are entering a work of legend, based on medieval tales of Britain's foundation and settlement that bear only a passing resemblance to 'true' history, but offer many other kinds of truths. I am not going to attempt to separate all the fact from fiction. You will encounter gory saints' lives, the haunting legends of the Welsh *Mabinogion*, the disturbing, enchanting tales of the *South English Legendary*, as well as Germanic legends of Weland the Smith and Havelok the Dane. These tales are more than words on parchment or paper. Moments from them were also carved into stone, ivory, and the wooden furniture of churches, painted into books and onto the plaster of domestic walls, woven into wall-hangings and stitched onto linen.

This is a journey through Britain and through time. Many of the places described here can be visited. Many of the stories include and account for monuments, landmarks and natural features that survive to this day. They are sacred places, beautiful and unexpected. And while they are too many to list here, they include prehistoric monuments like Stonehenge and Wayland's Smithy; towns like Grimsby and Leicester; mountain ranges and lakes such as Snowdonia and Loch Etive and rivers including the Ness, the Soar and the story-silted Thames.

In the commentaries accompanying the retellings, I will introduce you to some of the primary sources I've used and the circumstances of those sources' medieval production and influence. I have looked for stories that have political implications, as well as their complement of marvels. While folklore no doubt lies behind some of the tales, it is not the focus of this book. Similarly, while I have touched on Irish legends that in turn touch on Britain, I have not presumed to represent the wealth of Irish mythological material with this narrative. These are separate, if contingent, traditions. As for the stories that do feature, you may notice a bias towards the deep past of the British, as opposed to that of the Scottish and English. The impact of the *Brut* tradition (pronounced 'brute', the origin myth of the British, of which you will read hereafter) was far-reaching and the same kind of material was not produced in a consolidated way in Scotland until the later Middle Ages. One explanation is that the Brittonic Celts arrived on these islands much earlier than anyone else and represented, especially to later settlers, a kind of indigenous presence whose stories could be used to the advantage of those in power.

In the spirit of legend, it is time to shed modern views of universal chronology. Forget dinosaurs, forget evolution, forget the elusive Neanderthals. These are for a later age. Here, the story follows the medieval view of time, shaped by Classical and biblical traditions. We start between Creation and Noah's Flood, in an age when the earliest generation of giants, the children of Cain, or the progeny of fallen angels, walk the earth, then we proceed to the age of the Exodus, the Trojan War and on, until the birth of Christ, the *Anno Domini*, closing with the Norman Conquest of England. Writing in 1336, a historian from medieval England called Geoffrey le Baker believed he was living 6,445 years after the Creation of the world. He dated the Flood to 2865 BC and the foundation of Britain to 1300 BC, but exact numbers were matters to debate even then. This is the misty temporality of *Storyland*.

It is also time to shed modern notions of geography. Medieval world maps showed a circle divided into three unequal parts, surrounded by a ring of ocean (see the diagram opposite). Asia fills the whole upper half of the map (east, rather than north, is at the top), with 'paradise' located at the uppermost edge and Jerusalem in the centre. Beneath it is a band of sea in the shape of an 'L' turned upside down. That sea, which sits at the middle of the earth, is the Mediterranean. The short stroke of the 'L' separates Asia from Europe and Africa, which are in turn divided by the long stroke of the 'L'. To find the territories of Hibernia (a Latin name for Ireland used in its origin myth) and Britain, you would look to the very edge of Europe: the lower left-hand corner of the map. Members of these great civilisations were held by inhabitants

MEDIEVAL WORLD MAP (MAPPA MUNDI)

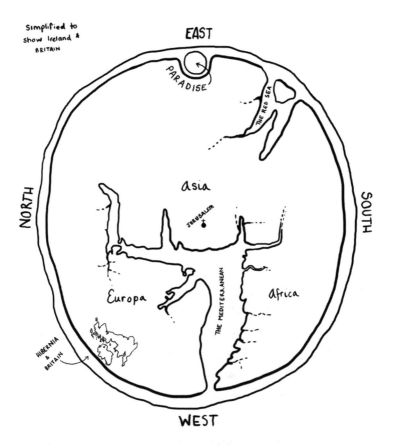

Simplified to show Ireland & BRITAIN

EAST

PARADISE

THE RED SEA

Asia

JERUSALEM

NORTH

SOUTH

Europa

THE MEDITERRANEAN

Africa

HIBERNIA & BRITAIN

WEST

of medieval Britain to have travelled from the East long ago and to have seeded new dynasties in these chilly but fertile climes.

I have retold the stories within a medieval temporal and spatial framework, but in a manner that I hope will feel relevant to a modern audience. Today, we are learning the limitations of our power over the natural world. We are learning, within that, about how we relate to each other and we have the opportunity to address our own mistakes and those of our forebears. These stories are grounded in genuine medieval narratives, but some elements are of my own invention. They pay greater attention than in most of the original sources to figures who are neither men nor kings, to characters' interior worlds and to the landscape. My illustrations, too, might take their subjects from the past but their style and emphases belong to today. All this I have committed to these pages within the bounds of my own understanding and any mistakes are my own.

May *Storyland* be a stepping stone into the powerful medieval mythscape – and perhaps beyond, to the rich seam of primary sources that have, by some miracle, survived. At the end of this book, you will find a list of all the texts on which I have depended and frequently cite, translated by a panoply of dedicated scholars, including Carolyne Larrington, Jane Bliss, Sioned Davies, Rachel Bromwich and the late Richard Sharpe. Their patiently applied skill means that any English speaker can now read these wonderful texts. I hope you are inspired to do so, if you haven't already.

Because it retells and reimagines old stories for modern audiences, *Storyland* is a 'new' mythology of Britain. I have written and decorated it for you, wherever you come from and wherever you are going.

Part One

In the Beginning

1

The Giants' Dance

Now giants were upon the earth in those days. For after the sons of God went in to the daughters of men, and they brought forth children, these are the mighty men of old, men of renown.

Genesis 6: 4–5

The giants' home – the hot, excessive regions of remotest Africa – belonged to the southernmost part of the map, south of the Nile, at the antipodean edge. There the great beings abhorred the night's lingering heat, not to mention each other, for they had blood like lava and tempers to match. Eons before the Flood, in the dryness of the desert, they cracked the stones from a rock-face unchanged since Yahweh wrought the land. From that rock-face, the giants would take the stones to a place where water would release their mineral virtues and soothe the giants' seething blood.

The largest of the group drove a wedge into a fissure. She struck once, twice, three times, with her hammer.

When the wedge had stuck, she inserted another, striking until, standing back, the stone groaned into her arms. Her skin, which was ember hot, was now the yellow of sand, now blue like the mudstone she cradled.

Without acknowledging her companions, who were driving in their own wedges and adding to the din, she heaved the rock onto her shoulder and walked away. Sweat hissed from her brow and dust desiccated her throat, but she journeyed for the rest of that night, pursuing the trace of a chill on the breeze: a whisper of colder climes. She drank deeply from rivers at daybreak and slept until sunset each day, disguised as a hill or sandbank. She did not disturb the creatures about her: herds of deer with swivelling horns, beings that shaded their faces with one enormous foot, or villages whose inhabitants' faces were located in their chests. Each night she bore her load onwards. Once or twice she saw a city, smoke rising from its rooftops, laughter and music from its streets. These she hated and avoided, striding on until she reached the sea.

The other giants followed with their heads bowed and their rocks resting on their backs. When they came to the great ocean, they felt the water like a balm. They travelled for weeks, plucking whales skywards for food. As they passed the gates of the Mediterranean, the Sirens saw them and covered their beautiful mouths.

As the giants waded, the heat abated, and soon they reached the part of the ocean where the clouds hung low and cold winds blew on even the warmest days. Then the lead giant saw an island and stepped from seabed to reef to cliff-face and onto the moon-illuminated meadows. Deep greens and blues rippled on their skin as the giants followed, striding over marshes, until scree rose to meet them. The air condensed and they felt the fires in their veins grow cooler. They made for the peak of the tallest mountain.

In later days the Irish called it Killaraus. And even later than that they said it had never existed at all. On its summit was a plateau, pillowed with thyme and veiled with cloud. When the giants assembled, moisture-beaded, they were in harmony. It was conducive to their bodies, this place of moss and mist; the unnatural accord this task allowed would last a little longer. They placed the stones in circles and topped them with flatter stones. Then they dug pits in the midst of the central circle, and watched as the rain that came and went pooled into them, flowing over the rocks.

When the stones were erected and the baths full, the giants encircled their structure in a great ring: a carol, a dance. One by one they dipped their heads below the water. Minerals entered and soothed their veins. All their hurts subsided. That would be enough for now.

The island was full of valleys and hollows perfectly suited to the solitary ways of giants. When they had washed, it was to these they retreated, returning to their dance when they were wounded or sick. Years later, there came a Flood. Many of the giants' original number were swept away for good, but their healing temple endured. The Irish called it 'The Giants' Dance', perhaps on account of the stately formation of its colossal stones, perhaps because the mist preserved some memory of a unique meeting. The stones stood there for many thousands of years; when at last they were moved, it was by the power of a child.

❖

A few years ago I took a cruise ship with a jazz band from Tilbury Docks to the Canary Islands and back again. For the first, and probably last, time in my life, I spent a fortnight floating on the Atlantic, watching a lonely East London sparrow orbiting the ship all the way to the Moroccan coast. In that time, I thought about Europe, Africa and the sea. These three things are connected in the story of the origins of Stonehenge, mentioned in Geoffrey of Monmouth's c. 1136 *History of the Kings of Britain*. The character of Merlin speaks of a monument known as the Giants' Dance, 'on Mount Killaraus in Ireland': 'many years ago the Giants transported them from the remotest confines of Africa and set them up in Ireland . . . they used to pour water over them and to run this water into baths in which their sick were cured.' The giants made a similar journey to the one being traced by my cruise ship. Travelling to Ireland, they might have tacked through the Atlantic, with

Africa to the east. They might have passed the mouth of the Mediterranean. Like me, they might have experienced a gradual transition from a desert to a temperate climate.

It's a compelling thought, this journey undertaken by stone-bearing giants. But why giants? Why Africa? And why Ireland? Of course, even now we don't know the whole answer to the real question of how all the monoliths that make up Stonehenge were transported to their current site. And in the Middle Ages, giants were a viable explanation; they even appear in the Bible. According to the Book of Genesis, giants walked the earth after rebel angels lay with human women, engendering the races of mighty men. In the Old Testament Book of Samuel, David fights a giant called Goliath. And in the Old English epic *Beowulf*, the narrator describes the monstrous semi-human Grendel as 'Cain's kin', and Cain is the murderous brother of Abel, son of Adam and Eve. In the Middle Ages, giants were real. Why not giants? They were the obvious candidates for the transportation of impossibly heavy stones.

However, Geoffrey of Monmouth also has Merlin claim that Stonehenge was carried by these giants from 'the remotest confines of Africa'. This requires some explanation. Again, looking to early texts reveals Africa's furthest reaches to be accepted as a likely homeland of giants. For instance, in the somewhat later legend of Guy of Warwick, a Danish army challenges Guy to fight a mercenary African giant. But why? Medieval European thought was steeped in ideas inherited from the Classical age. The far south of Africa was held to be a place of intense heat and, by extension, an incubator of monstrous beings. According to the Classical writers Hippocrates and Galen, the concentrations of the body's four humours (blood, black bile, yellow bile and phlegm) could be affected by extreme climatic conditions, leading to changes in physiognomy. Monstrous races found on the lowest edge of the world map included beings like Sciapods, who had one enormous foot apiece, the headless Blemmyes, whose faces were in their chests, near the seat of their appetites, and Cynocephali, who had the heads of dogs. All of these beings appear in drawings on the southern edge of the Hereford Mappa Mundi (a world-map, dated *c*. 1300).

Yet even with all this in mind, Geoffrey's backstory to the Stonehenge monoliths is enigmatic. Why did the African giants want to go to Ireland in the first place? I recalled the return leg of my ride on the cruise liner and the transition from the hot dryness of lands level with the Sahara to the chilly mists of the Thames estuary. What if the giants owed their excessive size to the hot, dry home of their birth? What if they craved a cold, wet place of respite? And what if the stones, the healing properties of which were best mediated by water, could enhance that longed-for comfort? And so the giants took their medicinal monoliths to a cold, damp island in the sea, and that is where they remained.

2

The Naming of Albion

They were daughters of a king so powerful that he was never subject to anybody. So, nor did they want to be subject to anybody, and nor did they want to have masters or be under any constraint. Each wanted to be absolute mistress of her husband and everything he possessed.

Des Grantz Geanz [Of the Great Giants] (c. 1250–1333/4)

In ancient times, God sent a Flood to drown the sinful races. But afterwards the survivors repopulated the world and learned to sin again. Kingdoms were re-established and proud kings ruled over them. In Syria, 3,970 years after Creation, stood such a kingdom, ruled by such a king. He lived in his marble palace with his thirty daughters, the eldest of whom was called Albina. Like their parents, his daughters were wondrously tall, but they held none of their father's imperial power. This was not at all to their liking. All the while they were trapped in marriage to his barons, they would be no better than slaves; they resolved

to murder their husbands in their beds and take over the kingdom. But the youngest among them could not suppress her guilt. She confessed to her husband and he went straight to the King. A brutal punishment ensued. The sisters, all except the youngest, were cast out to sea and left to the mercy of fate.

For weeks they drifted, rudderless, collecting water from the sails to drink, eating nothing, until a storm came upon them. For three whole days and nights the waves crashed on their ship, but the vessel endured. When the first morning came after the passing of the storm, they awoke to the sounds of birds and the slow crunch of waves on sand. They had landed, though they had no idea where.

The air was much colder and wetter than it had ever felt in Syria.

Albina landed on the seaweed-strewn beach, beneath the bone-white cliffs. She seized a handful of sand and pebbles and let them fall like beads through her fingers.

Together the women explored. In their hunger they ate acorns and sour crab apples, medlars and chestnuts. They might have found more, but what did they know of foraging? The rivers were full of gleaming trout, but they had never fished.

What was more, no matter how far they wandered, in search of food and shelter, or a town in which they might find lodging, the sisters encountered no one. They realised they were alone, washed up on a strange shore with none but themselves to rely on. 'This land shall be called Albion,' said Albina, and they accepted her as their queen.

So, Albina and her sisters were forced to learn how to survive, until they were no longer pampered queens but mistresses of root, stone and antler. First, they learned to gather berries and nuts, curbing their hunger with these. Soon, wanting meat, they devised traps and spears from wood, and rope from sinuous stems. Then, they practised with these tools, till they were cooking deer on open fires and falling asleep with their stomachs full. It was not without hardship that they came to live off the land, but live they did, and well. The sisters, already tall, grew plump as penny-bun mushrooms and strong as wild boar.

But there was still something missing; with their traps and snares and their growing hunger they caught more than meat. It came to pass when they began, whether on languorous summer evenings, around autumn fires or from warm winter caves, to long for sex, for their lust was soon detected.

The devil and his legion ascended to the deepest parts of the forests and caves, thickening the air and visiting the women after nightfall. When they saw the spirits' eyes in the darkness they knew their own hunger was as nothing to the hunger suffered by these beings. Their eyes were red from an eternity in the dark without touch. Their lips

were pale from the chill of ages of neglect. All at once the sisters ached with pity. And in the vessel of the night they enveloped the spirits with their tender touches and the spirits sowed their seed in them. In the consummation of dawn, the devils slid from the women's arms and back down into hell.

After a few weeks Albina and her sisters suffered violent sickness. Their bellies swelled – as if they were already full term – and by the time they had gestated for nine months, they barely escaped with their lives, as if some magic kept their outsides from splitting like overripe plums. When they finally gave birth, their screams sent eagles flapping from mountain-tops and knocked fish insensible in the depths of the northern lakes. When the pain finally passed, the mothers were intact and weathering the wails of their enormous, hideous sons and daughters. From devils and queens the giants of Albion were born and they suckled milk that was as fat as the land.

Albina and her sisters lived from the land until they were old. With their children they mined the earth and made golden idols to worship: bulls and swans and dragons. When they died, their white bones became part of the chalk downs and their flesh turned the hay gold. After this, their children grew huge, strong and ancient. The giants populated the land by means of one another, though they fought with more passion than they bred. Each giant claimed a territory and guarded it jealously from its neighbour; they worshipped the golden idols and they feared no invasion. For who would disinherit the devil?

❖

The legend of the thirty Syrian sisters is a prequel to the story of Brutus and the giants that you will read in the next chapter. It survives in both Latin and Anglo-Norman French versions. The latter is called *Des Grantz Geanz*, or *Of the Great Giants*, and dates to between the mid thirteenth century and the second quarter of the fourteenth. It places great emphasis on the sisters' ingenuity:

> But [Albina and her sisters] were clever and inventive, and put their minds to thinking of something; at last, with a lot of ingenuity they made a good number of devices. Using branches, they made nooses to catch animals; they made traps out of wood to catch birds. They made lots of such things, and set them cunningly, to snare game and also to take fowl. When they had got as much as they wanted, they prepared the game and made a fire by striking pebbles together – there were plenty.

Today, Albina and her clan read like heroes, but in the Middle Ages, their characters may have been more ambiguous. This has to do, perhaps, with their Syrian origins and their similarity to the stock character of the female Saracen. In medieval literature, Saracen women, especially princesses, are often portrayed as determined agents of their destinies, which, in the context of many a Crusader narrative, might well manifest itself in infatuation with a Christian knight (often one she hasn't met yet) and such a powerful desire to be with him that she may betray, injure or even kill members of her own household to satisfy it.

The Syrian Albina and her sisters behave with the quintessential hot-headed murderousness of literary Saracen princesses but without the saving grace of the Christian knight. They may have represented, like the East itself, both an allure and a threat to their original readership, and a lesson against giving women free rein. When the sisters copulate with the devil and his legion, the race of giants they deliver – which interbreed and interfight, guarding the land with insane jealousy – are all threat.

Some versions of *Des Grantz Geanz* include lines noting how in later years farmers tilling the soil found huge bones, shield-sized shoulder blades and the like. Hilltop fortresses smack of giant-work too, they say. All of this serves as evidence for the erstwhile presence of Albion's race of giants. Whoever the poet was, they were a storyteller of the highest calibre, with a vivid imagination and a sense of humour to match. We may never work out the true origins of the name 'Albion' or why it was believed to have been populated by giants. In the absence of another explanation, why not look to Albina?

3

Brutus Founds Britain

The Britons . . . transplanted from the hot and arid regions
of the Trojan plain, keep their dark colouring, which reminds
one of the earth itself, their natural warmth of personality
and their hot tempers, all of which gives them confidence in
themselves.

Gerald of Wales, *Journey through Wales* (c. 1191)

When the very first Britons arrived in Albion, they learned
of Albina from one of her descendants. He told the story
while tied up on the cliffs, his colossal knees forced to his
chest and his fists clamped before his massive, rolling eyes.
The giant's chin was dimpled and his craggy fingernails
were like oyster shells, undercut with moss. Despite his
great size and strength, he was a prisoner, and the corpses
of his kin were scattered along the coast.

The giant's name was Gogmagog.

Gogmagog proclaimed his right to the land, and to
the gold, silver and iron that ran in its veins. He insisted

on it with narrowed, restless eyes. The Trojans, led by Brutus, listened to what he told them, but they were not cowed. They did nothing more than laugh. All along the river, Gogmagog could see their settlements, but the puny inhabitants were newcomers, who would never call Albion home.

When Brutus, who was young and searching, had first set out for Albina's ancient kingdom, he had known that giants awaited him. This did not make him want to turn back. Born to a prophecy, he was the great-grandson of the Trojan Aeneas, the son of the goddess Venus. He had their courage and determination and he was in need of a homeland. Brutus had been exiled from Rome after killing his father in a hunting accident. Roaming the Mediterranean, he had stopped at the court of the Greek King Pandrasus, where he had found more Trojans, men and women, being kept as slaves. Identifying himself as their kin, Brutus led them in revolt, defeated Pandrasus and married his daughter, Ignoge. When they left, their ships weighed down with gold, Brutus watched her weep until she had no more tears. He put his arms around her with the tenderness of Venus until Ignoge seemed to sleep in his arms. He would build her a kingdom, if only he could find a home.

One evening the fleet docked at an island called Logice, where the men found a temple of the goddess Diana. When Brutus saw its marbled beauty, he chose twelve of his most trusted soldiers to perform a ritual sacrifice with him. They chased, killed and slaughtered a milk-white stag, cutting its throat, draining its dark blood into a bowl and mingling it with wine. Four times he circled the altar before the idol of the goddess, pouring the offering into the hearth. Then nine times he cried:

'Forest goddess, terror of beasts, power in the heights and in the deeps, reveal our destined homeland!'

Brutus laid his dark head down on the white hart's blood-mottled skin and fell asleep. The goddess opened her eyes.

Diana was moved. Not for centuries had anyone worshipped her. Half asleep she had stood since then. When the ships had docked, her mind had nodded towards the noise. When the men had entered the temple, she had felt a keening at her heart. When the one who she now knew was their leader had made his sacrifice, had spoken words of worship, had danced around the altar, all her intention had become bent upon him.

Brutus' dark form lay curled on the white pelt. Yes, she thought, I see Venus in the curve of that mouth and the glow of that skin. This boy is her progeny. Diana pierced Brutus' sleeping mind, felt around it with her fingers, caught at the nerves and sent pulses through them. How she wanted this young man to stay on the island! More than anything, she would have him warm her with that mortal energy. And yet she knew that he could not be

contained. For even as she searched in his being for a string she could pull to her own ends, she met the force of his resistance. Yearn as she might for his presence, he strove for a kingdom of his own. His ambition would kill him if she did not give her aid. What she did next broke her immortal heart. She felt the heat of his ambition flooding her stone-cold limbs, the fierceness of his determination charging her veins with life. Diana sensed the strength of this sinuous, dancing youth, and now that he was asleep she billowed over him.

That night Brutus dreamed that he saw the statue of Diana come to life, swelling in the fire's silver fumes to a vast and terrible size, swaying like a tree in the wind.

Her shoulders were muscular from the draw of the bow, and her face glared after some distant quarry. As her lips parted, he heard her speak. Her voice was like flames in the canopy:

> 'Brutus! Beyond Gaul is an island.
> Giants live there now,
> But it will become your home.
> There you will build a New Troy
> And found a royal line
> To rule the round circle of the earth.'

And as she cried her prophecy, she flung out her hand to the west, to the place where, just hours before, the sun had extended its last beams, and only when she had fallen silent, with the blaze of her skin still searing his eyes, did Brutus awake. Before him, in the pale gleam of dawn, the marble statue stood, unmoving. Rousing the men, he shared the vision. They were excited. They returned to the ships determined. 'Who's afraid of a few far-off giants?' they said, as the spirit of Diana grew cold.

The journey to Albion took Brutus through the Pillars of Hercules, his ships brushing Africa and enough pirates to test the mettle of his crew, though they escaped not only alive but having plundered the pirates' gold.

Then the voyagers found themselves on a true ocean for the first time in their lives. It must have been strange for even the bravest among them to see nothing to the west but sea and sky, while rolling depths sounded beneath them. And though their ships nearly sank with the effort, they resisted the song of the Sirens; all except Ignoge, who longed to join them on their rock, but was held captive on the ship.

After that, they raided the land to the east for food and riches, and there met more displaced Trojans. They were led by a warlord called Corineus. Brutus had heard of his fame as a giant-killer and invited him to join his fleet. Together, Brutus and Corineus laid waste to Gaul and defeated its king.

As the Trojan ships tacked north on the Atlantic, the weather darkened, clouds amassed above their heads and turned the ocean grey, while a melancholy note sounded on the wind. Now another land was on the horizon. Brutus had brought them here and they were surely lost, they were surely at the furthest edge of the world, in a realm of storms and cold. But Brutus, knowing he had come to the place described by Diana, directed the fleet further to the west, where they found an inlet in the coast. They passed upstream in silent procession. That was where they made camp and where the captain shared his plan. From his place above the crowd of Trojans, his dark eyes glinted, and his mouth proved as gifted in oration as that of Venus in her seductions.

He told them that the island would be renamed Britain, after himself, because it was theirs by Diana's decree and by the divine blood in his veins. Did they not see about them that the rivers teemed with fish, that its soil was rich and dark, and its forests full of game? The people, now the Britons, would build settlements and populate the land, and if the giants of which the goddess had spoken showed them trouble, they would kill them. He would divide Britain's regions between his men. Corineus would be lord of the region to the west, which would be called Cornwall in his honour.

For a short while after the arrival of the Trojans, the giants of stolen Albion let their skin take on the complexion of the earth, sinking into caves and hollows, burying their ancestral treasure of which the Trojans knew nothing. A few giants fell foul of Corineus' armies, as the region of Cornwall was especially full of their kind. But it was not until the newcomers held a festival at a port near Totnes that they struck. The day was radiant, the sky was thrush-egg blue, the sea and sand sparkled, the people danced and sang, and twenty giants crept over the headland. One was thin and grey as a fenland eel, another gorse-haired and bracken-red as Snowdon, and yet another was white and undulating as the downlands to the south. Their leader was like a boulder among pebbles on the plains. Gogmagog, it was said, could uproot an oak tree as if it were a whip of hazel.

With terrible aggression the giants attacked, killing Britons with swipes of their hands and crushing them with rocks. But Corineus and Brutus fought back and their warriors joined them. The air rang with the clash of metal, and the Trojans' fury and organisation overwhelmed their larger foes. Against all odds, they slaughtered the giants of Albion, all except the leader.

The soldiers bound Gogmagog, deaf to his roars. They drove iron pegs into the ground. They secured him there so he could only move his eyes and mouth. In the salt spray from the ocean, the soldiers gathered to interrogate their captive, for they liked nothing more than a story. He told them of his diabolical origins and he told them of Albina.

When the men had learned all they could, Brutus turned his bold face to Corineus, and challenged him to wrestle the captive. Corineus threw down his weapons and waved his bare hands in the air. It was like the old days in Gaul and Iberia, and the very air was breathless.

The jeering men encircled man and giant, while Corineus hitched up his tunic to show his muscular buttocks. He bounced on the balls of his feet, knees bent, his fists clenching and unclenching. Then Gogmagog was released. And at once they locked together and the men's laughter became shouts of encouragement, even of fear. Gogmagog may have been the stronger fighter, but surely Corineus was quicker? Surely he would win, the famous giant-killer? In the eye of the storm, in the straining cavity between the wrestlers' interlocked bodies, the

only sounds were Corineus' panting grunts and the giant's hideous growls.

But Gogmagog had the upper hand. He girded his opponent, squeezing and squeezing, till *crack!* With a sound like fire bursting rock, he broke three of Corineus' ribs. The Trojan screamed in agony and rage. And now his anger and his fear were so acute that he found strength within himself that he had never known. Corineus lifted the giant from the ground and charged to the edge of the cliffs. Teetering for one terrible moment, man and giant were frozen against the blue, then Corineus hurled Gogmagog into the sea. When the splash came, all other noise was mute. The Trojans walked to Corineus and peered over the edge. Below, the sea-foam was pink and the rocks were red. Gogmagog was gone.

After the extinction of the giants of Albion, Brutus built a New Troy on the Thames, which was called Trinovantum, though in the reign of Lludd it became known as London. The river where his fleet had docked would one day be called the Dart, and their landing place, Totnes. Brutus' wife, Ignoge, bore three sons, called Camber, Locrin and Albanac. When Brutus was old and dying, he divided the territories of Britain between them: Kambria, Loegria and Albany. One day those regions would be called Wales, England and Scotland. But even then, at the end of Brutus' reign, much was already as he had predicted. In those first years, Corineus ruled Cornwall, and the people multiplied, speaking the Trojan tongue or 'Crooked Greek'. They came to call themselves 'Britons' and the island 'Britain', after Brutus, their founding king.

❖

I have already mentioned Geoffrey of Monmouth's *c.* 1136 *History of the Kings of Britain*. While Welsh in spirit and allegiance, it was dedicated to an Anglo-Norman patron (Robert, Earl of Gloucester) and came in time, after various translations into the vernacular, to be seen as the deep history of the Kings of England, the region given to Brutus' eldest son, Locrin. What with Brutus' illustrious great-grandparents, the fatal hunting accident that killed his father, the procurement (kidnap) of Ignoge, the prophecy from Diana, the pirates, the Sirens and the giants, Geoffrey's patrons could hardly have asked for a more entertaining or illustrious history to absorb. It was translated into prose and verse in Welsh, French and English, and the story came to be known as the '*Brut* chronicle', after Brutus.

Geoffrey states in the *History*'s opening dedication that the work is a translation of an ancient book in the British tongue, presented to him by Walter, Archdeacon of Oxford. Any such book, if it ever existed, has not survived. It is more likely that Geoffrey's history was derived from numerous older texts, including works by such earlier historians as Nennius and Gildas, not to mention Bede.

Illustrated *Brut* chronicles, in whatever language or form, are rare, but when they do survive, they show us how medieval readers might have imagined the dramatic events of Brutus' arrival. For instance, one of the many later translations and adaptations of the *Brut* chronicle was Roger of Wendover's *Flowers of History*, copied into the *Chronica Maiora* (*Great Chronicle*) of one Matthew Paris, a polymath monk at St Albans Abbey in the thirteenth century. The first volume of the autograph manuscript in which it survives (Cambridge, Corpus Christi College, MS 026) is full of fold-out maps, marginal symbols and illustrations. Among them is an image of a figure standing on an ornate pedestal, with a cloth around her hips, antlers on her head and wings on her ankles. Before her lies the bleeding body of a deer, behind which stand four men. One steps forward, lifting up a bowl. The illustration shows Diana sending Brutus to Albion, where he will found a race of kings to rule the whole round world.

Though few know the story today, the far-reaching political and cultural impact of Diana's prophecy should not be underestimated. *Brut* chronicles were popular well into the sixteenth century. Many a civilisation has aspired to empire, and many factors give rise to its realisation, but in the rootstock of Britain's particular brand of imperium we might just hear the echo of a goddess's call to action.

4

Scota, First Queen of the Scotti

*Beyond Britain, also, in the ocean between it and the west,
is situated the island of Ireland, where the Scots first fixed
their abode.*

John of Fordun, *Chronicle of the Scottish Nation*
(c. 1385–7)

Some fifteen hundred years before the birth of Christ,
there lived a prince called Gaythelos, known for his beauty
and his wayward spirit. He was popular with the other
young men of the court, who wanted to be just as self-
assured and full of his boundless, searching energy. But
Gaythelos' manner was mistrusted by the elders, so much
so that, when he came of age, he learned he was to receive
no royal responsibilities from his father.

The walls of the palace courtyards were white and
mighty. The fig trees that grew up them were heavy with
fruit. There was a fountain, which kept the air cool, where
birds bathed, and the women, all of them beauties, sat and
embroidered panels of colourful cloth. But as Gaythelos

walked beneath the archways, in and out of the Grecian sun, he felt that all the beauty in the world would leave him cold if he were not free.

The injustice of the council's decision filled him with anger. He was too strong, too clever, to be told to stay at home. Now he longed to escape the white walls, the heavy, purple figs, the birdsong and the women. They weighed upon him like a yoke. Gaythelos gathered his companions. When night fell, they took to the stables and rode the horses out of the gates. Through the kingdom they passed, setting fire to barns and storehouses, destroying the judicial buildings. Together they caused so much mayhem that the King banished them for life.

Cast adrift, Gaythelos travelled to Egypt, to a city called Heliopolis, and offered his services to the Pharaoh. Pharaoh's line was one of the oldest in the world and in those days he was engaged in a dispute with his foster-brother, whose name was Moses, over the freedom of his Hebrew slaves. This was trouble enough, but at the same time, a band of warriors from Ethiopia had invaded, crossing over the mountains and reaching as far as Memphis. Gaythelos convinced Pharaoh to let him lead an Egyptian army against the invaders. He had waited for such an opportunity since childhood. He used all his cunning and fought with terrible aggression, driving the Ethiopians back. In thanks, Pharaoh offered Gaythelos the hand of his only daughter. Her name was Scota.

When Scota and Gaythelos were married, their love-making made the marble halls ring just as much as Moses' cries for deliverance. Like her father, she was proud, but not to the point of blindness. At first when she saw the Hebrew God's punishments – the Nile turning blood red – she thought it was the sunrise, but the sky was overcast. That day, the servants could not get the blood out from under their nails, which had become stained as they washed their clothes before daybreak in the shallows of the river. Then frogs had made those same waters boil: so many frogs that they killed each other with their collective weight and, seeking freedom from their own swarm, climbed the sandy palace steps, entering the bedrooms, hiding under pillows, in washstands and in shoes. When Pharaoh chased the Hebrew slaves out of Egypt and was swallowed by the Red Sea, the peasants of the land rose up against Gaythelos, driving him out along with Scota, his Greek companions and the remainder of the Egyptian nobles.

Thus it was that while Moses and Aaron sought the Promised Land, Scota and Gaythelos took their people west. They sailed away from Africa, having rested in Algeria, and sailed down the Mediterranean, through the Pillars of Hercules, until they were south of the Bay of Biscay. Full of the eagerness of youth, Gaythelos and Scota moored their ships in Spain and, finding themselves ill-received by the people of that land, hurried to build a fortified town in which to live. They called it Brigantia. The site was chosen for its coastal hill, on which they constructed a watchtower. Some claim the tower, which has never fallen, was the work of Hercules, or of the Romans, but it was built by Scota and Gaythelos.

In Brigantia, years passed and the exiles found no peace, suffering constant attack from their neighbours. Gazing across the ocean from his tower, Gaythelos longed now, as he had in his father's court, for freedom. Meanwhile Scota saw how every day their power dwindled. *These people are the cream of Egypt and Greece*, she thought; *they were born for more than this.*

Gaythelos sent scouts into the Atlantic, charging them with the task of finding somewhere they could live in peace and independence. He was old now, and took, trembling, to his shrines to keep vigil, fast and pray until the scouts returned. When they did, they professed to have found an island in the north-western ocean. It had generous harbours and its inhabitants were few. Gaythelos dared not hope. He sent his soldiers to the island, and they destroyed the minor settlements they found.

When the soldiers returned to Spain, they brought news that the island in the sea was ready for colonisation. But upon arrival in Brigantia's harbour, there were no smiles to greet them. In the time that they had been gone, Gaythelos had taken sick. It was believed that he was dying.

Scota and Gaythelos had two grown sons, whose names were Hyber and Hymec. They were together now, with Scota, at Gaythelos' bedside. She knew her husband was dying, but she was too proud to cry. Her shoulders were square and her charcoal-lined eyes were clear, though in the secrecy of her heart she was remembering their youthful passion. When Gaythelos began to speak, she directed her sons to listen.

'The gods have kept us safe here and shown us the way to a new home. Do not submit to oppression; it would be better to die. Go. For there is nothing more precious than a nation that has chosen to serve its own king, who rules by hereditary right.'

Scota remained at her husband's side as he died, but Hyber and Hymec led a fleet to the island. The air around them cooled as they went, until they saw it: jewel bright in the blue sea. Coming ashore, they routed the remaining tribes, though, unbeknownst to the invaders, giants remained hidden in the mountains. Then Hyber called the territory Scotia after his mother, who was the most noble of all their people, and her name, along with that of Gaythelos, was given to the Scottish and Gaels.

Hyber became king when his father died, and his people were willing subjects. He made frequent crossings between Spain and Scotia, giving his name to the Iberian Sea, the peninsula of Iberia, the River Ebro – and Hibernia, which would later be called 'Ireland'. His descendants would one day cross the sea to Albion and found Scotia. Though much else changed, and though they travelled great distances, there was nothing the Scotti prized more than freedom.

❖

Edward I traced his seat back to the character of Locrin, the son to whom Brutus was said to have given the territory of Loegria (later England). As the eldest of the three legendary brothers, Locrin and his successors were held to be the natural overlords of the rulers of the territories given to Brutus's other two sons – Kambria (Wales) and Albany (Scotland).

For the contemporary Scottish, the story of Scota and Gaythelos provided an origin myth to rival that of the English kings, who traced their line back to Brutus. In Medieval Latin, 'Scotti' meant Irish, and its modern counterpart reflects the Scots' roots in Ireland. The above myth comes from *The Chronicle of the Scottish Nation* by John of Fordun (died *c.* 1384), which may be based on a late thirteenth-century predecessor. It refers to 'Albion' rather than Britain, stressing that only the southern part was inhabited by the Britons and that the northern part, called 'Scotia', was colonised by the Scots from an early period. Fordun's text would be followed, a few decades later, by Walter Bower's beautifully titled and closely related *Scotichronicon*. Both chronicles stemmed from earlier Irish origin myth material.

In medieval terms, the tale of Scota is even more illustrious than that of the Britons; for one thing, Gaythelos is Greek, while Brutus is descended from Trojans, whom the Greeks defeated (though, of course, Brutus gets his own back by defeating the Greek King Pandrasus). What with his marriage to Scota, daughter of the Pharaoh from the Old Testament Book of Exodus, the Scottish people could claim descent from two of the most powerful royal dynasties of the Classical and biblical worlds.

The issue of the Scots' independence from the English (or any other) crown sits at the heart of this legend. Gaythelos' dying words to Hyber encapsulate the tale's political message:

It is both pleasanter, and more praiseworthy, for us to suffer death bravely in battle, than, barely dragging on an ignoble existence, to die daily, miserably fettered under the burden of an execrable subjection. For he, on his neck, as on that of the ass, is imposed the yoke of continual slavery, is by no means worthy the name of man. Now, therefore, my sons, gratefully accept the gift the gods offer you, and go without delay to the island prepared for you, where you shall be able to live noble and free; for it is the highest nobleness of man, and the one delight, of all things most desired by every gentle heart, nay, the one gem which deserves to be preferred to all the jewels in the world, to endure the sway of no foreign ruler, but to submit voluntarily to a hereditary power of one's own nation.

John of Fordun had lived through the Second War of Scottish Independence. The Scota and Gaythelos myth turns Egypt, Spain (especially the Tower of Hercules in 'Brigantia', today the town of A Coruña) and Ireland into stepping stones that bypass southern Britain, cutting out Brutus and his sons altogether, rendering the English claim to ancient overlordship obsolete. It sets the Scots' royal heritage apart, rejects the advances of the Norman Kings of England, and refuses 'the burden of an execrable subjection'. It characterises a Scottish nation that is both 'noble and free'.

5

Woden and the Peopling of the North

Near the middle of the world was constructed that building and dwelling which has been the most splendid ever, which was called Troy.

Snorri Sturluson, *Prose Edda* (c. 1220)

The sun flooded the city beyond as the Queen of Thrace brought her baby to her breast. She had sent the servants away, still too unfamiliar. There was yoghurt, meat and warm bread for lunch and she had brought quinces from the larder to steep in honey and wine. Her afternoon with her son, Loridi, would be a peaceful one.

He looked just like Thor, with those sapphire eyes set in skin like polished silver. Perhaps he would inherit his father's strength as well. She still could not believe she was here, lifted from the chill poverty of her youth. Thor was the grandson of Priam, once King of Troy, and his uncle was Hector, who had fought Achilles, best of the Greeks, in that famous last stand for the city. At the age of twelve Thor had lifted ten bear-skins from the ground. Then, when he had come of age and risen to the throne of Thrace, he had travelled around the world, fighting monsters and defeating a dragon. Thor had found her in the northern lands and had married her for her beauty. He had called her by the name given to her in the temple of prophecy: Sibyl, or Sif.

Now Loridi had stopped feeding and his breathing was growing deep. His cheeks were red and his hair was sticking to his forehead. Sif laid him in the cradle, stood up and padded to the fire. Beside it were the quinces, already peeled and boiled, bathed in lemon juice to preserve their mellow colour. She sat cross-legged before the flames, pouring wine and honey into the pot and hanging it where it would boil. Then she added mace and cloves from bowls left out by the servants. She was absorbed in her work, delighted by it. But then, distracted by a cough from Loridi, she dropped a scroll of cinnamon. It fell into the flames and emitted a plume of smoke. The pungent odour, mingling with that of the sweet alcohol, plucked at her senses. Lights danced in the space behind her eyes and images blossomed there . . .

A child, asleep in his cradle, with the towers of Thrace outside his nursery window. The same child playing in the familiar gardens of the palace. Now a pale adolescent, seated with the shamans, burning incense, lost in spells. A man leaving Thrace with his wife and clan, crossing

mountains, penetrating luminous lands, entering forests that towered over the black lakes and the thick-furred beasts who watched from coniferous shadows. Sif recognised her northern homeland. Then she saw the same man walking alone through the dark pines, the floor white with snow, as a roaring wind blew; the snow and the trees deeper and darker, and no shelter for him but a long grey cloak. The man alone in a leafless tower, approaching a swinging noose, looping it round his neck. Sif saw him fall, watched the sun wheel about as his eyes bulged, sapphire blue. Nine times the sun set, turning him nine times to gold. And the wind howled like a wolf, till on the ninth night he screamed. Screaming, he hung till dawn was in the sky and all around was blue. Then the rope snapped and the man fell through the night, through the wind, through the snow, into the bedrock of the forest and down to the waters beneath. And now Sif saw the man on a throne, with a raven on each shoulder. One of his eyes was missing, but the other shone like two. His beard flowed to his lap. Warriors were feasting in his hall and they raised their cups to Woden. He was king and he was shaman. And as she looked into his one sapphire eye, she saw herself reflected there.

Sif awoke to the sound of Loridi wailing. The wine had boiled to a paste. Her legs were numb. She crawled to the child and gathered him to her. Never had she seen so vividly. And in that moment, as the child nuzzled her breast, she knew Loridi would not take after Thor. Her gift would pass through the baby now in her arms, then on down the generations, water through rock, till it came to the one they would call Woden. And he would return to the North and his descendants would be unnumbered.

❖

You have read how Albina founded Albion and engendered a race of giants, how Brutus arrived at Totnes and established the kingdom of Britain and how Scota and Gaythelos gave rise to the Scotti. Later you will read how those Scots, along with the Picts, colonised the North of Britain. But now we are among the tribes of Scandinavia and Germany. Some of these will soon be crossing the North Sea to settle all over Britain, and come to be called the Saxons, Vikings, Danes and Normans. All will one day be known as the English.

There is no single origin myth that all these cultures would have recognised. Indeed, in the high Middle Ages the English royal line effectively appropriated the ancient history of the Britons. However, these various Germanic groups did have shared cultural roots; they wrote in runes, spoke related languages and worshipped a related pantheon of gods, led by Odin (or Woden, as he was known in Old English, hence 'Woden's Day' or 'Wednesday'). In histories about these societies, largely composed well after their conversion to Christianity, primary gods like Woden and Thor are rationalised as mortal patriarchs (a process called 'euhemerisation').

The above story of Sif, Loridi and Woden is my own invention, built from elements of the thirteenth-century Prologue to the *Prose Edda* by the Icelandic historian Snorri Sturluson and an Old Norse Eddic poem called *Hávamál*. The *Prose Edda* and the *Poetic Edda* represent much of the corpus of texts preserving the stories and creed of Norse paganism. However, they should not be seen as an unadulterated snapshot of its belief system. For one thing, by the time the *Prose Edda* was written, Iceland had been Christian for two centuries, affecting its author's treatment of the narrative. Snorri Sturluson justifies his prose retelling of the pagan Norse myths by proposing that the gods in question were ancient nobles of such fame that 'they were said to be more like gods than men'. He elaborates that Thor was the grandson of Priam, King of Troy, and that Odin was a descendant who travelled to found the northern kingdoms:

The name of one king there [in Troy] was Munon or Mennon. He was married to the daughter of the high king Priam; she was called Troan. They had a son, he was called Tror; we call him Thor. He was brought up in Thrace by a duke whose name was Loricus. When he was ten he inherited his father's weapons. He was as beautiful to look at when he came among other people as when ivory is inlaid in oak . . . He took possession of the realm of Thrace . . . Then he . . . travelled through many countries and explored all quarters of the world and defeated unaided all beserks and giants and one of the greatest dragons and many wild animals. In the northern part of the world he came across a prophetess called Sibyl, whom we call Sif, and married her. No one is able to tell Sif's ancestry. She was the most beautiful of all women, her hair was like gold. Their son was Loridi, who took after his father; his son was Einridi, his son Vigenthor . . . his son Finn, his son Friallaf . . . He had a son whose name was Woden, it is him that we call Odin.

Odin had the gift of prophecy and so did his wife, and from this science he discovered that his name would be remembered in the northern part of the

world and honoured above all kings . . . and whatever
countries they passed through, great glory was spoken
of them, so that they seemed more like gods than men
. . . And they did not halt their journey until they
came north to the country that is now called Saxony
. . . There Odin put in charge of the country three of
his sons; one's name was Veggdegg, he was a powerful
king and ruled over East Saxony; his son was Vitrgils,
his sons were Vitta, father of Hengest . . . Odin's third
son was Siggi, his son Rerir. This dynasty ruled over
what is now called France.

This twelfth-century Icelandic text hints at an origin myth
for the Saxons – note the mention of Hengist, whom you
will later meet, along with Horsa – and perhaps even the
Normans, who are sometimes called the Franks. Similar
genealogies already existed in the work of the Venerable Bede
(eighth century), as well as Norman histories of the Saxons.
And as for the Normans (or Norsemen), Roger of Wendover,
a historian at St Albans Abbey, offered a genealogy of the
Norman dukes in his early thirteenth-century *The Flowers of
History*. He writes how the Norman dukes 'often boast that
the Trojans proceeded from their stock, and that, after the
fall of the city, Antenor fled for his treachery, and arriving
in Germany reigned subsequently in Dania or Denmark, to
which country he gave his own name'.

I have offered one story of the many that might be spun
from Snorri's words, giving Sif centre stage. She represents

the northern connection, having been found there by Thor and brought to Thrace. What is more, it could be inferred that it was her prophetic powers that passed to their progeny. I have imagined what it would be like if the prophetess Sif foresaw her descendants' journey back to her homeland and the life of the man who would be called Woden.

Finally, in this retelling I have allowed the mortal Woden (or Odin) to meld with the one-eyed, self-sacrificing god of the Norse mythological tradition. He is forever seeking knowledge, trading his eye in return for a drink from the well at the base of the World Tree, Yggdrasil, hanging himself from its branches for nine windy nights to absorb the knowledge-bearing runes in its roots. This moment is described in an Icelandic Eddic poem called *The Sayings of the High One* and constitutes some of the most haunting lines in all of medieval literature:

> I know that I hung on a windy tree
> Nine long nights,
> Wounded with a spear, dedicated to Odin,
> Myself to myself,
> On that tree which no man knows
> From where its roots run.
>
> No bread did they give me nor drink from a horn,
> Downwards I peered;
> I took up the runes, screaming I took them,
> Then I fell back from there.

6

The Naming of the Humber and the Severn

He had a cave dug beneath the town of Trinovantum and there he shut Estrildis up . . . for despite everything that had happened he was determined to make love with her in secret.

Geoffrey of Monmouth, *The History of the Kings of Britain*

(c. 1136)

When Locrin became king, he promised he would marry Gwendolen. He was Brutus' eldest son and she was the daughter of his dearest friend, Corineus. She was extravagant and quick to anger, just like her father, though there were no giants left for her to fight. The King promised to marry her partly out of fear of Corineus and partly out of fear of Gwendolen. The agreement was made before the invasion of the Huns, led by King Humber, when everything changed for Locrin.

King Humber invaded Albany, Britain's northern kingdom, which took its name from Albanac and would one day be called Scotland. Albanac was Locrin's brother. Humber slaughtered Albanac in battle and all the people of Albany fled south, to the kingdom of Locrin, which was called Loegria, not-yet-England. Upon receiving this great wave of refugees and hearing that Humber remained in Albany with his troops, Locrin called upon Kamber, his third brother, who ruled Kambria, not-yet-Wales. The two brothers took their troops north to avenge Albanac and expel Humber from the island. They met on the banks of a mighty estuary, flanked by flat marshes green with samphire. Fired by their grief and anger, they beat Humber back to the waters, till he had no escape. The foreign king sank, weighted by his armour, and his eyes did not leave Locrin's face till they were filled with the muddy tide. From that day to this, the estuary has borne his name.

Now, Humber's ships were in the estuary and the Britons searched them for gold and silver. Locrin admired the craftsmanship of their fittings and the beauty of the treasures within. Among them were three women, who were prisoners from an earlier raid. One was the daughter of the King of Germany and her name was Estrildis. Locrin was captivated by her high, narrow waist, her slender face and her deep-set, mournful eyes. He had never fallen in love before, but as soon as he saw her stepping from the darkness of the ship's hull, he knew he had to possess her, to marry her if he could.

Corineus, though old, had been at the battle and soon heard of the King's intention. He was even more enraged at this than when Gogmagog had broken his ribs. The grey-headed Lord of Cornwall surrounded the King with his men and waved a battle-axe in the air. He railed against Locrin for coveting another woman when he had promised himself to Gwendolen. If she were abandoned now, Corineus would seek his vengeance; he would use whatever strength was left in the hand that had once choked the life out of giants from here to Italy. By the time he had finished his speech, men who counted themselves friends of both parties interceded on Corineus' behalf and Locrin knew he had to concede.

Estrildis stood on the boat, her hands still bound at the wrist. She did not understand what the men were saying, but she had seen the one in the crown looking at her and knew the significance of that look. Since being taken from her father's house she had known some man or other would have her. At least if it were a king, she would enjoy some comfort, wouldn't she?

After Corineus had gone, Estrildis was taken back to the New Troy. She was kept in a secret part of the palace, where she would be seen by none but the servants. The women she had been with must have been sold or given away, for she did not see them again. And though she was given good food and a soft bed, she missed their company. They were her last link to the life she had lost.

One day she looked out of the window to see a great pageant beyond the palace gates. The King was marrying a woman who stood at least a head taller than him. Estrildis wondered at the wedding and what it might mean for her. That night she was taken by guards down into the bowels of the palace, through a trapdoor and down into a tunnel. The tunnel meandered, its vaulted walls bearing the marks of pick-axes. Then they entered a chamber, with dim torches on the walls and a richly dressed bed in the middle of the rush-strewn floor. There was food in one corner and a washstand. A wooden clothes chest stood at the end of the bed. Without a word, the guards left her. Estrildis could hear her breath echoing from the walls. And as she looked about her she realised she was not in a chamber, but a cavern. Its roof, only just visible in the dim light, was pitted and undulating, sending down long stems of rock that tapered to milky droplets of water. And as her eyes drifted to the furthest reaches of the light, she saw that where it had seemed to end was in fact no more than an area of deep shadow, continuing for what could have been forever.

After a time, enough time for Estrildis to think it must be evening, the King arrived. He had been running, despite the weight of his nuptial finery. He took her shoulders, pushed her onto the bed and, saying some words she didn't understand, proceeded to make the walls ring with the echoes of his efforts. Estrildis stared at the stony ceiling, waiting for him to stop, and long after he had smoothed down his clothes and hurried from the cave, she continued to lie there and stare. At some point she visited the wash-stand, then she returned to the bed and fell asleep.

A year passed and Estrildis did not – could not – leave the cave. She was maintained by Locrin's servants and he visited her most days, avoiding discovery by telling his wife that he was going to the temple. Estrildis felt as though he came down with some of the light of the city still gleam-ing on his shoulders. She desired that light more than anything, and though she walked the dark caverns when she was alone, she found no passageway to the surface. He was her only hope of escape.

When Estrildis discovered that she was pregnant, she did not know that, far overhead, Gwendolen was pregnant too. When Estrildis gave birth to a daughter, she named the child Sabrina. And, in that dismal place, she was brighter to her than any sun. In the palace, Gwendolen called her son Maddan. As soon as he was weaned, she sent him to live with Corineus, from whom he would learn to fight. In the gloom of the cave, Estrildis sang to Sabrina of the world above: of how there were such things as plants, which held their palms up to the sun and drank in the light like wine. There were such things as birds too, that wheeled in open skies and sang their song to the heavens. Some years had passed and Sabrina had grown old enough to talk and play, which she did happily enough in the darkness. She knew

off by heart the chill labyrinth of tunnels and chambers that wandered out from the one in which they slept.

It all changed when Corineus died. Locrin feared Gwendolen, but he had feared her father more, and without him he felt courage enough to proclaim his love for Estrildis. He ended his marriage and brought his new queen to the palace. Estrildis, who had for seven years craved the heat of the sun, now wondered if she would rather return to her cave. What did this man think would happen? Did he not know how she hated him or see what harm he had done to their child by keeping her underground? Had he no fear of the great queen he had rejected, whose father had wrestled and defeated giants?

Estrildis was no fool, but she could not get away, surrounded as they were by the mute servants and guards of her captor king. Their daughter Sabrina was quiet, averse to light and the company of others. She held her hands to her face when they were borne through the sunlit city, she clung to her mother and wept if they were parted for even a moment. Her mother could do nothing but wait and see what their fate would be.

Indeed, Gwendolen had not surrendered as Locrin believed. She had returned to her father's domains, the Duchy of Cornwall, and mustered an army. When the King heard, he rode out to meet her near the River Stour, beholding on the battlefield a woman who was every inch her father's daughter. As she wielded her battle-axe he felt he might have been back on the banks of the Humber, buckling to the will of Corineus. She ordered her troops with the expertise of a warlord, and Locrin had hardly the time to utter his battle cry before he was struck in the chest by an arrow. The daughter of Corineus killed the son of Brutus and named herself Queen of the Britons. She installed herself in the region and sent for Estrildis and Sabrina.

Estrildis implored the soldiers to take them by night, so that her daughter would not fear the glare of the out-doors, but they did not listen. For the whole journey the child buried her head in her mother's cloak. If Estrildis knew they were travelling to their execution, she did not let her daughter see her fear.

Gwendolen was waiting for them on the banks of a great estuary: not the Humber, where Locrin had found Estrildis, but a river-mouth in a deep and wide valley, flanked by distant ridges of hills. Mother and daughter had their hands bound and were lifted from the wagon. Then they were pulled towards the water. Sabrina kept her face to Estrildis' cloak, who knew that the silver light on the water must hurt her like a burning brand. She was grateful that Sabrina could not see the grim faces of the men, or the cruelty in Gwendolen's eyes. They were led to a boat and Estrildis helped her daughter in. Then they were rowed out into the middle of the eddying current. It was wide as the sea, Estrildis thought, this river-mouth, and just as treacherous. She could see gulls circling overhead and white egrets waiting for fish in the branches of far-off trees. *Such beauty there is in the world,* she thought, *and such danger.*

Then the men seized woman and child and threw them into the churning flood. Estrildis cried out at the shock of cold, but would not be overcome; she had to take hold of Sabrina. But where was she? Spitting water from her mouth, she looked about her, unable to find a small hand in the flow, panic causing her to swallow muddy mouthfuls and breathe in gasps. No matter how hard she looked, she could not see a waving hand, nor a curl of tawny hair on the surface. When her legs finally grew tired of kicking and her arms could do nothing but float in the water, her head slipped beneath the waves.

No one knows for certain what happened to mother and daughter then. Perhaps Estrildis knew only darkness at first. Perhaps she saw her daughter in the gloom. Did Sabrina have her eyes open? Were they shining and jubilant? Perhaps Estrildis saw a creature with her. An otter. The pair were playing: twisting and turning with the current, with rippled light dancing on skin and fur. Perhaps Sabrina swam towards her mother, a smile on her pale face, and it dawned on Estrildis that they could be happy here, alone but for the creatures of the river and far from the too-bright sky. Perhaps Sabrina looped her fingers through her mother's, and led her into the dark.

Whether or not in the centuries that followed mother and child found wonders in the wandering tendrils of weeds, the long lives of eels and the strange habits of dragonfly nymphs, since that day the river has borne Sabrina's name, though, by some corruption of speech, it is now called the Severn.

❖

The naming of the Humber and the Severn is given in Geoffrey of Monmouth's *c.* 1136 *History of the Kings of Britain*. Sabrina is given the Middle Welsh name Habren, which he converts to its Latin form at the end. The tale is a tragic conclusion to the friendship between Brutus and Corineus that led to the foundation of Britain, but it has the parallel impact of presenting a woman, Gwendolen, as the third ever monarch in Brutus' line. Female succession is an issue close to Geoffrey's heart and one to be explored more over the coming chapters. She reigns for fifteen years, then passes the sceptre of the realm to her son Maddan. He proves to be a good and just king. Geoffrey dates this period to the reign of Samuel in Judea and the life of Homer, traditionally around the seventh century BC.

So how familiar is Britain now? The Trojan Britons, to us the Brittonic Celts, have settled the island, though invasion of Albany by the Huns has pushed the population south, out of the North and into the regions that will become Wales and England.

Meanwhile, a people have established themselves in Ireland who are called the Scotti. This was the name given to the Irish in the early Middle Ages. In time, having formed an alliance with a people called the Picts, they will cross the Irish Sea and make settlements in western Albany.

This leaves the Germanic tribes who will come variously to be called the Vikings, Saxons, Danes and Normans. According to the Christian genealogies, which transformed pagan gods into mortal patriarchs, Woden has left Thrace and journeyed to the North-West of mainland Europe, founding a royal line that will give rise to the Saxons and Franks. Before long they will have filled the North and will set out in ships for new homelands.

But for now the Scotti and the progeny of Woden will stay in Ireland and on the Continent, and the Britons will have the run of Albion. We enter an age of magic: of necromancers in Bath and dragons under Oxford, of kings brought low and old women with more courage than their battle-hardened sons.

Part Two

Prehistory

7

Weland the Smith

And their skulls which were under the hair,
He chased with silver.

The Lay of Völund, from the Poetic Edda
(tenth/eleventh century)

Weland believed Hervor had meant it with all her wandering heart, the love she had sworn to him on the ground.
But now he knew that in the sky, where she belonged, she
felt only the cold strength of the Valkyrie, called to bear
the dead to Valhalla.

Nine years ago, he and his brothers had found Hervor
and her sisters spinning flax beside Lake Wolfdale, their
swan-feather capes, which they wore in order to fly, drifting on the moss. When the women saw Weland and his
brothers, they longed to grasp the men's warm flesh, so
used were they to the cold. Hervor had seen no one like
this man; his goldsmith's hands, calloused at their fingertips

and stained with metal, were not made for fighting. She swore she would love him forever.

But Valkyries and goldsmiths are not alike. Weland's brothers had married Hervor's sisters, but the swan-maidens flew away in time. Hervor waited for as long as she could, for nine winters, though she yearned ever more to travel, to visit in sleet and snow the corpse-strewn plains of battle and undertake her work. She begged Weland to join her, but he stayed in his fire-warmed forge, bent over filigree, setting exquisite gems. At the close of many a crisp afternoon, finding him thus, she would play at his elbow, teasing him, and ask him to come with her to the pregnant fields of her labour, but this would just make him mutter, frowning, until he sank once more into work. Afterwards, he regretted this neglect.

The day she left, Weland had awoken without knowing what to make. He went to his chest and looked through his ingots, scraps and pouches of stones, but nothing inspired him there. No new pendants hung in his mind's eye: no new combinations of precious metal and coloured gems. This was not a familiar feeling. Outside, he could hear Hervor singing as she spun, as she always did, those endless skeins of yarn, and weaving yard upon yard of identical sheets of linen. He stepped into the daylight and shared his predicament. She stopped spinning, her spindle wheeling on its axis, and faced him with shining eyes.

'Oh!' she said. 'Then I will take you with me and you will see what the wide world holds!'

Weland lowered his gaze. 'I don't want to,' he muttered.

'What?'

'I don't want to go. I'm scared.'

The spindle roved, a pendant of wood and fibre.

'Hervor,' Weland said, 'I will never be like you! I sit every day in my forge, crafting intricate things. I am not made for great voyages or scooping up cadavers in my arms. Hervor, heights fill me with fear.'

'So,' she said, 'you will never come away with me?'

Weland swung his gaze to the sky, then quickly back to his feet. Then he turned his back on her and traipsed into the woods.

That morning, he checked his snares. One had caught a stoat, which he skinned for its fur. He didn't hear Hervor leave. He didn't hear her because all she had to do to abandon him was fetch her swan-feather cape from under their bed, draw it across her shoulders and walk to Wolf-dale lake. From there, she ran across the water, beating her wings until she was airborne. She cried all the while but her tears were lost to the vanishing scar left in the water by her racing feet and in the gulf that widened beneath her as she rose into the air, and soon she had disappeared over the dark trees, battle in her heart.

When Weland discovered Hervor gone, he hoped that she would come back that evening. She did not. Then he hoped she'd be back the next day, but she was not. Nor the end of the week, nor the month. He took to staring at the sky and praying he would see her, but his eyes were not used to sunlight, and swan-shaped blots were conjured by the glare, mocking his fear.

When his brothers' wives had flown, which they had in the end, the men had set out in snowshoes and deer pelts to find them. But Weland stayed at home. What was there to be gained by pursuing her? She had chosen to leave him. He was not, he had never been, enough. Heavy with sadness, he dreaded each slow day, the brief, low passing of the sun that did not show him his Valkyrie love, a being who had chosen life with the slain over a living, breathing man. To pass the time, he started, once more, to work. He didn't need to look for inspiration this time. He thought of Hervor's patience, spinning and weaving while she waited for him to join her. He would make her a ring while he waited, he would make her hundreds of rings. When she came home, she would know his devotion.

Weland toiled like no maker before him or since, forging ring upon ring, obsessed, oblivious. But the world was not ignorant of him. For as he worked, a king by the name of Nithad heard tell of the skilful Weland, the smith all alone in the woods.

They were greedy, the King and his wife. They coveted Weland's treasure. When they reached the smith's home, the waning moon was high and the land mute in icy darkness. Had Weland been there to meet them, he would have seen hostile rows of shields and sword-hilts, but he, as it happened, was out. That day his snares had caught a bear, and he was in the forest, removing its heavy pelt and carving its flesh into portions.

Nithad and his wife had brought their daughter, Bothild. She was young and beautiful, without the guile of her mother. Finding themselves and their retinue alone, the family pushed open the door of the hall. Then their eyes filled with stars far redder than any in the sky outside. Strung between the beams were more rings than they could count. Bothild's parents moaned with longing.

Gold speaks darkly to people. Inflamed by the sight, Nithad unwound the ropes. One. Two. Three. Four. He slipped the rings from the fibres and passed them around, till all their hands were heavy with treasure. They orgied, silent and sick, until the last ring slipped from its rope. This ring he gave to Bothild with a kiss. Then he replaced the others and wound the rope back across the beams.

When Weland got home, the family was gone. He wandered into the empty hall with his bear-skin, ready to lay it out beside the hearth and fall asleep. Then his heart began to pound. One of the rings was missing: one of the rings for Hervor.

He laughed. His wandering love had come home! She had seen what he had made and she had delighted in it. Even now, she was twisting the ring on her beautiful finger, marvelling at its gems and at the fineness of each coil and bead of metal, each made for love of her. His heart swollen, he checked the forge and the lake and the place where she had sat at her loom. Where was Hervor? He peered into the canopy. He checked the rafters of the hall. She was nowhere to be seen, but that did not mean she was not close. He would wait. That night he sat on his bear-skin, staring into the gloom, straining his ears, just in case she came to him, the ring on her Valkyrie finger, forgiveness in her smile.

But, at first light, it was Nithad who returned to the hall, along with his wife and Bothild. They found the smith on his bear-skin beside a barren hearth. Though he sat upright, his blue lips were parted and his red-rimmed eyes were closed in sleep. The men worked with stealth and speed.

Weland stirred. He made to move his benumbed limbs, but his feet and hands were too heavy. They were fettered.

'You stole our gold,' lied Nithad. 'You owe us service.'

Weland croaked, confused, 'My gold is from a place far from the Rhineland; it is from the mines of my ancestors.'

But then his clearing eyes noticed the sword-hilt at Nithad's waist. It was his own sword. Then he saw the red gold ring on Bothild's finger. The agony of realisation tore his heart in two. Hervor had not come home. The token of his love was stolen. He pulled at his fetters and screamed. He stared a razor edge at Bothild.

Quiet as a cat, Nithad's wife stepped forward and crouched before the prisoner.

'Look how he bares his teeth when he sees the sword at your waist, husband. And see how his eyes shine like a snake's at the sight of Bothild's hand. He will hurt us when he can. Cut his sinews. Take him to the island.'

Her warriors advanced, unsheathing their swords and slicing through Weland's hamstrings. Blinded by agony, the goldsmith knew no more.

The kidnappers took him east and imprisoned him in a smithy on an island called Sævarstadir, alone but for seabirds, seals and lupins. Everyone except the King was forbidden to approach the island. It was Weland's prison, and he lived there in solitude, setting gems for the King, tormented by the loss of Hervor and the red gold promise he made for her love. But soon he would make the finest ornaments of his life.

The King's two young sons rowed their boat stealthily to the island, hoping to meet the smith. They found him to be docile, propped harmlessly on crutches, not at all monstrous as their father had said. Entering his smithy, they pointed at a wooden chest in the corner and asked for the key, which he gave to them without complaint. Peering inside, they saw, or thought they saw, piles of jewels, wires of gold, ingots and all the materials of his trade. Their eyes filled with light.

'If you come back tomorrow, I'll make you something,' Weland said, 'but don't tell a soul.'

Promising to return, the brothers raced back to their boat, whooping, sliding in the bird-mud, cracking the stems of the lupins and pushing each other with glee. Weland set to work.

When, the very next morning, they craned their necks over the chest, he cut through their spines with a new-forged blade.

On the mainland, people realised the boys were gone. A few days later, the boat was found further down the coast, knocking gently on the rocks. Weland's island was searched, but nothing found. They did not look in the mud under the smithy. The King's sons had come to grief at sea, they said.

Weland had removed the crowns of the boys' skulls and made cups, scooped out their eyeballs and fashioned earrings, and pulled free each of their teeth for brooches. The cups, earrings and ornaments he gave to the King and Queen and to the Princess Bothild, generous gifts to soften their grief as they wept at the boys' empty pyre. Weland saw the flames reflected in Hervor's gold, from its place on Bothild's hand.

It came to pass, after the death of her brothers, that Bothild dislodged one of the ring's gems. Fearful of what her father would say, she stole secretly to the island.

Seeing her approach on the dawn waves, the water clear beneath her, Weland concocted a draught. If Bothild had known her crime, she would not have drunk it when she entered the smithy. She would not have been drugged by its power. She would not have felt so weak that she fell to the floor, or have been unable to scream as he dragged himself onto her chest. She would not have been helpless to resist him as he forged within her an uninvited life.

It was evening by the time Bothild awoke, bruised and smeared, and Weland was nowhere to be seen. She wrapped herself in torn clothes and ran back to her boat over the island's broad rocks, though as she ran through the twilight she kept losing her footing on the droppings of wild birds. Her father would punish her for this. Sliding down the boulders to the boat in the waves, shaking with cold and fear, she grappled for the oars, hardly able to lift them in her stiff, naked hands. She dreaded returning, but she could not stay. Then a voice spoke out of the darkness.

'Stop, thief, and see what I've become.'

In the rising moonlight she could discern him, some way off, a pearl on the grey earth. He was holding himself on his arms. They looked wrong. They were too big somehow, too dark.

'I must thank you, Bothild, for making me fearless.'

And with that he rose into the sour air, arms aloft, feathers splayed, fanning out in symmetry, the grey plumage of the island birds black-tipped with rancid mud.

And Bothild tried to row, but Weland no longer cared about her. He knew where he wanted to be. His legs hung beneath him as he ascended and flew to the diamond-encrusted sky.

Later he would hover over Nithad and mock him for all he had lost, confessing to the murder of his sons. Then later Bothild would bear his son, Widia, who would become a hero. And later again Bothild would hear the story of Hervor and how she had left Weland and was living the noble life of a Valkyrie. Then she would dream herself back to the slick and stinking boat, where the goldsmith had blamed her for all the wrong he had done. And this time, this time she would say:

'I didn't know I had stolen from you. I didn't know that the ring on my finger was made for another, with whom you'd rather have had a child. But even if I had known, what you did to me was too great a punishment. What have you gained? The poets will sing of my suffering and of your Valkyrie love; she doesn't know who I am and doesn't spare a thought for you.'

❖

There is something about the high craftsmanship of a time before modern machines that sets the imagination whirring. It is against this hum that we should enjoy tales set in an age when artistry and dark magic were two sides of the same, spinning coin. Once upon a time the skills of their architects and artisans transcended those of ordinary mortals. I speak of legendary architects and artisans, of course, though part of me thinks the real ones were superhuman too. Whenever I go to the British Museum, I try to spend a few moments before the Sutton Hoo shoulder clasps, whose makers had magic in their fingertips; for the delicate ornaments, unearthed in Suffolk in 1939, are some fourteen hundred years old and yet sparkle as though new. Dating to the late sixth or early seventh century, they are made of gold, inlaid with garnets from southern Asia, and each stone is cut to fit a tiny golden cell. Together the cells form a pattern, part snake, part beast, part geometry, with each garnet curved, following the camber of the clasp, and overlaying a sheet of waffle-textured gold. The gold is designed to reflect a shimmer of oxblood-tinted light. When these jewels, or others like them, graced the shoulders of a living prince, watching him move by firelight must have been mesmeric. Similar encomia could extol the finesse of the Tara Brooch from near-contemporary Ireland, with its filigree and embossed spirals in a vivid, vibrant, vibrating interplay of gold and silver, around pools of dichromatic enamel.

Such objects from the distant past are like flashes of light, an archaeological *aurora borealis*, scattering shadowy notions of the 'Dark Ages'. They whisper of networks of trade and cultural exchange, joy in beauty and skill, and glimpses of gorgeously arrayed individuals whose names are long forgotten.

Germanic tribes will not arrive in Britain for a few centuries, so I include this story here as background. It serves to demonstrate the heritage those tribes will bring when they do arrive. In today's Oxfordshire, there lurks a prehistoric barrow called 'Wayland's Smithy', which occupies a wooded glade, like a brooding, grey-skinned troll,

its gaping mouth a window onto shade, a void to be filled
with stories. And the tale invoked by its name makes the
air ring with the tap of the goldsmith's hammer.

The earliest reference to the barrow as 'Welandes
Smiððan' is in a tenth-century English charter, but the
name may be much older than that. Indeed, the legend of
Weland must have been in Britain from at least the early
eighth century, given that it is depicted on the Franks
Casket, a beautifully wrought whale-bone box of that date,
now in the British Museum. It is likewise alluded to in Old
English poetry, though the fullest version may be found
in the Old Norse alliterative poem *The Lay of Völund*, on
which the story you have just read is based.

The Lay of Völund from the *Poetic Edda* may be found in a thirteenth-century manuscript, but, like many of its neighbours, it probably has roots in a much more ancient oral tradition. It ends with Weland landing on the roof of Nithad's hall and revealing the fate of his sons and the rape of Bothild. The King wishes he could strike Weland down if only he weren't so high in the air, though voicing his wish only causes the smith to rise yet higher, laughing all the while. Bothild is absent, though she enters the hall once Weland has gone. She confirms the rape with these words:

> I should never have done it.
> I did not know how to strive against him,
> I was not able to strive against him.

Other sources have Bothild and Weland become the parents of Widia, a hero. In the poetic fragment *Waldere*, Widia grows up to save the life of the King of the Ostrogoths. Where Weland went after tormenting Bothild and Nithad is anyone's guess. In *Thidrek's Saga*, he returns with an army, killing the King and marrying Bothild. One can only imagine how that made her feel. In the Old English poem *Deor*, preserved in the tenth-century Exeter Book, we glimpse her secret grief:

> To Beadohild her brothers' death was not so sore upon
> her as her own situation,
> in that she had clearly realised that she was pregnant.

74

Never could she confidently consider what needs
become of that.

That passed away: so may this.

The final words of this stanza – 'That passed away: so may this' – are repeated after six of the poem's seven stanzas, until the whole thing becomes a rhythmic meditation on the transience of life, its hardships as well as its joys: typical of the oft-moody but always wonderful corpus of Old English poetry.

We can infer that colonising Germanic tribes brought stories with them to Britain from survivals like the Franks Casket, *Deor* and the name of Wayland's Smithy. Visit them all if you can, especially the last, and Weland may make it worth your while. It is said that if you leave your horse and a shilling there overnight, you will find the beast new-shod by morning and the payment taken by the smith.

8

Bath and Bladud's Fall

> His son was called Bladud;
> He was a most busy man.
> He was strong and huge,
> Rich he was and mighty.
> He knew the craft of evil,
> So that he spoke with the fiend
> And would do whatever it said.

Layamon's Brut (c. 1190–1215)

In the days of the Prophet Elijah, Bladud held himself to be the greatest sovereign that had ever lived. His young son Lear believed him. Why wouldn't he? There was no questioning his father's abilities. He had built Bath, nestling its edifices in a wooded valley, channelling lava-warmed waters into ordered pools and decorating them with pillars, pediments and vaults. He dedicated the baths to his patron, Minerva, and ignited perpetual fires in her honour. Lear had heard it said that these fires became balls of stone when they cooled. He also knew that Bladud was a necromancer, using magic to speak with the dead, crouching beside the heated pools on cold nights, steam rising from the water, mingling with the smoke from the fires. Lear's father burned herbs and recited incantations, summoning spirits, harnessing powers to divine the future. The boy, dressed in his princely nightclothes, would peer around the door and watch with fascination, though he went unnoticed.

Bladud's magic was borne by his priests into the cities and countryside, until all the people could summon the dead. It was an evil age, though Lear did not know it. Bladud was triumphant, for he was a mighty king, great and darkly powerful. He had built a city with his bare hands. With his magic, he had found the underworld and brought it under his sway. Now he longed to ascend as far as he had descended. He could do anything he wanted to do. And Bladud wanted to fly.

That summer, the court was in Trinovantum, the New Troy. Prince Lear went with the slaves to the River Thames, where they collected the feathers needed for his father's scheme. It was late August, which is when the swans shed and regrow their plumage. Lear gathered armfuls from the buzzing banks, now compacted from the padding of webbed feet and slippery beside the fast-flowing water. He was careful to choose only undamaged feathers of various lengths and shapes, obeying his father's instructions to the slaves. Sometimes, to reach the best ones, he would venture too close to a brood of cygnets and the parents would hiss him away, their barbed tongues exposed, their wings arced. He thought that, if they had teeth, they would be bared.

The prince collected more feathers than anyone else that day and, as night fell, he rode proudly back to his father's palace. Bladud met them, checking the feathers, nodding his approval and turning, without noticing his son, to leave. Lear ran after him, clutching a handful of the best plumes, wanting to tell him how he had obtained them despite the hissing of the swans and the dangerous rushing of the river, but Bladud took his wrists in one enormous hand, and snatched the feathers with the other.

'Don't touch these,' he hissed, his teeth bared in the lamplight, and Lear was too awed to speak.

He did not see his father for the whole of that autumn. Bladud was shut up in the room he used for councils and his own private studies. The slaves took him food and hushed the boy if he made too much noise. On the cold, bright afternoon when Bladud finally emerged, the whole palace held its breath.

The King stepped onto the ledge of the palace's largest window. Wings were strapped to his arms, whooshing as he swung round, hoisting himself onto the roof. The building was the highest in the city and everywhere the citizens stopped in the streets or looked up from barges and rafts. They could not help but gaze in wonder. Then the King

opened his arms wide. From where Lear stood – he had been playing in the courtyard – his father was a silhouette. He could not wait to see him fly. Bladud would be so happy when his ambition had been achieved, and Lear might sit beside him at the feast.

Bladud leapt. The watchers had known he would, and yet the act, so sure of itself, so confident in the success of an untested invention, brought a sigh from both sides of the river. For a moment the King was caught in the sun's last light, framed in a halo of fire. He could have been a god. But Bladud was flesh and blood indeed, and the spectators saw both with their own, half-shielded eyes. His shoulders whipped back as he fell, which he seemed to do slowly, then he twisted round, his hands clutching at nothing, his face upturned, till the last thing he knew was the retreating brightness of the sun.

Lear watched. When would he start to fly? Why was he playing this trick? His disbelief remained as he watched his father crash onto the sun-warmed roof of Apollo's temple, strike the tiles with a snap and lie still. And though the ragged wings were splayed in a white V against the red of terracotta, in a widening pool of blood, the boy went on waiting for Bladud to stand. It was not until the slaves carried Lear away, tears on their weatherworn cheeks, that he asked if his father was dead.

❖

The ancient Kings and Queens of the *Brut* chronicle were once accepted, even beloved, characters from Britain's heritage. Bladud's son is usually called Leir in these versions, and the story of his reign underpins that of Shakespeare's *King Lear*. In my retelling, I have imagined the Bladud legend from the child's perspective, even though he first appears as an adult in both the *Brut* and in Shakespeare.

Bladud is said to have been responsible for the construction of Bath, in Somerset. Today, the city consists of Regency town houses encircling a complex of ancient Roman baths built to receive the water from nearby thermal springs. The town sits in a valley and sometimes, on wintry mornings, can be completely submerged by a pool of mist. It can feel unlikely, when seen from the wooded hills, that there is a city there at all.

Given the magnitude and beauty of the Roman architectural remains, it is no surprise that medieval people wondered at the city's origins and what great ruler had ordered their construction. The awe inspired by Roman ruins is expressed by one early English writer, whose work survives in the tenth-century Exeter Book:

> Wondrously ornate is the stone of this wall, shattered by fate; the precincts of the city have tumbled and the work of giants is rotting away . . . There were bright city buildings, many bath-houses, a wealth of lofty gables, much clamour of the multitude, many a mead-hall filled with human revelry – until mighty Fate changed all that . . . the city rotted away: those who should repair it, the multitudes, were fallen to the ground.

The Ruin, the modern title for the above poem, is believed to refer to Bath. The poet suggests the crumbling walls were the work of giants. We can sense a similar idea in the much later story of Bladud. In Layamon's Middle English *Brut*, Geoffrey's Bladud is 'strong and huge'. And both authors give him giant ambitions.

In many ways, Bladud is a stock character: the maker-architect who is brought low by his own craft. Geoffrey must have been aware of the legend of Daedalus and Icarus; Ovid's *Metamorphoses* was widely read in the Middle Ages.

Daedalus underestimates Icarus' ambition, and when they escape the court of Minos on wings made of wax and feathers, the boy flies too close to the sun, melting the wax and falling to his death. Daedalus is undone by his greatest achievement. In the legend of Bladud, the sun god's temple breaks the King's fall, breaking his back in the same instant, punishing him for his pride. Evidently, the warning was not heeded by Eilmer of Malmesbury, an eleventh-century monk who, having also read of Daedalus, attempted flight from the roof of Malmesbury Abbey and broke both his legs.

Geoffrey's sources for the legend remain obscure, and it is tempting to assign them to personal, or at least second-hand, experience of the archaeology at Bath. For instance, there really was once a Romano-British shrine at the springs dedicated to Sulis-Minerva, and curse tablets discovered at the site by today's archaeologists agree strangely with the necromancy practised by Bladud. Bring in the survival of a first-century pediment depicting the sculpted face of a male gorgon, with snakes in its beard and, importantly, wings above its ears, and the temptation is yet stronger. But the sculpture was underground when Geoffrey was writing. It is more likely, and has been well-argued by scholars, that Geoffrey looked to Classical textual sources for his information on the Roman city.

Despite now being less famous than his son King Lear, Bladud had a long afterlife in Bath. In the city's Regency heyday, the architect John Wood the Elder (died 1754) designed crescents and promenades of town houses for the Londoners who came to take the waters. He knew a version of the Bladud legend in which the legendary king was educated in Athens, which accounted for his architectural skills and was where he contracted leprosy, hence his desire to be near the healing springs of Bath upon his return to Britain. Wood seems to have believed the story of Bladud, though it had been widely discredited by his time. He suggests the King was the pupil of none other than Pythagoras. And while Wood never went so far as to make himself wings, he may have seen himself as an heir to this legendary British architect.

9

Cordelia and the Soar

*They did not want to take any ransom, but had her so long
that she killed herself in prison from sorrow, a foolish deed.*

Wace, *Roman de Brut* (*c.* 1150)

Cordelia stood alone in the tomb; alone but for the body
of her father. Lear lay in state before her, illumined by
the flickering bronze light of an oil lamp. Blossoms were
caught in the silk of his white hair, and one petal clung to
his eyelid, relics of his procession through the city. Now
that the crowds had gone, she wanted time with the body
of her father, a moment before the start of things. She
had entered the passageway and descended into shadow,
accompanied by the gush of the River Soar which flowed
overhead as she passed beneath a lintel carved with the
two faces of Janus: one looking back, one looking forward.
Then the amber-coloured walls had opened out to form a
chamber. Now, falling to her knees, she rested one hand on

his forehead. How slim a barrier his skin had become; she felt only skull beneath her fingers. Cordelia shut her eyes.

Lear's fragile form – and the soul it had enclosed – had once been gigantic in her eyes. When she was a child, he had founded the mighty city of Leicester and named it after himself. The people had built their homes in its walls and felt safe. She remembered how he and his knights used to leave the city to hunt, charging through the gates, and how once, afterwards, he had lifted her to his shoulders and carried her to the larder to show her the carcass of a stag. It was hanging upside down from the ceiling, reeking and swaying, and its antlers had been wider than she was tall. Cordelia was level with the beast's pelvis, where a trail of yellow drops had stained the hairs of its flank: the remnants of a stream provoked by fear or death, though it made no difference which. Both had been her father's doing. Yes, how mighty he had once been.

But when she had reached adolescence and her father was entering his dotage, Lear had asked Cordelia and her sisters, Goneril and Regan, a question.

He had brought them into the presence of his barons and had asked, 'How much do you love me?'

With that question, and all it implied, he had diminished before her. It was like an involuntary expression of frailty, like the yellow stain of the stag. Her sisters had intermingled praise with whispered devotions, declaring that their love for him was too great, too immeasurable, to express. Cordelia, repulsed by their wiles, had said:

'I love you as a daughter loves a father, and no more.'

He had cut her off and had sent her without a dowry to marry King Aganippus of Gaul. Goneril and Regan were given to the Dukes of Albany and Cornwall. For many years, Lear had ignored her, living richly with his knights in his preferred daughters' homes. But as time passed, the women and their husbands stripped him of his knights and all his royal privileges, and he had come to learn his mistake. When he had lost everything, he at last understood Cordelia's answer. She loved him as a daughter loved a father, not as a sycophant loved a king.

He set out to the court of Aganippus and Cordelia, and they received him quietly, with tears and embraces. She took him into her home, hiding his poverty and giving him a new company of knights. Then, for as long as it took Aganippus to win back Britain, Lear was granted management of Gaul.

Crossing the narrow sea and flowing onto the land like a tidal wave, Aganippus' armies soon overthrew Regan and Goneril. In the final battle, Lear and Cordelia rode together at the front of the troops and defeated the ones that had robbed them. When Lear was restored to his throne, there were festivals in towns across the kingdom and the King was to enjoy a time of peace with his daughter. In his last years, he learned to love her as a father loves his child, and to accept her love in return. They were a long way from the warm waters of Bath and the court of his father, where little had been known of such things.

Three years later, both Lear and Aganippus died, and Cordelia returned to Britain. Her father's body was carried through the streets and brought to a barrow beneath the Soar that she had ordered to be built. Dedicated to Janus, it became a place where the craftsmen would go at New Year to undertake their first labour.

Still kneeling in the bronze light of the tomb, Cordelia raised her hands and lifted her new crown from her head, observing how the light was multiplied, multicoloured, within its many gems. Her father had been a child when first he had worn it, wiped clean of the blood of his father. She imagined how he must have felt and longed to console that child and be consoled in return.

The new Queen kissed the dead Lear's temple, young bones stooped over old, beneath the flowing of the river, and let her tears fall. Then Cordelia stood, replaced the crown on her head and turned towards the image of Janus, the past at her back, her sovereignty before her, the Queen of the Britons imagining herself gigantic.

For five years Cordelia reigned. She worked hard, arbitrating disputes, maintaining her knights and levying fair taxes. She might have kept her throne for decades had it not been for her sisters' sons, Marganus and Cunedagius, who were grown-up now, and covetous. Insidiously, knowingly, they seeded doubt in the minds of the British. Was it right to give a woman power? They said it would bring trouble, as it had in the days of Locrin. The brothers spread their suspicions in halls and fields. Fighting men joined the cousins and the rebellion thorned and tangled.

Cordelia found she could neither deny her sex nor counter their complaint with weapons. The last battle ended when she was pulled from her horse, her sword torn from her hands, and chains thrown about her. She was taken to a dungeon and held there with just enough food to survive.

While Marganus and Cunedagius established themselves as rulers of Britain, time passed over Cordelia like the Soar over her father's royal bones. Neither moon nor sunlight reached her. At first she tried to stay clean, should her ransom be paid. She washed by wetting her hands in her water supply and rubbing them on her skin. But in time the skin of her hands cracked and her nails grew long. Her teeth furred and ached. Her hair grew bedraggled and bloodstains covered her legs, the involuntary expression of her fatal womanhood. She missed her father more than ever at that time and she mourned her hard-won kingdom.

There was a piece of flint in her cell, which, when sheared against another, could be given a deadly edge. One night – or was it day? – Cordelia slid the blade across her wrists. And the blood that condemned her drained, and all her strength diminished, and the Soar, the Severn, the Humber and every river in the land went on roaring to the sea.

❖

The story of King Lear and Cordelia first appears in Geoffrey of Monmouth's *History of the Kings of Britain* and was retold in the many translations and adaptations of the *Brut* legend. In the hands of Shakespeare it achieved the height of its fame. However, at the time of its composition it was intensely relevant to the political situation. Geoffrey's text is generally agreed to have been written in around 1136, and this was a time during which Matilda, Holy Roman Empress by marriage, was herself fighting for the English throne. She was Henry I's legitimate heir, and he had compelled his barons to accept her as his successor. However, when he died in 1135, a baronial *coup* placed Stephen of Blois on the throne. This was largely because there had, at that point, been no Queens of England.

Scholars have suggested that Geoffrey invented or included Cordelia's story in order to explore the question of precedent when it came to political decision-making. He may even have endorsed female rule. For instance, several generations later in his genealogy, Geoffrey arrives at the reign of King Guithelin, who he says is married to a noblewoman called Marcia, skilled in the arts and composer of a legal text called the *Lex Martiana* (which Geoffrey explains becomes the 'Mercian Law' under King Alfred, a real historical document). When Guithelin dies, their son is too young to succeed him. Marcia therefore rules Britain as Queen Regent until her own death. 'For this reason,' Geoffrey writes, 'his mother, who was extremely intelligent and most practical, ruled over the entire Island.' In Geoffrey's own time, Empress Matilda strove fiercely to gain sovereignty but was unsuccessful. She lost the throne to Stephen.

It would be anachronistic to call any medieval author a feminist. However, female characters may well be active, political and sympathetic. Cordelia's independence of spirit is clear from a pen-and-wash illustration in the margins of Matthew Paris' thirteenth-century *Chronica Maiora*, which also depicts Diana's prophecy to Brutus. Cordelia is shown standing apart from her sisters, who make flattering gestures towards Lear. She holds a scroll, which reads, '*Tant as, tant vauz, tant te pris pere*' ('Such as you have, such as you are worth, so I take you, father'). Lear's journey to wisdom is initiated by his daughter and, in the hands of Geoffrey of Monmouth, she lives to see herself understood by her father, if not by her rebellious subjects.

10

Conwenna saves Britain

*Remember the womb of your mother, in which the Creator of
all things fashioned you . . . bringing you forth in the world
while the birth-pangs tore at her vitals because of you.*

Geoffrey of Monmouth,
The History of the Kings of Britain (c. 1136)

Cordelia's nephews split the kingdom between themselves.
The realm north of the Humber came to be governed by
Marganus, and the southern part by Cunedagius. However, within a few years, Marganus, who was the eldest,
wanted to be King of all Britain. To this end, he invaded
Cunedagius' kingdom. On their journey south, his soldiers
razed every village they passed to the ground. News came
to Cunedagius as smoke on the wind and he rode out with
such force that Marganus fled to Wales. Cunedagius caught
him, killed him and took his throne.

Those were the days of the Prophet Isaiah, and when
Romulus and Remus founded Rome. Some generations

after Marganus and Cunedagius, another pair of brothers made war. Their names were Belinus and Brennius.

They say blood is thicker than water, but it flows thin for a crown.

The troops advanced across the plain, drowning out the sounds of lambs and birds with the clanking of their weapons. Trepidation hung in the air like mist. In the fear of it all, no one paid attention to an old woman slipping between the ranks. She was wearing a hooded cloak, so at a glance she looked like one of the peasants who collected fallen arrows. If any of the soldiers had looked under her hood, he would have seen tears creeping from her eyes, though her gaze was steady and her jaw was set. She would not be stopped. Conwenna was making her way to the middle of the field as fast as her arthritic legs could carry her.

The rule of the Britons had passed to a man called Belinus. He was beautiful like a lark. His younger brother, Brennius, was beautiful like a raven. And while both men were trained in body and mind for battle, where Belinus was placid, Brennius was tempestuous. And just as they had fought when they were children, so they fought now: because Brennius had started it and would not back down.

Belinus was king because he was the eldest. But Brennius was jealous. He waged war against his brother and it lasted many years. Soon their friends asked to negotiate for peace.

They decided that King Belinus would primarily govern the regions that are now England, Wales and Cornwall. Brennius would rule over the region that is now Scotland, and recognise Belinus as his overlord. The treaty held for all of five years.

Brennius once again grew jealous of his brother's supremacy and began, once again, to pitch battles against him. As before, Belinus fought back; Brennius was expelled from Britain and exiled to Gaul, but he did not stay there long. While Belinus oversaw the construction of great roads interconnecting all the cities, on which he decreed that no violence could be committed, Brennius ingratiated himself with a Gaulish king and married his daughter.

With the resources of that kingdom now at his disposal, Brennius mustered an army and brought it to the shores of Britain. This time, he knew it would be different. This time, he brought with him the might of Gaul. He was right, of course: it would be different, but not in the way he expected.

The men had stopped marching now and were holding their formation. Somewhere a horn was being blown, readying the troops for battle. In their ranks, Conwenna was the only moving thing: a brown beetle wending its way through a field of iron spears. Ahead, Belinus and Brennius were striding towards each other. When were fewer than twenty paces apart, they stopped and drew their swords.

At that moment, the small, cloaked figure broke out of the first row of Brennius' troops. She cried in a thin voice, and threw a hand forward, gesturing to them to wait. The brothers stared over in surprise, staying guards who had sprung forward at the sound. The brothers knew that voice. When Conwenna reached Brennius, she pulled his helmeted head towards her and began kissing his bare skin, his cheeks, his eyes and his chin, sobbing in earnest. He did nothing to resist. Around them, his soldiers exchanged looks.

Then the old woman stepped backwards, threw back her cloak and tore open her dress. Short as a child she stood, and naked to the navel, the mushroom flesh of her stomach pushed against her waistband, the skin of her breasts soft below her aged face and hands. She spoke to her younger son and her voice was like a dove.

'Brennius! Think of the breasts that soothed you. Think of the womb that formed you and the tearing agony I suffered to bear you. Think of all the worry I will have wasted on you, if you do not make peace with your brother. You have no case against him. You started this fight without good cause. Now I am telling you to end it.'

Brennius stood still in Conwenna's rheumy gaze. He could not remember ever seeing her naked. She had always been proud, silk-clad and distant, nothing like the vulnerable woman before him, at the very moment of war. Ever so slowly, he sheathed his sword, raised his hands and pulled the helmet from his head. Behind him, his troops followed suit, with a noise like a waterfall. With steady steps, he walked towards his brother.

Belinus was wary, with good reason. He did not at first loosen his grip on his weapons. But once they were standing face to face, a familiar expression passed across his younger brother's features. And they were back in their childhood home, stained with mud and tears. The downcast eyes, the pressing together of the lips. The furtive nod. Now, as then, it was momentous. An apology.

Belinus threw down his sword, pulled off his helmet, and the lark and the raven embraced. Conwenna's sons looked at her once before disappearing in a mass of men, but she needed no thanks. She shivered, drew her cloak around herself and, picking her way back through the thousand redundant spears, took herself away.

❖

As the *Brut* tradition would have it, the reconciled Belinus and Brennius go on to share the crown of Britain. Together, they conquer Gaul, followed by Italy and Rome. It is said they both build monuments that bear their names. Belinus builds Billingsgate in the walls of the New Troy, while, according to the later fourteenth-century *Romance of Fulk Fitzwarin*, Brennius builds a castle on a hill beside the River Dee and calls it Castell Dinas Bran.

Brennius' name preserves the Celtic noun *Bran*, meaning 'raven' or 'crow', and appears frequently in Celtic history and myth. Brennius may be inspired by the historical Gaulish chieftain Brennus, who captured Rome in the fourth century BC. As for Belinus, it has been suggested he is a mortal iteration of the Celtic god Belenus, honoured by the Celtic May Day feast of Beltane, evidence of whose cult, closely bound to that of the sun god Apollo, has been found across Romano-Celtic Europe. Alternatively, a Welsh translation of Geoffrey's *History* uses variants of the names Belinus and Brennius that suggest they are euhemerisations of the rival Celtic gods Beli and Bran. It may well be that, in Geoffrey's hands, or in those of earlier historians and bards, the deities were made mortal in the same way as the

Norse gods were under Snorri Sturluson. Whatever the case may be, by the later Middle Ages, Geoffrey's treatment of the warring royal brothers Belinus and Brennius placed them firmly in the canon of legendary British kings.

That the kings and queens of the *Brut* tradition were not once as obscure as they are to us now is shown by the casual allusions to them in contemporary poetry. For instance, a fourteenth-century poem called *St Erkenwald*, set during the episcopacy of Erkenwald, Bishop of London until 693, tells of the discovery of an ancient sarcophagus under the foundations of St Paul's Cathedral. The tomb is made from white marble, with gargoyles carved at its corners and a cryptic inscription in gold lettering on its surface that none can read. Upon opening the tomb, its finders behold the incorrupt body of a man in costly robes. Erkenwald is called upon to decipher the mystery. The dead man wakes up and tells him that he was a judge, good and fair, in the days of King Belinus. He moans with sadness, because he missed the journey to heaven made by all the good pagans who had been languishing in hell in the years prior to Christ's resurrection. Upon hearing his testimony, the Bishop Erkenwald weeps and prays, inadvertently baptising the dead pagan. The judge is redeemed and his body turns to dust.

The *St Erkenwald* poet indicates the corpse's goodness in life by identifying him as having been a judge in the age of the just King Belinus. In Geoffrey's *History of the Kings of Britain*, Belinus is said to have 'ratified the laws which his father had drawn up. He proclaimed that justice should be administered fairly throughout the kingdom.' Evidently the later *St Erkenwald* poet assumed an audience familiar with the legendary Kings of Britain and their defining characteristics.

Medieval readers must have remembered, too, the audacity of Conwenna (or Tonwenna). Only one artistic depiction of her survives (*Brut* texts are rarely illustrated): in a thirteenth-century copy of Geoffrey of Monmouth's *History of the Kings of Britain*, in Clare College, Cambridge (MS 27). The sprightly marginal scene on folio 36 shows her wearing a crown and a wimple. Her right arm encircles Brennius' neck and her face is held to his. She is pulling open her robes, revealing aged breasts. Both she and her wayward son wear an expression of consternation. Behind them, good King Belinus is gesturing, the mittens of his chainmail hanging loosely at his wrists, his helmet, sword and shield abandoned on the floor. Soldiers on horseback, still holding their weapons, flank the family. All the salient details of the story are present in this scene: her royalty, the incongruity of her act with the modesty of the noblewoman, the proximity of battle, Brennius' confusion and resignation. It is characteristic of the way in which medieval artists could distil textual narrative into dynamic visual vignettes.

There is a significant parallel to the Conwenna episode in Book 22 of Homer's *Iliad* (630 BC, or before), when Queen

Hecuba halts her son Hector on the ramparts of Troy, uncovering her pacifying breast and pleading with him not to fight: 'Hector, my child, this is the breast that fed you: respect and pity me.' Conwenna, the most noble women in the land, in Geoffrey's *History of the Kings of Britain* makes a comparable plea:

> With trembling steps she came to the place where Brennius stood, threw her arms round his neck and kissed him repeatedly with all a mother's love. She bared her breasts before him and in a voice broken with sobbing she spoke to him as follows: 'Remember, my son, remember these breasts which once you sucked.'

But the women's deeds are shocking not because their breasts are obscene or sexual. They are shocking because here are two mighty queens revealing the intimate humanity of their motherhood. The breasts of Hecuba and Conwenna are not the bawdy bosoms of the medieval *Fabliaux Erotiques* or *The Canterbury Tales*. Their breasts are the means by which the women once soothed their sons in infancy and, now, when the anger of adult men threatens to consume them, and all their people besides, they have become their last political resort. However, unlike Hecuba, whose son ignores her plea and is killed by Achilles, Conwenna's maternal bosom saves Britain from civil war.

11

The Throne of Scone

He accepted the stone as a precious gift bestowed on him by
the gods and as a sure omen he would be king . . . as if they
had absolutely handed both the kingdom and the crown over
to him. He also received a prophecy about it from his gods . . .

> *'If destiny deceives not, the Scots will reign 'tis said*
> *In that same place where the stone has been laid.'*

Walter Bower, *Scotichronicon* (c. 1437–49)

The coast of Hibernia was approaching, and Simon Brecc
had the anchor dropped and the boats readied to take the
people to shore. They were the last of the Scotti who had
remained in Spain since the days of Scota and Gaythelos
and their son Hyber. But in all that time they had never
known peace from their neighbouring kingdoms. They had
sailed to Orkney, where they had met Gurguint, the son
of Belinus and King of the Britons, and he had told them
to come here, to the island where their ancestor Hyber
had founded a new kingdom, many generations before.

But as they readied to disembark, the winds began to rise and the green sea to turn brown. Foam amassed in ridges and waves rolled in from the horizon, butting the hull like frothy-headed rams. The gulls cawed in warning as Simon Brecc seized the anchor chain. He had to sail the ship out of the shallows, into the calmer deeps.

The crew joined him at the chain, but the anchor was hard to move, as if an unseen force were pinning it down. They had heard of monsters at sea and their fear rose with the wind. But the passengers came to help and they dragged on the chain as one, feeling the anchor lift, until, at last, it was leaving the seething water and crashing against the ship. When it swung into view, they saw what had made it so heavy.

The object dripping through the air before them, darker than the slate-grey sky, encrusted with barnacles and garlanded with kelp, was a magnificent marble throne. Despite the crashing waves, the battering of the wind and the unchecked movement of the ship, the company watched in wonder, keeping desperate hold of the chain, guiding it gently and setting the throne down on the deck. Calm was returning to the sky and to the waves, and as the sails were unfurled and the ship steered towards the safety of the sound, the throne shed squirming creatures, hermit crabs and shrimp, onto the sodden boards.

When they brought the marble throne onto the land, Simon Brecc felt the same deep calm that Hyber had felt at the sight of an island designated for his people. And in the days that followed, in which the throne was set on the Hill of Tara, he heard a prophecy from the gods. It promised that, wherever Simon Brecc's throne stood, the Scotti would rule. And the prophecy was never forgotten.

❖

How the marble throne discovered by Simon Brecc ended up in the sea in the first place is not fully explained by the textual record. Both late medieval chronicles of Scottish legend, John of Fordun's *Chronicle of the Scottish Nation* and Walter Bower's *Scotichronicon*, suggest that it was among the pieces of furniture brought from the palaces of Egypt by Gaythelos. Within the fiction of the narrative, we might imagine the dark grey Egyptian marble thrones, inscribed with hieroglyphics, as depicted beneath seated figures in Ancient Egyptian sculptures. We might imagine it toppling overboard during one of King Hyber's trips between Iberia and Hibernia. Whatever the origins of the throne, however, it is associated with the Throne of Scone, or Stone of Destiny, used in the coronation of Scottish monarchs for generations. In 1296 it was removed to Westminster by Edward I and not returned to Scotland until exactly seven hundred years later.

We come now to a period in which the populations of Hibernia (Hyber's people) start to have designs on the north of Albion (as it is called in the Scottish chronicles). After the arrival of Simon Brecc, ships full of a people called the 'Picts' arrive in Hibernia (Ireland). They say they come from Aquitania, fleeing war, and that they are seeking a homeland. The Scotti reply that their own land is full, but the northern coast of Albion is empty. If the Picts settle it, promising to choose their kings from the maternal line, they may take their choice of wives from among the Scotti. The Picts accept and depart for Albion, foreign wives in tow.

The British account of the same legend casts the allegiance of the Scotti and Picts in a less innocent light. Geoffrey of Monmouth's *History of the Kings of Britain* describes how the Picts are invited to help the Britons defeat a usurper. At the last moment, they treacherously switch sides, and the usurper, victorious by their aid, gives them lands in the north. According to the British record, the presence of other principalities in the far north of Britain is thus little short of an invasion.

What the stories agree on is that the Picts sought wives from among the Scotti of Hibernia, bringing the descendants of Scota to the northern reaches of Britain.

12

Dragons under Oxford

The second Fortunate Concealment: the Dragons in Dinas
Emrys, which Lludd son of Beli concealed.

The Welsh Triads

(written down in the thirteenth century)

In the days of King Lludd, the Britons had been invaded by
a fairy race with such good hearing that they could detect
any words caught by the breeze. Try as the people might,
they could devise no plan to expel them without being
found out. Even worse, the invaders were one of three
dreadful plagues afflicting the Britons, each as terrible as
the last.

King Lludd, a good king, sought advice from his
brother Llefelys, who ruled Gaul and who possessed marvellous wisdom. They met in the middle of the Channel
and to avoid detection, Llefelys whispered the solution to
each of the plagues down the barrel of a horn. That way,
his words would be protected from the breeze.

Lludd listened, taking care to cover the mouth of the horn, so the sound went only into his ears. At first, he could only hear insults, but upon pouring wine into the mouth of the horn, they expelled a demon that had been altering his brother's words. Once that obstruction had been cleared, Lludd learned everything he needed to know. The siblings waved each other farewell and Lludd crept back to the Thames.

Following his brother's advice, the King of the Britons trapped and dried magical insects. He bruised their shells with a pestle and stirred the dust into water. Llefelys said the potion would be safe for the Britons but deadly to the fairy race. So Lludd called everyone to an assembly, as if to broker peace, but instead he poured the insect water over the assembled masses. The Britons gasped and spluttered. The invaders blistered and died. Thus the first plague was defeated, but still two more remained.

The second plague had arrived years earlier, on the eve of May Day. It came as a scream, which struck the air and rushed into the cracks in people's ceilings and walls. They pressed their hands over their ears, not knowing up from down, and some felt their hearts would rupture from the noise. The strongest men became feeble, and pregnant women miscarried in the street. Up and down the land the same damage was done to the young of animals and the chicks in birds' eggs. Blossoms, unvisited by the bees, fell to the ground and dead fish breasted the surfaces of rivers and lakes from Orkney to Land's End. The same scream returned each year and no one had any notion why.

But Llefelys (who was wise) had whispered the answer down the horn. The scream was coming from a dragon being attacked by another dragon: a foreign invader. Her injuries were terrible and that was why she screamed. So Lludd set a trap beneath the ground in Oxford, at the very centre of the land, as his brother had instructed him to do, sinking a vast cauldron into the earth. Then the two dragons, the screaming native and the attacking foreigner, appeared suddenly over the heart of Britain, twisting in the sky with wings of scales and lightning breath. Lludd had filled the cauldron with mead and covered its mouth with a concealing cloth, so that, as the beasts fell from their fight, they did not see the cloth, nor the honeyed trap beneath, and that was how he caught them.

By the time the dragons had gorged the last drop of mead, they were curled in the cauldron like kittens, their sticky eyelids closed. Lludd watched from beneath his brows as the pair submitted to sleep, transforming into pigs.

At this, Lludd climbed into the vessel, like a bee in a nectarous flower that would eat him whole if he put one foot wrong. He folded the cloth around the sleeping pigs, which until recently had been dragons. Then he heaved them to the surface. They grunted. He paused. They slept on.

Lludd stowed the pigs in a wagon and drove them west, into wilderness. This was far from his city, once the New Troy, but which he had renamed London after himself. Crossing the Severn, the home of Locrin's daughter, he entered the land of Eryri, of wooded peaks and weather that was wet and windy. Then, following his brother's advice, he passed roaring waterfalls and forded torrential streams, making for the hill called Dinas Ffaraon Dandde, or the 'Fort of the Fiery Pharaoh'. He reached the summit and saw before him the covering of a tomb. Placing the pigs in two stone chests that stood beside the tomb, he located the mouth of a pit and threw them into the abyss. As he sealed the opening, the rock beneath him shook, but

Lludd thanked the gods; the dragons' mouths were muffled by the hill's stony hand.

Lludd struck out for home, for London, where the final plague awaited him. He passed through the countryside, lashed by rain, and wondered whether he would survive this last ordeal. Llefelys, who could see things others could not, had told him what to do, but this time his instructions were more daunting than ever. Lludd set his beetle brows and made his way. When he arrived in the city, people were lighting their lamps and climbing their stairs to bed, but Lludd would not be sleeping.

He had always been a generous king, sharing his food with the poor, but one night, some years earlier, just after his stores of food and drink had been refilled, all the food had disappeared. His servants had replenished the empty barrels. But again, after just one night, the supplies vanished. The guards stayed up to watch for an intruder, but they reported neither thief nor vermin. They insisted the food was being swallowed by the air.

Still sticky from the mead, damp from the mountains and exhausted from both, Lludd reached the palace. He instructed the guards to stand down. This time, he would keep watch. Following his brother's advice, he fetched a barrel of water. Then, settling himself in view of the food-stores, he waited and he peered. According to Llefelys' words, spoken down the barrel of the horn, the guards had not seen the thefts because a spell was putting them to sleep. And indeed, as the night deepened, Lludd's mind began to swim. Soporific music threatened to close his eyes. But whenever these visions arrived, he plunged his head into the water, emerging awake and dripping. So the night went on, so he remained wakeful, until he saw the thief.

A huge man entered the larder, carrying a basket and decked head to toe in armour, so that little of his skin could be seen. With ease, he scooped up handfuls of grain, singing and chuckling, tossing whole hams in his mouth and swigging from flagons of wine.

Lludd leapt out, his sword drawn, and ordered the giant to stop. Peas tinkled from the thief's hand.

And Lludd sprang towards him, and he dropped his basket of food. Then they fought among the onions and grains. They battled so ferociously that sparks flew, reflected in glass and metal. Lludd felt like a minnow in combat with a pike. But he ascended a pile of sacks, which toppled and threw him forward, and he caught the giant by the neck. He pressed his sword against it.

Lludd agreed to spare the giant's life in exchange for his service. And that's how the Britons became free from the plagues. And Lludd reigned in peace till he died and was buried by London's city wall. The place that was known thereafter as Ludgate.

❖

The tales of the *Mabinogion,* on which the above story was based, blend history with dream vision, myth, folklore and more besides. They are among the most disarming, vivid, mind-bending pieces of vernacular literature to survive from medieval Britain. Take, for instance, the Prince of Powys encountering other-worldly hounds while hunting in the forest:

> And of all the hounds he had seen in the world, he had never seen dogs of this colour – they were a gleaming, shining white and their ears were red. And as the whiteness of the dogs shone, so did the redness of their ears.

Llefelys' description of how Lludd will capture the dragons is no less mind-bending:

> When you get home, have the Island measured, its length and breadth, and where you find the exact centre, have that place dug up. And then into that hole put a vat of the best mead that can be made, and a sheet of brocaded silk over the top of the vat, and then you yourself keep watch. And then you will see the dragons fighting; and finally, when they are exhausted . . . they will fall onto the sheet in the shape of two little pigs, and make the sheet sink down with them, and drag it to the bottom of the vat, and they will drink all the mead, and after that they will sleep.

Like Beli and Bran, Lludd may be a euhemerisation of the Celtic deity Lugh. The mortal Lludd, as the one described above, is held to be the subject of prophetic poems dating to the latter part of the eleventh century, entitled *The Great Eulogy of Lludd* and, more prosaically, *The Short Discussion of Lludd*. This places his story among some of the earliest surviving writings in Welsh. From the twelfth century, 'Lud' appears in the *Brut* tradition as a descendant of Brutus, and gives London his name. From the mid-thirteenth century, the story of the plagues and Lludd's brother Llefelys features in Welsh translations of the *Brut* known as the *Brut y Brenhinedd*. He also crops up in *The Welsh Triads* (*Trioedd Ynys Prydein*): a kind of mnemonic for storytellers, clustering fragments of stories in groups of three. Finally, we find the fullest version of the story of Lludd and Llefelys in the aforementioned *Mabinogion*, which survives in two manuscripts, the White Book of Rhydderch, dated *c.* 1350, and the Red Book of Hergest, dated between *c.* 1381 and 1410 (held in the National Library of Wales and the Bodleian Library respectively).

The notion of dragons, drunk under Oxford (by some magic, the centre of the land) is wonderful. But the dragons' fight ties into a more serious theme that runs through many of the stories in the *Mabinogion*: that of invasion. Most of the stories are set in an age before the coming of the Saxons, but written when the British, by then known in English as the Welsh, had already been subject to dominance from

Rome. All three of the plagues defeated by Lludd manifest themselves as some sort of invasion. The fairy race, called 'the Coranians' in the *Mabinogion*, are all-hearing, an invasion into the world of private counsel. It has even been suggested that the Welsh name for them, the *Coroniaid*, is a confusion with *Cesariaid*, the name for the Romans. At the same time, the dragons constitute a kind of medieval ethnic cleansing, with the scream of the native dragon causing the women to miscarry. Finally, the giant strikes at the heart of the kingdom's staple resources, stealing stores of food. The Britons are, symbolically, left without privacy, heirs or sustenance. Whether inspired by Saxon, Roman or some other incoming force, the tale expresses the collective trauma of conquest.

The three deeds of Lludd – the drowning of the Coranians, the burial of the two dragons, and the subjugation of the giant – restore the kingdom to peace and plenty. But the dragons are not dead, and the Fort of the Fiery Pharaoh does not stay sealed forever, as you will read in time.

13

Deirdre Flees to Albany

But their number was also increased by an endless succession
of criminals, because anyone who was in fear of incurring
penalty of the law went off to live with the Picts scot-free.

Walter Bower, *Scotichronicon* (c. 1437–49)

The woman now sitting in a chamber of Emain, her head
on her knees, had screamed in the womb. Her scream had
inspired a prophecy that she would be the most beautiful
woman in the world, a woman like a flame, for whom men
would die. All the courtiers had pleaded for the infant to
be killed, but Conchobar, King of Ulster, had coveted her
future beauty. At her birth, he had given her to foster-
parents and raised her in the court, reserving her for his
pleasure. Now, many years later, the men had died just
as the prophet had foretold, but not on account of the
woman. Their deaths had been ordered by the King, and it
was she, not the court, who mourned their loss the most.
Deirdre sat, her food untouched, her bed not slept in.

She had not eaten for weeks. She was waiting for her own death now.

At that time, Albany in Northern Britain was a place to which the Scotti could flee when home was no longer safe. It was to there that Deirdre had escaped with Noisiu, whose hair had been black as the crow, whose skin had been white as the snow, and whose lips had been red as blood. She had found him on the ramparts of Emain, the nephew of the King, and had used all her skill to seduce him. They had left that night in a company of three hundred men and women.

At first they had stayed in Ireland, fending off Conchobar's attacks. It had been a time of fear and narrow escapes, until they had boarded ships, crossed the brimming sea, and learned the ways of the hollows and hills they found there; she wished she could have stayed forever. Each day, Noisiu and his brothers would lead the men in raids for food and mead, and she would work with the women, gathering bog myrtle from the banks of the loch, cradled by the arms of the mountains. And as each evening came, she would gaze into the forest, watching for him like a child.

When the day ended, the thrum of male voices would be heard beneath the women's conversation. Deirdre would run to the woodland edge, sending goldfinches fluttering to the sky, and there she would see the sons of Uisliu – Noisiu, with his brothers, Ardán and Anle – striding ahead of the other men, who had been gathering provisions: mountain game, mead from a farmstead, livestock if the forests yielded nothing. Noisiu, his dark hair lifted by the wind, and his cheeks flushed, would be carrying a barrel or a flask; Ardán would bear the carcass of a stag or a boar; Anle might be shouldering a roll of woven cloth or some other treasure. The glimmer of Noisiu's smile beneath the canopy of birch, the agile shadows on his face, would fill Deirdre with joy. He would see her, and while his brothers continued their jokes, his eyes would not leave hers. Each night, Deirdre and Noisiu would fill a pit in the forest with embers from the fire, bury the wrapped meat, and drag the earth back over it. They would confine the warmth and light to the ground as the hawthorn blossom fell, as if they were burying an angel. After that, she would wash him beside the fire, he would kiss her forehead, cheeks and lips, and they would escape to their tent. By the time they emerged, there would be bread to quell their hunger, fresh leaves and meat. Later, the mead would be shared, while Noisiu and his brothers sang. All could find their part by listening to their voices, but Deirdre would dance with her bare feet on the pebbles of the shoreline. To her, Noisiu's voice was like a wave of love and she adored him more than anything. When they at last went to bed, nourished by food and music and warmth, she would sleep in the crook of his body, with her head on his left arm and

his right hand enfolded in hers. And when he got up, she would watch him dress beside the birches.

That had been the time of beauty, Deirdre thought now, from her place on her knees, remembering Noisiu's kisses on her forehead. It had not lasted, for one day the men were caught stealing cattle and the whole company taken to the King of that part of Albany, which was the name of the land. Noisiu had offered himself and his men as soldiers to compensate for the theft, telling Deirdre to keep hidden, and the King had accepted their service. They made a new camp at his court.

Deirdre had stayed in their tent, with no more gold-finches, lakes or stars. She had counted the sewing loops in the canvas and the twists in the ropes that ran in and out of them. She had rejoiced when Noisiu returned for a night, only to brood with fear and frustration when he was sent away again to battle. Each day she would dress, cook, eat, wait, undress again and sleep, between her memories and her dreams, waiting for the hemmed-in days to pass.

They had been betrayed in the end. Deirdre did not know that the King's steward had been asked to spy on Noisiu, nor that the man saw her with him one night through an opening in their tent. When the steward had described her beauty to the King, he had wanted her for himself. Every day, the King would send her messages, asking for her to be his wife. Every day, she would refuse, and return to dressing, cooking, eating and sleeping, more fearful than ever before.

Soon she realised that the King would rather kill Noisiu than let her go, so she convinced her lover and his brothers to lead them in flight. Away they stole, till they had reached an island in the sea. But they were running into danger. Conchobar had hidden spies on the island, who alerted him at once, and he sent his barons as guarantors of peace, asking his nephew to return to Ireland, bringing the lovely Deirdre. She told Noisiu not to trust him, but Noisiu bore great faith in the old oaths and customs, and he insisted they go, despite her warnings. Was there anything she could have done to prevent what followed?

As their protectors departed, so Deirdre's dread deepened, for she detected the influence of the King.

Conchobar had Noisiu meet him at dawn, and so he did. As the first light fell, the women assembled on the ramparts and the men upon the green. Deirdre stood at the front, where, in the open, she was able to see Noisiu, flanked by Conchobar's men. Noisiu stepped forward to greet the King, and his shadow reached towards her.

A hand covered her mouth at the same moment that Noisiu's shadow broke in two. It had broken like a mast in a storm, like a twig under a wheel. One of the men with him had lunged out with his spear and thrust it into his spine. She tried to run forward, but even as one of Noisiu's allies shielded her lover's body with his own, pushing them both to the ground, the King's traitor thrust his spear in again, driving it through both their chests and holding it there till they were still. Deirdre was dragged away. And now here she was. The memories churned in her head and she ground her teeth in anguish. Every day had been the same since then.

She had been at Emain for many months, and King Conchobar had done everything in his power to restore her to happiness. He had taken her to see the troops returning to Emain, with trumpets and pipers playing wild, military songs. He had brought her the best mead, a favourite drink of his son. He implored her to do as the other women did, to stain her fingernails red and greet visitors to their court. She had refused. Deirdre knew he would never understand, because he had never seen beauty as she had. Lifting her head from her knees, she would sing to herself of Noisiu:

> I used to wash him clean by the fire
> And I used to watch him dress by the forest
> And we used to cook our meals in a hollow
> And we had nothing; and we had everything.
>
> Now you say beauty is in the music
> And in the metal of war,
> In troops and cavalry; you're deluded;
> I preferred the sea and I preferred the trees.

> Bring me the one with the hair as the crow
> And the softest snow-white skin.
> Show me lips as red as blood
> And I will show you love.

One day, Deirdre found herself being led out of her room to a chariot. She would be going to a fair, she was told. A king called Eogan, ruler of another part of Ireland, and King Conchobar were sitting ahead of her. On the journey, they laughed about who would take her in the end. She said that no men would have her now that Noisiu was dead. And Eogan replied that she had no more power than a ewe between two rams. Deirdre did not answer, for she had seen a great stone on the roadside.

As they drew near, she threw herself from the carriage. The stone was as hard as she had hoped it would be. Such was the force of the blow that her head was smashed to a mess of bone and blood, and Deirdre ended her suffering.

It is said that the loch beside which Deirdre and Noisiu lived and loved was called Etive, and the site of the camp was called Cadderlie. Perhaps they live there in death, where his song and her dancing feet may be heard on the shoreline. Or perhaps it is the wind over the waters. Or perhaps it is just the burn over stones.

❖

The legend of Deirdre and Noisiu (pronounced *Nee-shuh*) is traditionally set around the dawn of the first century AD and, for our purposes, represents an early example of the cultural communication between Northern Ireland and north-western Britain in medieval legend. The same is true of another Irish tale, *Buile Suibhne*, the protagonist of which is the son of the King of Ulster. Cursed with perpetual flight, he spends time on Ailsa Craig, off the coast of north-western Britain, and then travels to the mainland, where he lives for a year with a wild man of the forest.

In the Ireland portion of Deirdre's legend, the action centres on Emain Macha, a Bronze Age ring barrow in County Armagh now known in English as Navan Fort and long associated with the legendary Kings of Ulster. Tradition has it that, when Deirdre and Noisiu fled to Albany, they spent their time in Glen Etive, in west Scotland. There are place-names in Glen Etive that recall characters in the story. For instance, in some versions of the legend, Noisiu, son of Uisliu, is called Naoise, son of Uisneach. This iteration of his father's name is given to the island Eilean Uisneachan and the fort Dun Mac Uisneachan. There is also a wood to the south of Loch Etive called Coille Nathais, meaning 'Noisiu's forest'. Similarly, a burn and meadow known as Cadderlie lies on the northern shore of Loch Etive and has been so called since at least the fourteenth century. The name is believed to be Gaelic for the 'Burn at

Deirdre's Garden'. These are mysterious connections – hard to interpret or date with any precision – but they suggest that the story of Deirdre, like Deirdre herself, was not confined to Ireland.

On my visit to Cadderlie I discovered a tumbling burn of cold, peat-yellowed water, which a crease in the bed-rock funnels into the immense waters of the loch. There is a bothy in the woods beside the burn where you can stay the night, and a rope swing hangs from one of the moss-mantled trees, speaking of summers well spent. I met one or two visitors from Northern Ireland there, who like me had followed Deirdre to Glen Etive.

Deirdre is one of the most famous characters of the rich Irish mythological tradition. There are other versions of her tale. I have used the one given in the early cycle of myths concerning the Kings of Ulster: the *Táin Bó Cúailnge*, or 'Cattle Raid of Cooley'. It is more simply called *The Táin*. It is early, found in Irish manuscripts dating from the twelfth century. In *The Táin*, Deirdre recites a song, list-ing the many beauties she enjoyed while with Noisiu and the emptiness of those things valued by Conchobar. The freshness of the song's emotion, conveyed over so many hundreds of years, is, to me, a miracle. I would urge you to seek out the translation.

For our purposes, this legend marks the beginning of the movement of the descendants of Scota across the Irish

Sea. In the chapters to come, we will turn our attention back to the Britons, travelling from the first to the sixth century AD. We will witness the arrival of an Apostle and the resurrection of the red and white dragons, we will meet a child magician, and we will run with Arthur's hounds.

Part Three

Antiquity

14

Joseph of Arimathea

And since it was the first church in this land, the Son of God
distinguished it by fuller dignity, dedicating it in his own
presence in honour of his mother.

John of Glastonbury,
The Chronicle of Glastonbury Abbey (c. 1400)

When Christ was taken down from the cross, a tomb was
offered by a rich man called Joseph of Arimathea. Few
know now that this same Joseph travelled to Britain during
the reign of a king called Arviragus, or that the bones
of this same Joseph lie beneath the mists and willows of
Avalon. His grave was beside the wickerwork church that
he and his followers had built there.

When the community had assembled for the funeral,
his coffin was carried to the altar by four men and placed
on a trestle. When they lifted the lid, light mantled the
body, along with dampness from the shower of spring rain.
And this was seen, beyond the walls of the church, by an

old man who was watching, squinting through a gap in the wattle wall, and holding his breath. No one knew he was there. As one of the monks began to read Joseph's words from a book, he listened with all his might.

'It was the evening after our Lord was crucified. For burying him on the Sabbath, I was jailed, and I said my prayers in my cell. Then, though it was the middle of the night, I saw rays of light piercing the narrow fissures in the walls. By bringing my face to those fissures, I could see the wings of angels. Impossible though it seemed, they were carrying my prison to the sky. Then it seemed a man was standing before me. He held my hand, embraced me and cleaned the grime from my face with the corner of his robes. Then, again he kissed me, and said, "Don't be scared, Joseph. Can't you see who I am?"

'"Rabbi Elijah?" I replied.

'"I am Jesus, the one you buried."

'"Let me see the tomb," said I, for I did not believe it.

'The man took my hand, and we were back in the sepulchre.

'"Here is the shroud," he said, "and the cloth you wrapped round my head."

'I remembered. We had pressed down the flesh as we embalmed him. We had picked off the flies. Even after he had been washed, his forehead and temples were flayed, shining pink by the light of our lamps. His executioners had done their worst. And then I knew the man beside me was him, because I knew the profile of his skull from washing it. I knew his hair from combing out the blood. I knew his hands from folding them on his chest and touching the wounds that pierced them. I used Scripture because my own words had left me.

'"Blessed is he who comes in the name of the Lord."

'Jesus took my hand again, and transported me to the house of my childhood.

'"Hide here for forty days and don't be scared, for all will be well. Now I must go to my disciples."'

Still spying through the wattle wall, the old man was rapt. He did not belong to the community. He was just a Briton of the Avalon marshes. But he had been fascinated by these holy men since childhood, and especially by their leader, Joseph. As a boy he had witnessed a shining figure descend to him from the sky, in robes the colour of milk, and land at the base of the Tor. Having rushed to that place through the reeds, he had seen Joseph kneeling, his head bowed. Above him, hovering on wings of vapour, the messenger had instructed the community to build a place of worship and dedicate it to the Mother of God. Then, as Joseph had wept his gratitude, the being returned to the sky.

Ever since, the spy had come back as often as he could, hiding, watching and learning, and many years had passed and now he was old. In that time he had learned that the community ate modestly. They prayed constantly. They tended their garden and they cared for their sick. There were women among them. Women whom they treated as wives, but who lived with prayerfulness and modesty. More than once he heard talk of a secret treasure, perhaps the secret to their sanctity. But in all these years he had never discovered what it was. He hoped today would be different.

The reader was speaking now of how they had travelled to Britain with Joseph, sent by the Apostle Philip to spread the Word of God. They had sailed across the sea and King Arviragus had recognised their piety, though he refused to give up his gods. He had given them a place called the 'Glass Island', or 'Avalon'.

Then the angel of the Lord had come and given the company instructions, and they had gathered willow and woven the first church in Britain. They had pushed in stakes, bent whip and thatched the roof. Then Christ himself had appeared and dedicated the church to His Mother. The Risen Lord had stood among them, just as He had stood beside Joseph on the night of his death. His feet had pushed moisture from the turf, making the very water of Avalon holy. As the spy listened, his fingers on the willow, he thought he could feel vital blood pulsing under the bark.

And now the reader was closing his book and turning to open the Tabernacle, and the old man was pressing his eye so hard to the wattle that it was digging into his cheek. And as the reader reached up, the monks were praying in tongues and easing to their knees, until their bodies were obscuring the view. The spy searched for another hole in the willow, hoping to see what was to emerge from the depths of the Tabernacle, but, when he finally found one, it was too late. Whatever had been brought out had already been placed in the coffin, and now, with much chanting and burning of incense, the lid was being lowered. Tears spilled down his cheeks.

The next day, they buried Joseph beside the church on a sacred line in the soil, but none present knew what had happened the night before. The spy had stolen into the church and approached the lonely coffin with a lantern.

Full of trepidation, he had prised open the lid. And when he saw what lay inside, beside the body of Joseph, he had opened his eyes and mouth wide and hurried from the church. From that night until the night his soul left his body, the old spy uttered no more sound than a slow worm.

After the death of Joseph and those who had accompanied him to Britain, the group dispersed, finding homes among the Britons. Joseph's nephew had children, and their children bore children, until one came into the world who would give birth to a king, and that king would return to Avalon.

❖

A summer settlement, Somerset is still a marshy landscape, of reeds and willow. In winter, prior to modern drainage, the conical hill in the flat plain, called the Tor, would have stuck out of the wetlands like a knee in the bath. And by the late Middle Ages, the magnificent profile of Glastonbury Abbey would have been visible beside it. Today, upon entering its grounds, you are confronted with ruins so extensive that you would be forgiven for thinking the fragmentary walls ahead of you were two buildings end to end. In fact, they were one massive structure toppled during the sixteenth-century Dissolution of the Monasteries.

The grounds of Glastonbury Abbey contain gravesmarkers to lost monuments. At the north-west end of the ruin, in a navel in the grass, is a modern plaque. It reads: *Site of column set up to indicate the eastern limit of the original wattle church.* Joseph of Arimathea's legend has no discernible historical basis, but we know with some confidence that a wattle church once stood on this site and burned down in 1154. Archaeological excavations have revealed evidence of a settlement on the site by at least the sixth century. The fragile wooden structure may have dated from this period.

Whatever the real origins of the wattle church, the later monastic community at Glastonbury held it to be the earliest church in Britain, built by their legendary founder, Joseph of Arimathea, and dedicated by Christ himself. The source for my retelling is a history of Glastonbury Abbey, written *c.* 1400 by one John of Glastonbury. Partaking happily in a venerable tradition of making things up, I have inserted the character of the spy.

John of Glastonbury claims to have derived his material from the Gospel of Nicodemus, found, he says, in the council chamber of Pontius Pilate. He likewise cites a prophet called Melkin when giving the location of Joseph's grave: '[Joseph] lies . . . next to the oratory's southern corner, where the wickerwork is constructed . . . Joseph has with him in the sarcophagus two white and silver vessels, full of the blood and sweat of the Prophet Jesus.' A more significant source for John was Robert de Boron's thirteenth-century Continental French story of Joseph of

Arimathea, the *Estoire dou Graal* (or *History of the Grail*). It follows the journey of the Holy Grail from the place of the crucifixion of Christ to Britain's mythical Isle of Avalon, which came to be associated with Glastonbury Tor. John of Glastonbury doesn't say whether he thinks the two vessels buried with Joseph are the Holy Grail. So popular was the notion of the Grail Quest by the early fifteenth century that he did not have to.

After Joseph's death, Christianity is said to have fallen away until the reign of King Lucius (in the middle of the second century AD), while the place of his burial returned to being a haunt of wild beasts. The Tor was Joseph's headstone, and his church no more than a willow web in a wilderness. But his line endured, according to legend, generation giving way to generation, until the birth of a girl called Igraine. She might have passed into obscurity had she not attended a feast at the court of Uther Pendragon, as you will soon read. But there is some way to go before that story, for soon the Saxons will be crossing the North Sea and, with a weak king on the throne, much will be at stake for the Britons.

So why not locate the Grail at the foot of Glastonbury Tor, where the Chalice Well gushes and the fragments of an ancient wattle church imbue the marshy soil? Why not look to the Somerset Levels, with their murmurations of starlings and stands of osier's willow? If I were to hide the Holy Grail, I would certainly hide it there.

15

The Red and White Dragons

Then one of them said: 'I can't make seed or conceive a child in a woman, but there's one among you who could, and I know a woman who's somewhat in my power. Let the one who can take the shape of a man do so in utmost secrecy.' And so the demons plotted to conceive a man who would work to deceive others.

Robert de Boron, Merlin (c. 1200)

The story of Merlin could be said to have begun nine months before his birth, in the closed cell of St Peter's, Carmarthen, with a girl sitting on her bed waiting for darkness to fall. She was the daughter of the King of Dyfed, and that night her actions would change the course of history. As with so many like her, her name has been forgotten.

Maybe she would tell you it started earlier, when she entered the convent as a child, before her body and her mind changed. When they did, she felt desires of which she was neither able nor permitted to speak. It followed that there was a time when she thought this hunger would melt her away to nothing. The meals, the prayers, the shelter, the vocation: they were not enough. She yearned to be close to another human in ways her community did not allow. But it was only when her lust – for that was what it was – had reached such a pitch of fever that she feared she would die, that the impossible happened.

She had entered her cell one evening, had said her prayers and extinguished the light, when by the meagre beam of the moon she had seen him. He walked across to her, stooped and kissed her neck and shoulders, and, although she had dreamed of such kisses, she was startled and pushed him away. At this he had disappeared. All the

next day she cursed herself for her fear. If only she had let the vision stay.

But all was not lost. The vision returned that night, but this time only as a voice speaking gently out of the darkness. She found herself much comforted by their conversation. He promised to come back the next night, and the night after that. And that is what he did.

Pushing from her mind the caresses of their first encounter, the girl told herself he was a vision sent by God to save her from her loneliness and longing. Each night she returned to her cell and found his voice answering her there, appearing only once the doors were locked and the darkness deep. She poured out her heart to him, telling him of her royal childhood, raised away from the streets and forests in which the other children played. She told him of when her parents had left her in the convent. She told him, in whatever words she could find, of how it felt to grow up and know her desires were ones she could never fulfil. By speaking to him as she did, she found that each day she was able to perform her religious duties more fully. Surely he was sent by God. She asked him if it was so.

And then the visitor had begun to tell his story. It started in heaven, he said, where there was no such thing as want. Everything had been overflowing, but none were as high as the Most High. They taught themselves to want His throne. Then there had been a war in heaven. The rebels had lost the war, and then they had been sent to hell.

Just as heaven had been plentiful, so in hell, the visitor said, there was nothing but longing. If you longed for food, you would hover on the edge of starvation. If you longed for a loving touch, you would know nothing but neglect. He had known nothing but neglect since he had fallen from heaven.

The girl, who thought she knew suffering, heard in the visitor's voice a pain that hers could never equal. The pity it roused within her caused her to reach out into the darkness, hoping to grasp his hand, but she felt nothing there. Still, above the beating of her heart, she discerned his stifled weeping. And whispering, trembling, she told him to come back tomorrow. She would be ready for him then.

And so it was that the very next evening she sat on the edge of her bed as darkness fell. And so it was that, on that night, and for many nights after, she shared herself with a spirit. And so it was that Merlin was conceived.

Some ten years passed, and Merlin was playing a ball game with his friends outside the walls of Carmarthen. These were the days of King Vortigern, the new summer was hot and the sun was squinting down on the town like the eye of a tyrant.

Behind them a troop of soldiers were resting from their travels. They were finely dressed in colourful clothes, and their horses' bridles were trimmed with gold. The soldiers heard the children taunting the smallest among them for having no father, repeating the taunt, leaving the soldiers in no doubt. This is what the men had been searching for.

The soldiers went over to the child with no father and asked bystanders if what his playmates said was true. They told them it was so, and that the child's mother, daughter of a king, lived with a community of nuns in the church of St Peter's. The soldiers soon obtained the town governor's permission to take both mother and boy to the King.

The pair travelled north with the soldiers, and around them the hills grew hillier and the sky cloudier. Streams fell in skeins from precipices, fracturing the dark skyline, while the trees craned their branches away from the unrelenting wind. Merlin's mother wondered what the soldiers could want with her son.

When he was born, she had pleaded with the nuns not to throw them out. She had confessed his demonic origins, arguing that to raise him outside the House of God would be to give the devil free rein with his soul. The women had been convinced, and had raised a boy who was good and kind, though there was no denying his powers, nor his ungodly fascination with wild things, nor his mischievous nature. Now he was riding in watchful silence, taking in the towering pines and the banks of mountains ahead. Whatever lay in store for him now, his mother would have to trust his ingenuity to see him through.

After several days they reached the foothills of a great mountain. One foothill stood apart from the others, a lonely hillock beside a lake, and could be approached via a sloping path that passed before roaring waterfalls and over tumultuous streams.

They reached the top of the hill, where bony oaks receded, giving way to thin grass and bare rock. Everywhere about them were strewn building materials and the apparatus for moving them. In the midst of them all were the beginnings of a tower. Beside that stood a colourful tent. The effect was incongruous. Its red panels flapped, a circle of bright streamers cavorted from its apex and an armoured guard glittered at the door. The soldiers took them inside.

King Vortigern was nothing like his trappings. The dyed furs across his shoulders and the rich blanket over his legs made his face look as grey as a puddle. Once, he must have been handsome. He still had a strong, angular jaw, but his eyebrows hung low, as though his crown were too heavy for his face.

He beheld his visitors. Then he asked Merlin if he were indeed the boy with no human father. A scribe stood behind the King, with an ivory stylus and tablet clamped to his chest. His fingers tightened.

Merlin replied that he was, and upon further questioning his mother parted with the story of his conception.

Scratching his throat with his stylus, the scribe, whose name was Maugantius, confirmed her tale with words from Apuleius' *Demon of Socrates*.

'Between the moon and the earth,' he said, 'is a realm occupied by spirits called incubi. They are partly human, partly angelic, and can assume human form and lie with women.'

Then Vortigern began to laugh, his forehead pleating under his crown. He was building a tower, he told them, but each night the day's progress would be swallowed up by the earth. Each night the tower would crumble to the ground. His magicians had sent for a boy with no human father, because, as they said, only by spilling the blood of such a boy would Vortigern's tower cease to collapse. And now he was relieved, because it seemed they had found the boy. Merlin's mother cried out in horror at Vortigern's words and at the thought of spilling her dear son's blood, but the soldiers dragged her away, taking her back to Carmarthen.

Merlin was not intimidated. He challenged Vortigern's magicians, asking them why, for all their glittering robes and bejewelled fingers, they could not divine the real cause of the crumbling tower. He said that it would be found if Vortigern had his men dig below the foundations. Curious to see if the boy was right, Vortigern consented to follow his instructions.

Now the boy and the King stood at the edge of a deepening pit and Vortigern was feeling uncomfortable: not just because of his gout, or the prospect of what lay beneath the foundations, but because events were reaching a culmination that had been set in motion many years ago. Sharpening his sword at the edge of his mind was the figure of Aurelius Ambrosius . . .

Vortigern had not inherited his crown. As a young man, he had entered the court of Aurelius' father, King Constantine. He had learned how to be a baron. He had learned the art of flattery. When Constantine died, Vortigern formed a plan. He encouraged the eldest son, Constans, to succeed his father. The boy was reluctant, because he was a monk, and monks were not meant to be kings. Then again, his younger brothers, Aurelius and Uther, were only infants.

With carefully chosen words, Vortigern won Constans round – his was a limp soul, fond of praise. And because Vortigern could find no bishops willing to perform the coronation, he was forced to do it himself. And King Constans came to depend on Vortigern. He trusted him. He relied upon him. He relinquished his power to him. He did not wonder how it was that the older barons of the court had begun to disappear or die in recent months, leaving only a band of greenhorn youths to resist Vortigern's slow ascent. In time, Constans agreed to sign over all his treasure to Vortigern's care, to better protect it from the threat of outsiders. Vortigern fabricated a tale of a Danish and Norwegian invasion, which scared Constans more than anything. He told him that, to deter the invaders further, they should swell the ranks of the court by bringing in a company of Picts.

Constans wept at the prospect of a Norwegian attack and thanked Vortigern piteously for his counsel. As for the Picts, of course, he bid them come. When they did, he showed them all the hospitality he could offer. And Vortigern obeyed. He threw the mercenaries feasts at which their cups were never empty. Night after night, they proclaimed him 'kingly', even in the streets, which they roamed after nightfall.

One evening, at yet another feast, Vortigern stood up beneath the embroidered hangings. The Pictish revellers fell silent. They watched him, marking the mournful look in his eyes. Vortigern had not touched a drop of wine that night, though he pretended he had. He raised his cup and swayed. As he spoke, his voice cracked.

'It pains me to say that I will not see you again, dear Picts. I must depart Britain in search of a better life. My income from the King is not enough even to maintain fifty knights. Indeed, I can no longer maintain you. It is a tragedy, but I find myself forced to leave.'

There was uproar. One man stood up and shouted, 'Your "king" doesn't know he's born!'

Another said, 'It should be you on the throne!'

'Leave it to us!' they cried together, with murder in their eyes.

Vortigern bowed to them all and shortly afterwards he left the feast altogether, though if the Picts could have felt the excitement in his gut, they would have known they had been used. They only discovered their folly when, having ambushed and killed poor Constans, Vortigern had them rounded up, condemned and beheaded. Vortigern's head took the crown. He screwed it in place himself.

At the accession of Vortigern, Constans' younger brothers, Aurelius and Uther, were taken to Brittany, which the Britons had long ago populated, to be raised in the household of its king. And Vortigern knew he would have to protect himself from them in time, but he could no longer depend on help from the Picts. Thus it was that he came to accept the help of the Saxons, led by the royal brothers, Hengist and Horsa, though in the end they only augmented his problems.

Let me tell you about Hengist and Horsa. They are remembered for their fine clothes, their height, their fair hair and their skin, so much paler than that of the Britons. Hengist and Horsa were descended from Wecta, King of East Saxland and the eldest son of Woden, who had come to the North from Troy with his second sight and great ambition. Elegant and kingly, migrants from an overpopulated country, Hengist and Horsa offered their service in exchange for land. Greeting them from his court in Canterbury, Vortigern let them in. When they helped him win a war against the Picts, outperforming the Britons in the army, he bestowed on them much of the territory of Lindsey. And by other tricks and wiles, Hengist won more land for his people.

One evening, as Vortigern sat on his colourful throne, the Saxons at his side, Hengist's daughter Ronwen walked naked into the room. She approached, barefoot on the rush matting. Then she raised a golden cup.

'*Wassail.*'

Be well.

This was a customary greeting among the Saxons. An interpreter leant close to Vortigern's ear. 'You must reply with *Drinchail.*'

Drink well.

'Then you exchange kisses.'

Vortigern said the customary words and drank from the cup. Then Ronwen stepped forward and kissed him.

So enraptured was he by Ronwen that Vortigern did not care that she spurned the Christian God in favour of Apollo, Mercury and Jupiter. He wanted to marry her and sleep with her that night. He asked Hengist if it could be so. In return for her hand, her father Hengist requested the province of Kent, and Vortigern agreed without hesitation. And that's one of the ways in which the Saxons took root, but it was only the start of all the trouble that would ensue.

After they were married, Ronwen turned against Vortigern. She and Hengist used their new power to bring more of their people to Britain. And when Vortigern's son led the unhappy Britons in revolt, even seizing the throne for a short time, Ronwen had him poisoned. Vortigern, caught between the two factions, was fearful of war, and his only alternative was to foster peace. He invited both sides, Saxons and Britons, to a feast near the town of Amesbury.

Many hundreds of warriors intermingled on the benches, and the young barons of Vortigern's court, whose fathers and uncles had disappeared or died when Constans had first taken the throne, picked with suspicion at their food. Then, at a shout from Hengist – 'Take your knives!' – the Saxons seized daggers from their waistbands and plunged them into the bowels of the men beside them. Of the Britons at the feast, only Vortigern and the Earl of Gloucester escaped alive. Earl Eldof got out fighting, killing many Saxons as he went. Vortigern's life was spared because he relinquished as many castles and fortresses to the Saxons as they asked for. Then the Britons were buried in that place, and Vortigern went to Wales, far from the Saxon strongholds.

And this was why he was here in Eryri, on the foothills of a mountain, beside the child Merlin, building a fortified tower.

Below him, one of the workers cried out. Then more cries, followed by the splash of rocks in water. Vortigern leant over the precipice, his crown creeping down his brow. Merlin was leaning too. A pool had been revealed at the bottom of the pit. The boy told the King to have it drained.

For the rest of that day, and the next, they watched as workers dug a gully in the summit of the hill, causing the water to run slowly into the lake in the valley below. Slowly, two stone chests began to emerge. When their lids were pushed away, the onlookers saw the spines of two great creatures. One was white, like a pale salamander, while the other was red, like an earthworm. As their backs dried, they began to writhe, lifting up their heads on long, winding necks, and biting at the air. And then the dragons started to fight, released from the captivity they had endured since the days of Lludd. The milky one charged forward and the red flew back in fear. Then she coiled back round, snapping her jaws, till the white one was forced to retreat. With terrible speed, the pair clawed their way out of the hole and flew into the sky. Vortigern cowered as the twisting monsters ascended, watching them vanish among the clouds. He asked the boy what it meant, and, turning to face Merlin, saw that he was crying.

Merlin explained that the red dragon represented the British nation, which would be taken over by the white dragon. The white dragon represented the foreign race to which Vortigern had given territory in this land. Merlin whispered that, because of the Saxons, the mountains would be made into valleys, the rivers would run with blood, the faith would be destroyed and churches would be ruined.

He did not stop there. Sitting on that precipice, tears weaving down his cheeks, Merlin described many strange portents: a hedgehog hiding apples in Winchester, and women miscarrying in the street. He saw the red dragon weeping at the furthest edge of the drained lake. He saw wolves with no teeth, and an eagle on a mountain-top nest. And all the while he saw the white dragon attacking again and again, until there was no hope. Vortigern listened till the boy had fallen silent, long after the sun had set.

Then Vortigern asked, exhausted, just how he was going to die.

The child told him that the brothers of Constans were travelling from Brittany to reclaim their inheritance. 'If the Saxons don't get you first, the Britons will burn you alive, trapped inside your tower.'

So Vortigern fled to another of his castles, not far from the River Wye, while the younger brother of Constans – Aurelius – arrived, and was crowned in London. Supported by the Britons, the Earl of Gloucester mustered an army and, together with Aurelius and Uther, marched west from London to the mountains. There they found Vortigern, holed up in a keep. The troops surrounded the keep and stacked wood about its base. That evening, while motes danced gold above the river and deer watched from the

banks, the soldiers lit the pyre. Soon, flames were feeling into the windows and catching at the furniture within.

Vortigern climbed upwards, a spider fleeing the gathering flames, emerging high on the battlements. From where Merlin was watching at the forest margin, he could see the King had no escape. The flames were nearly at the parapet, which he clutched like a child.

It was the crown that hurt first, the gold growing hot from the flames. It blistered his forehead, scorching a circle of skin. And now the stone was blistering his hands, and a veil of red mist was descending, turning into a halo of blackening blood. The last thing Vortigern saw, beyond the brothers, beyond the army, a point of brightness before the trees, was the small figure of the boy with no human father. King Vortigern breathed in to shout, but his lungs filled up with smoke.

Far below, Merlin felt the gaze of the traitor strike him, like an arrow made of air.

❖

After burning the treacherous Vortigern to death, Aurelius Ambrosius wins back Britain. He then meets Hengist in battle, who is captured by Earl Eldof and decapitated, and his sons imprisoned. Though the Saxon inroads into Britain are curtailed by this defeat, the descendants of Woden do not completely lose their hold in the east and are never fully expelled.

An early account of a child prophet and the red and white dragons may be found in the ninth-century *History of the Britons*, attributed to Nennius. The child's mother confirms that he has no mortal father, but does not elaborate, and the interpretation of the dragons is concise:

> The pool is the emblem of this world, and the tent that of your kingdom: the two serpents are two dragons; the red serpent is your dragon, but the white serpent is the dragon of the people who occupy several provinces and districts of Britain, even almost from sea to sea: at length, however, our people shall rise and drive away the Saxon race from beyond the sea.

The boy gives his name as Ambrosius and asks Vortigern for lordship of the city on the hill. Vortigern agrees, granting him dominion of all of western Britain.

In Geoffrey of Monmouth's later version, the character of the child bifurcated. Ambrosius becomes the name of the rightful King of the Britons, Aurelius Ambrosius, while the fatherless, soothsaying child is renamed Merlin, inspired by the name of another prophet of Welsh legend called Myrddin Wyllt. In contrast with Nennius' version, in which Merlin's mother denies ever having slept with any being, in Geoffrey, Merlin's prophetic powers are attributed to his diabolical father. His mother's words are these:

> When I was a full-grown novice, some thing – I don't know if it was an apparition – often came to me and kissed me intimately. I heard it speak like a man; I felt it as if it were a man. It lay with me and I conceived. I knew no other man.

When Merlin interprets the dragons, he does so as part of a great stream of crypto-prophetic utterances, among them: 'those who have had their hair waved shall dress in woollen stuffs of many colours'; 'a tree shall spring up on the top of the Tower of London'; and 'a hedgehog loaded with apples shall rebuild the town'. Medieval scribes would copy and recopy these prophecies, which were perceived to have real political import, often annotating them with commentaries by later writers.

There is a hill in north-west Wales called Dinas Emrys, which means 'The Fort of Ambrosius', and which scholars associate with the myth of the red and white dragons, as well as the prequel legend of how they got there in the earlier story of King Lludd and his brother Llefelys, though there it is called Dinas Ffaraon Dandde, or the 'Fort of the Fiery Pharaoh'.

Wooded and small compared to the surrounding mountains, Dinas Emrys seems, from the ground, an unlikely place for such a momentous tale. When I walked to its summit, the summer was waning; the air was humid and the rain poured. It was like wading through a tropical other-world, with ferns visible under the expanses of standing water either side of the path, their fronds open like green corals, as every leaf and every mossy branch overhead dripped. Then there was the roaring of not one but two waterfalls, just like the dragons, the thunderous fallout of which was only traversable via a bridge made of narrow slabs of granite.

If you have read about Dinas Emrys elsewhere, then you will know to expect a pool and some remnants of ancient building activity once you reach the top, but they are well hidden. After roaming the bare summit, you will find a ridge and, beyond it, a deep hollow, ringed with spreading, lichen-papered oak trees that extend their leafy branches to create a quiet, secluded haven. On my visit, I found the grass to be long, green and luscious, parted occasionally by plump boulders. At the deepest part of the hollow was an oval pool, darkly reflecting a single, nodding foxglove. Not far from the pool were the low ruined walls of a tower. The strange sanctuary on Dinas Emrys has an enchanted atmosphere. It might quite easily have been the site of a muddy altercation between two dragons, the pit long since healed by the progress of turf and tree.

Excavations in the mid-1950s revealed the pool to be the result of a man-made cistern, dated to the early Roman period with adaptations made in the early Middle Ages, while the ruined tower was dated to as late as the twelfth century. Evidently there was occasional human activity on the summit of the hill, both at the time in which the myth is set and the ages in which it was written down and revised. Make of this what you will. For me, the various iterations show how successive writers and interweaving textual traditions gave rise to a story that transformed a handful of buildings on the summit of a Welsh hill into the focus of the Britons' fight for political independence. Myths hold the echo of collective emotion, whatever they reveal of events.

16

Stonehenge

Merlin obeyed the King's orders and put the stones up in a circle round the sepulchre, in exactly the same way as they had been arranged on Mount Killaraus in Ireland, thus proving that his artistry was worth more than brute strength.

Geoffrey of Monmouth,
The History of the Kings of Britain (c. 1136)

After witnessing the death of Vortigern, Merlin retreated to the Springs of Galabes, where he could browse the plentiful cherries and tender leaves of early summer. He spared no thought for what would happen when winter came; that was in the future. Each day he ate, ambling along the woodland edge, birds, deer and rodents for company, until darkness fell, when he slept behind a fire. In the morning he was woken by birdsong and the first beams of sunrise, or diffuse light through cloud. Here he might happily have spent the rest of his days, had it not been for the coming of the riders.

The sound of metal – a horseshoe striking rock – cut a crimson gash through the everyday sounds he had come to know. Merlin climbed up a tree when he heard it, and saw, beneath the canopy of dark leaves, a troop of soldiers entering the clearing on horseback. They were beautifully arrayed. Everything about them was crafted. Merlin gripped the branch.

The soldiers called his name, but Merlin did not answer. Then they called again, telling him they were envoys of King Aurelius. Merlin hesitated for a breath, then he climbed down and stepped into the clearing.

At that moment, King Aurelius was in Winchester. Young, slender and radiant, his coiling hair fell bronze about his shoulders and gems shone at his ears and fingers. A Briton of Roman descent, progeny of Brutus, he was rightfully king and the true heir to the throne. The Britons were glad to be ruled by him, believing that a great wrong had been righted in their lifetimes. At last Vortigern was dead, Hengist had been beheaded by Earl Eldof of Gloucester, and the Saxons driven back across the sea, or to strongholds in the north-east. Aurelius would be celebrated forever. But one terrible wound festered in the people's memory: Vortigern's feast and the Saxon massacre of the Britons.

The bright Aurelius had wept to see the graves of all those barons on the Salisbury Plain, every man betrayed by Vortigern and the Saxon invaders. These were men he might have known and loved, had he not spent his childhood exiled in the courts of Brittany. No amount of vengeance would counter the depth of the suffering that traitor had caused, but the dead ones could be honoured. A memorial was needed, a monument to stand forever.

Aurelius had called together the best artisans in his kingdom, asking them for designs that would befit his purpose. Woodworkers came with tannin-stained hands, stonemasons with dust-grey faces. Some drew plans on the floor, some fashioned models in wood or clay, others sketched on wax. But nothing they presented was worthy; they even admitted it themselves. It was then that the Archbishop had suggested they find the child who had saved Vortigern's tower. Now Aurelius was in the hall alone, surrounded by broken plans and models, waiting for the seer.

Merlin and the soldiers had barely exchanged a word on the journey to Winchester. When they arrived, Aurelius had already made his way to the city gates with Eldof. The latter, who had rarely been seen without a breastplate since the massacre of the Britons, was middle-aged, barrel-chested and stern. Aurelius greeted Merlin and led him into the palace.

Merlin was not what Aurelius had expected, not least because he was so small. When he pressed the child to give a prophecy, Merlin frowned and refused, telling Aurelius that the spirits that granted him foresight would leave him if he prophesied without good cause. Once in the hall, the barons and bishops likewise asked to hear their futures, but the King put them straight. He then presented his problem. What could serve as a fitting memorial to the Britons slaughtered by the Saxons at Vortigern's feast?

Merlin replied at once.

'Such a structure already exists. It is called the Giants' Dance and its stones are so heavy that no one living is strong enough to lift them. It may be found on Mount Killaraus in Ireland. If we could bring it here, then it would certainly stand forever.'

Aurelius laughed, and said they had big enough stones in Britain, didn't they? The others began laughing too. Even the servants were smiling into their hands.

But Merlin said they were fools, telling them these were not just any stones. The stones had been quarried in Africa and carried all the way to Ireland by giants. He described their healing virtues. And he said that, even when all the world's cities had fallen, these stones would remain standing.

Merlin told Aurelius to send his troops to fetch the Giants' Dance back over the sea and rebuild it on the Salisbury Plain. There it would be seen and remembered forever. It was the only monument worthy of the men killed at the feast. The King had been persuaded.

Not long after that meeting, men were sent across the Irish Sea. Soon, Merlin was sent to join them. Aurelius' army had found Mount Killaraus and had defeated the Irish King in order to obtain the stones, which stood in two great circles on the misty peak. But when the men had come to lift them, not one had been strong enough. Now, the child climbed the mountain and walked among them. Like the barons and servants in the hall, they smiled behind their hands; the soldiers were the biggest in the King's army and this boy barely came up to their navels. Still, Merlin sat down on a mossy knoll, breathing in the scent of thyme, and asked to see their technique.

'We shall see which is better: brute strength or artistry and skill!'

They demonstrated how they rocked onto their haunches, embraced the rocks, or wound their hands around ropes, and, taking deep breaths, exerted their efforts on lifting the stones into the air. They demonstrated by trying once again, with all of their strength, determined not to be outdone by a child. Everywhere Merlin looked – nearby and receding into the mist-bands – he could see men purple in the face, their veins bulging, their calluses bursting against the rock, their feet pushing into the muddy turf. When it was clear that nothing they could do would shift the stones, the men walked panting over to the child. Now it was his turn to laugh.

The boy's bony arms poked from his tunic and he seemed too weak to lift anything heavier than a bird's egg. But he stood up and placed his hands over his face.

Those nearest heard him muttering words under his breath. Some wondered if he were praying, but others knew he was not.

The small child stood motionless on that mountain, but a change was palpable in the air. It was as if the weight of each stone were tiptoeing out of its crystalline core onto the droplets of the ubiquitous vapour. It was as if the strength of the rock was passing from those droplets into the bodies of the men. Fingertips twitched. Muscles rippled. Jaws clenched. Pupils dilated. And suddenly, as one, each man turned towards the stone with which he had previously contended, and placed his arms about it.

After the Giants' Dance had been carried down Killaraus, placed in ships and erected on the Salisbury Plain, it regained its former weight and the men their former frailty. And though the monument had only then been set in place, it appeared to have been standing there for centuries, the surface of the rocks pitted and comely as the plump arms of a matriarch, elbows planted in the soil. None who witnessed the feat ever again put brute strength above all other powers.

After his death, Aurelius would be remembered by the Britons for this glorious memorial, but it would also be his undoing. One of Vortigern's sons had allied with the Irish King, who resented the theft of the stones. At his behest, an assassin was sent to Winchester, where King Aurelius was sick with fever. The intruder put on doctor's robes

and visited him in his chamber. Receiving medicine from the man, the bronze-haired Aurelius drank. But it was not medicine in the cup, it was a toxic draught. It burned him inside out.

They laid Aurelius to rest beside the slaughtered ones in the midst of the Giants' Dance. One day, his brother Uther would be placed beside him. In time it would come to be called the Hanging Stones, and thereafter Stonehenge. And though much is written about it today, few remember it as the tomb of the Britons betrayed at the feast, nor the grave of legendary Kings.

❖

Were you a medieval visitor to Stonehenge, brought up on the *Brut* chronicle tradition, you would not have seen the stones as having first stood in Pembrokeshire's Preseli Hills, but in remotest Africa, whence they were carried across the sea by giants, and erected on a mountain in Ireland. You would have learned that the stones arrived in Salisbury Plain not by means of timber rollers or some other mechanism, but by the magic or skill (depending on which medieval version of the story you read) of the child Merlin. You would have been taught that they arrived not in the depths of prehistory, but comparatively recently, serving as a memorial to the victims of a Saxon betrayal of the cream of Britain's nobility. All this you would have believed had occurred in around the fourth century AD. To you, Stonehenge would have been the grave of Aurelius Ambrosius and his brother Uther Pendragon. Perhaps the rooks and jackdaws colonised the stones then as they do now, like the souls of as many heroes.

The massacre myth – sometimes called 'the treachery of the long knives' – enters British legend by the ninth century. But there was an existing tradition of historical writing that stressed the trauma suffered by the Christian Britons during the pagan Saxon invasions that took place between the fourth and sixth centuries. Take, for instance, the vivid imagery used by a contemporary British historian called Gildas:

The root of bitterness grows as a poisonous plant, worthy of our deserts, in our own soil, furnished with rugged branches and leaves . . . inhabitants, along with the bishops of the church, both priests and people, whilst swords gleamed on every side and flames crackled, were together mown down to the ground, and, sad sight, there were seen . . . sacred altars, fragments of bodies covered with clots, as if coagulated, of red blood, in confusion as in a kind of horrible wine press . . . for the vineyard, at one time good, had then so far degenerated to bitter fruit.

In the eighth century, Bede reiterated this passage, describing how many Britons fled overseas, and how those that remained 'led a wretched existence, always in fear and dread, among the mountains and woods and precipitous rocks'.

As a mythic trope, the massacre at the feast may be seen as a powerful catalyst for all the hostilities that will follow between the Britons and the Saxons. It demonstrated the Saxons' cunning determination, the consequences of the weakness of usurpers like Vortigern, and the imperative to stay true to the rightful royal line. Now that the Saxons had a foothold in Britain, the Britons' future would depend on a sovereign with all the steadfastness, strength and pedigree of Stonehenge. And a leader is about to be born with every one of these gifts.

17

The Deception at Tintagel

When the king saw her there among the other women, he was immediately filled with desire for her, with the result that he took no notice of anything else, but devoted all his attention to her. To her and to no one else he kept ordering plates of food to be passed, and to her, too, he kept sending his own personal attendants with golden goblets of wine.

Geoffrey of Monmouth,
The History of the Kings of Britain (c. 1136)

There are dreams in which people aren't quite themselves. Whether they become kinder, or more cruel, or whether they suddenly attract or repulse the dreamer in ways they never have in waking, they leave a strange taste in the mouth. It was just like this for Igraine, only Igraine was not asleep.

That night, she had been sitting in bed, listening to the bard tell a story over the ocean's suck and heave, when she heard the doors of the keep being opened. Someone had been allowed over the bridge. A friend, then. Igraine dismissed the bard and crept to the entrance of her room. She discerned a servant's footsteps and men's voices. One she recognised as the voice of her husband, Gorlois.

Igraine threw a robe over her nightclothes and hurried down the stairs. Gorlois was already in the hall.

'What has happened?' she cried, running towards him, and he met her with open arms, pulling her to his chest.

'My love, my Igraine,' he said into her hair, stroking it with one hand, holding her waist with the other, 'I had to know you were safe.'

She inhaled his familiar smell and thought how tenderly he held her. He was speaking again.

'I am sorry it has come to this. As long as you love me, Igraine, I'm yours.'

He stepped back, and she looked up into his face: still those familiar lines, still the curl of his grey eyebrows.

'Come to bed,' he said.

She nodded and kissed him. Then she led him up the stairs and into the rooms where she had, only moments ago, been dreaming of another. Yet, before he could reach out his hand, she was undressing him. Full of an unexpected desire for her gentle husband, she refused him nothing. And that night he asked for more than was usual.

At the moment of Aurelius Ambrosius' death, a star had appeared in the sky. From the doors of their threshing barns or bent over sickles, the astonished people saw a dragon soaring from its fiery core. The flames belched by the dragon stretched over many lands. Merlin, who was with Uther when the portent appeared, made this prophecy: Aurelius was dead, Uther must take the throne, and his progeny would be emperors. Uther took the dragon as his sign.

Newly crowned, Uther Pendragon had held a feast in London for all the nobles in the land. Among them was Gorlois, Duke of Cornwall, who had brought his wife Igraine. Rumours of her beauty were plentiful. From the moment she took her seat among the other women, Uther saw the rumours were true and kept his hungry eyes upon her.

While the attention of the venerable Gorlois was elsewhere, Uther had his attendants send platters of food to Igraine, as well as ewers of the best wine. She blushed with each offering, but kept her eyes downcast.

Uther persisted. His attendants took her more food and, despite her reserve, he could see she had drunk a good deal. In time, Gorlois' attention turned to the servants passing between his wife and Uther, and his old face creased with a frown. He stood and approached Igraine.

'We have to leave,' he said.

When Uther saw what the Duke was doing, he warned him that to leave would be the gravest insult and would not go unavenged, but Gorlois pulled Igraine up by the arm. The hall was very quiet. Everybody stared as he led her from the room. Uther shook with anger.

Igraine was angry with Gorlois and spoke little for the journey home to Tintagel. When they arrived, he did not dismount. He knew the King's army would not be far behind and he had to muster his men. In the twilight, Igraine could just make out the lights of the castle and the slate blue of water.

'I will be at Castle Dameliock,' he said. 'You can write to me there.'

With that, the sight of Gorlois and the thud of his horse's hooves were swallowed by the turf and fog. So he would imprison her here with no one but servants for company. She led her mare down the cliff-path to the bridge and, leaving the horse with the guard, crossed over onto the island.

Igraine did not write to Gorlois. The next day she sat in the window of her room, watching the sea, now brilliant beneath the summer sky. She was fond of her husband and their marriage was not unhappy, but now she was imagining being married to Uther. Oh, to be rescued by him from this boulder in the sea! To be rescued from the protective old man who called himself her husband.

But Uther was not on his way to rescue her. He was at Dameliock, where his armies were besieging Gorlois' castle. Reinforcements were coming from the Duke's allies in Ireland; they had provisions and could wait for months if they needed to. But there would be no waiting. The King was too sick for Igraine. As she dreamed of his affections, he wondered what she was doing, what she was eating and whether she thought of him.

Uther called his baron, Ulfin, to his tent and confessed, not for the first time, the terrible depth of his emotion. It was possible, he intimated, that he would not survive if he did not soon have Igraine. But, to Ulfin, this was all wrong. When the comet had appeared, it had issued a beast with a crest of glowing spikes, with ruby eyes and breath of blue flames that stretched over Ireland and France, dividing over their regions, disappearing like meteors beyond the horizon. The soothsayer Merlin had announced Aurelius' death to Uther, and the youngest brother, already tall in stature, had risen to the throne in glory, heralded by a dragon. Was this king destined to do no more than plunge the country into civil war?

It was Merlin whom Ulfin found to bring the King an answer.

'The solution is this,' said Merlin. 'By means of special medicines, I will disguise you as Gorlois, and Igraine will sleep with you. Then you will end this war.'

From behind the web of his fingers, Uther's eyes shone.

At Tintagel, Igraine was still indulging in fantasy. As the sun beat down, she took herself to the rocks, where, surrounded by seabirds, her toes in the cropped grass, she imagined what would happen if Uther were to win his war with Gorlois. She imagined the young King approaching the castle on the rock by ship. She imagined his smile, tilted up at her from the deck. He would discover her there, by chance, as she stood on the weathered cliffs. She would have only her shift on. Then he would scale the rocks and guide her down. He would enclose Igraine's narrow hand in his great one, and she would notice the calluses on his skin from sword and bridle. Perhaps they would take wine from the ship, row to an island and lie together in the grass . . .

It troubled her only slightly that Gorlois would have to die for this dream to come true, but she made his death a quick, heroic martyrdom, if her imagination strayed onto it at all. She found it easiest to let it be pushed aside by the thought of her future with Uther.

It was only later, when a man who seemed to be her husband came to Tintagel, passed the guards at the gate and embraced her in the hall, that she came to regret her unfaithful thoughts. As they entwined with more pleasure than Igraine had ever known, she half wondered if this could indeed be her husband.

So it was that, even as she kissed the likeness of her spouse, the real Gorlois' life was in danger. Uther's besieging army, without a leader and impatient for action,

had attacked the walls of Dameliock. Gorlois rode out to fight them off, but Uther's soldiers pulled him from his horse and chased his followers away. In the flames of his fallen stronghold, even as their king slaked his lust, they slaughtered the ageing Duke. Then the army looted his castle, fighting between themselves over treasures and leaving with whatever they could carry. A messenger fled for Tintagel. He had to warn Igraine.

It was morning when he arrived at the island and was let in by the guards. When he entered the main chamber, he was amazed by what he saw. Gorlois, whose remains he had just abandoned at Dameliock, was there, eating breakfast with his wife.

'I have come to tell you that Gorlois is –' the messenger faltered – 'that you are . . . dead.'

For a moment Gorlois looked shocked, then he laughed.

'I'm not dead! You must have been seeing things. But does this mean Dameliock has fallen? Then Uther will be coming here now with his armies. I must go and broker peace.'

He stood up, kissed Igraine and left the room. She watched him go, love and confusion on her face.

As soon as Uther was out of Tintagel, Merlin lifted his disguise. Together with Ulfin, the three men rode back to the camp. Though furious with his army for abandoning their orders and killing Gorlois, Uther was nonetheless eager to seize Tintagel and make Igraine his wife. Beside him, Merlin said nothing. For he knew something about the woman for whom the King had started this war: she was descended from Joseph of Arimathea. He knew too that she had conceived a child in the night. And he knew that the people's faith in their leader was broken and that, when the child came to his throne, that faith would have to be restored.

❖

If you travel to Tintagel today, you will see a bronze statue of Arthur on the headland, his sword rested point-first in front of him, his hands crossed on the hilt. Forming the abundant flora of the surrounding cliffs are stands of thrift, foxgloves and common toadflax. Falling away either side of him are sheer walls of slate, receding into sea caves or disappearing into the blue of the north Cornish sea. Not far inland, you will find Tregeare Rounds, a site of Iron Age earthworks associated with the legendary Dameliock, where Gorlois is said to have met his death. The bond between Tintagel and King Arthur is deep-rooted. And what more mysterious, ancient and beautiful place of origin could there be for the redeemer of the Britons?

In 1233, Richard of Cornwall, a powerful nobleman and son of King John of England, built a new castle on Tintagel. It had little defensive function, but, arguably, exploited the prestige of a legendary connection to King Arthur. This echoes contemporary enthusiasm for Arthur, the story of whose life took recognisable form in Geoffrey of Monmouth's twelfth-century *History of the Kings of Britain* and received embellishment later in the century in the hands of such writers as Chrétien de Troyes and Marie de France. While there is mention of a British warlord called Arthur in earlier British sources, it was doubtless the appeal of these more developed tales that captured the popular imagination and lent political utility. After King Edward I of England defeated Llywelyn ap Gruffydd, Prince of Wales, and conquered Wales in 1282, the Welsh presented Edward with 'King Arthur's crown'. In Edward's eyes, the precious relic would have symbolised his rightful dominion over the British.

As with many stories of great heroes, Arthur's conception takes place in supernatural circumstances. But even to Geoffrey of Monmouth, in whose *History* it first appears, Uther's methods are treated with a certain ambivalence:

> Who, indeed, could possibly have suspected anything, once it was thought that Gorlois himself had come? The King spent the night with Ygerna [Igraine] and satisfied his desire by making love with her. He had deceived her by the disguise which he had taken. He had deceived her, too, by the lying things that he had said to her, things which he planned with great skill. He said that he had come out secretly from his besieged encampment so that he might make sure that all was well with her, whom he loved so dearly, and with his castle, too. She naturally believed all that he said, and refused him nothing that he asked.

As for Igraine, she is an unstable character in the medieval sources, but never anything other than oblivious to the true identity of the man in her bedroom. Is it really plausible that anyone would be completely taken in by the advances of a stranger in the guise of a long-term partner? I suspect not. Meanwhile, in some other universe, there is a statue of Igraine on the Tintagel cliffs, wondering whose bed she will share.

18

The Sword and the Anvil

The queen was relieved to hear him grant her freedom to speak; and she told him how a man had lain with her in the semblance of her lord – the story that the king knew so well. And when she had finished, the king said: 'Make sure no one learns of this, for it would bring you great shame. And since this child is rightly neither yours nor mine, I want you to give it to the person I choose, so that it stays forever secret.'

'Sir,' she replied, 'I and all I possess are at your command.'

Robert de Boron, Merlin (c. 1200)

Night held the town like a spell as a beautiful man walked silently over the cobbles. He rocked the sleeping bundle in his arms, but his eyes stared straight ahead. Beyond, in the darkness of an eave, a tall shadow shifted. It stepped into his path and spoke.

'Merlin, I know it's you.'

'It has to be done,' Merlin said from his disguise, side-stepping the King and walking on. Uther followed.

'Is there no other way?'

The two proceeded across the square, towards a part of the town that Uther hardly knew. Merlin spoke.

'The people have no faith in their leader. We must set it right.'

'But must I give up my son?' The King's eyes pleaded through the darkness.

'It is the only way.'

'What did Igraine say when you took him?'

At this Merlin stopped and faced Uther. Igraine knew she had conceived her child with someone or some being other than her husband, and was full of guilt.

'She put up no fight.'

They were approaching a house, modest but not poor.

'And they are good people?'

'Yes. The foster-father, Entor, knows the boy's true parentage and has agreed to find another woman to nurse his own son in the meantime.'

Then Merlin gave the bundle to Uther.

'Say goodbye.'

As the King held his son, Merlin approached the wooden door, knocked, and spoke to the man within. The man stretched out his hands and Uther gave him the child. Then, murmuring his goodnight, the man shut the door and Merlin led Uther away.

Within the house, Entor lit a lamp and climbed the stairs to his bedroom. Their son had been taken that morning and now his wife sat on the bed, weeping, her nightdress stained with milk and tears. She gestured for the child.

'Has he been baptised?' she said.

'Yes,' Entor answered, 'and his name is Arthur.'

'Come here, little one,' she sobbed, drawing the bundle to her breast.

Some fifteen years later, Uther Pendragon died without an heir and Merlin's plan began to take effect. It was decreed that, on Christmas Eve, as part of a day of tourneys and games, a rightful successor would be found. One young knight in town, whose name was Kay, was eager to try his hand, having been knighted on the feast of All Saints. But his younger brother Arthur, who was responsible for looking after his armour and weapons, had forgotten to give him his sword. The boy had rushed home to fetch it, only to find the house locked and the servants absent. Then he had returned to the snow-dusted square in the hope of finding some friend who might lend him a sword so that Kay could take part in the tourney. He had heard that, only that morning, while he had been busy with chores, a special ceremony had taken place in the square and it had been full of people. Now, it was deserted.

The boy, tall for his age, with hair the colour of coal, looked around, searching for someone who might help him. Then he saw it. He could hardly believe he hadn't

noticed it before. In the middle of the square, in front of
the west door of the church, was a boulder, speckled with
holy water, which had frozen in the cold air. Planted on
the boulder was an anvil. Deep in the anvil was a sword.

A sword!

Arthur ran towards it, climbed onto the stone and
gripped the hilt. It was encrusted with many jewels, and
inlaid with gold and silver, and the blade was pattern-
welded, its surface shimmering like marble. Arthur pulled
harder than he needed to and, when the blade slid out of
the iron, he almost fell. As he jumped down, he pinned
the weapon to his side and ran in the direction of the
field behind the church, where all were assembled. In
his hurry, he did not read the inscription on the side of
the boulder.

At the edge of the crowd he saw Kay. Slowing, panting,
he proffered the sword to his brother.

'I couldn't find your sword, but here is another.'

As a flock of starlings ebbed and flowed in the field
behind them, Kay grasped the handle, and frowned.

'Where did you find this?' he asked.

'In a stone outside the church.'

When Entor saw Kay, and saw what he concealed, he
knew that he was powerless to prevent fate from taking
Arthur, his best son, from him. Much sadness in his heart,
he asked where the boy was. Once they had found him,
craning to watch the games, they led him back to the

square. Entor instructed Arthur to put the sword back where he'd found it. This Arthur did. Then Entor invited Kay to remove it, just as that morning hundreds of contenders for the kingship had tried to do.

Now, Arthur thought, Kay would slide the sword out just as he himself had done, the grim expression on his father's face would lift, and they would return to the tournament. But to his surprise he saw his brother heave on the hilt to no avail. Now it must be Kay who was pretending. Arthur laughed and a passer-by laughed too. But Kay's red face was set. Then Entor turned to Arthur.

'What good will it do me if I make you king?'

His eyes were full of tears. They moved from Arthur to the words inscribed on the stone, which at last the boy read:

WHOEVER REMOVES THIS SWORD
WILL BE KING OF THE LAND,
BY CHRIST'S WILL

'As much good as my father deserves,' Arthur said, his ears growing hot despite the wintry air.

Then Entor knelt and bowed his head. He enclosed one of Arthur's hands in his own.

'I am not your father, Arthur, but have merely fostered you from birth.'

Around them, the square was filling with people. They were watching Entor. Arthur felt tears prick his eyes. There must have been a mistake. He was not, as Entor was saying, a foster-son. It could not be true.

'If you become king,' continued Entor, 'I only ask that you make Kay your vassal and that his position is protected, no matter what wrong he does. My wife nursed you and gave him to another woman. That made him the way he is.'

Though Arthur wished he was standing safely with the crowd, he heard himself agreeing. Ahead, he saw the Archbishop approaching, as well as the knights and barons from the tournament. And now he was being invited to climb onto the stone and draw the sword once more from the anvil.

This time, when Arthur climbed up to where the sword stood, the wheeling starlings reflecting in the gems and inlay of its hilt, he gripped it without conviction. He felt caught in the gaze of all the people, the churchmen and the barons, and pulled with slow reluctance.

No one in that chilly square could believe their eyes. All those full-grown barons and knights of the morning were being outdone by this long-limbed, coal-haired youth, who seemed no more royal than they were. The moment the sword-point broke free of the iron, catching the low sun like a minnow in a kingfisher's beak, the crowd drew breath as one. Mothers squeezed their children's hands. The elderly patted their hearts. And Kay wondered if it was his imagination, or whether Arthur's shoulders

had broadened and his chest widened as he straightened and beheld the crowd. The barons felt uneasy; they knew nothing of this boy and nothing of his family.

The Archbishop stepped forward, gesturing to the clergy, who gathered around the stone and guided the new King onto their shoulders, bearing him into the church just as they would a reliquary on the feast day of a saint. And Arthur let himself be carried, realising that somehow this had always been his fate.

It took time for the barons to accept Arthur as king. It wasn't until early summer and the feast of Pentecost that they conceded, and then only because of two things. First, Arthur had refused to be crowned without their approval, which made them think him wise. Second, whenever he received gifts, he shared them, which showed his generosity. The Britons had gained a leader in whom they trusted absolutely. As the crown touched his dark head, the thronging nave let up a shout. Merlin was there, of course, and it was only then that he, having achieved his purpose, shared Arthur's true parentage with the barons. And so it was that not one person in the cities, or in the hills, mountains and plains of all the country, doubted Arthur's right to be king.

❖

Arthur's early life is passed over in the *Brut* tradition. We are told that Igraine and Uther were happily married and engendered Arthur and his sister Anna, who later marries King Loth of Lothian. In Robert de Boron's *c.* 1200 *Merlin*, the eponymous soothsayer takes the infant Arthur from Igraine and hands him over to foster-parents, Entor and his wife. Merlin does this, he claims, to atone for the death of Gorlois:

> 'My lord,' Merlin replied, 'Ulfin is absolved of his sin in arranging the affair between you and the queen. But I'm not yet absolved of my part in helping you with my trickery and in the conception of the child she bears, whose fathering is a mystery to her.'

We are told that the nurse who gives the child to Merlin does not recognise him. She sees only a very handsome man. We are not told why the character of Igraine parts with her new son so easily, but her confusion as to the circumstances of his conception may suffice.

Robert de Boron is responsible for the first 'sword in the stone' narrative, in which the young Arthur, diligently helping his newly knighted brother find a weapon, seizes the sword from the anvil, unaware of his royal father, and unaware that the act marks him out for kingship. There is great pathos in Arthur's reaction to his discovery that Entor is not his true father:

> And Entor said to Arthur: 'What good will it do me, if I make you king?'

And Arthur answered: 'Such as befits my father.'

Then Entor said: 'I am not your father; I have only fostered you.'

When Arthur heard this, he wept.

Once Arthur is on the throne, extraordinary tales follow. Geoffrey of Monmouth, Chrétien de Troyes, Marie de France and Robert de Boron, as well as the anonymous authors of the tales of the *Mabinogion* and the Vulgate and Post-Vulgate Cycles, are all instrumental in forming what we now think of as the Arthurian legend. The last pair, both in French, went on to become a primary source for Thomas Malory's 1485 Middle English *Le Morte d'Arthur* (*The Death of Arthur*), the title of which only refers to the last volume and was originally meant to be called *The Whole Book of King Arthur and of his Noble Knights of the Round Table*. Most modern retellings of the Arthurian legend draw on the Vulgate Cycles and Malory, but I have remained with the earlier material.

In the sources up to and including Robert de Boron in the early thirteenth century, the Round Table is born; Sir Kay becomes a hero, his name spoken in the same breath as those of Sir Gawain and Sir Lancelot; Arthur marries Guinevere, who in turn seduces Lancelot when he crosses the sword-bridge to rescue her. And the courts of humans and fairies mingle when Guinevere loses her temper at Sir Lanval, who says his lover is more beautiful than she is. Living up to his reputation as the Britons' defender, King Arthur suppresses the Saxons at the Battle of Mount Badon, the image of the Virgin and Child on his shield. Then he increases his domains, conquering thirty realms, Scotland, Denmark, France and Rome among them, and becomes an Emperor.

Around 1340, when Edward III claimed the throne of France, a manuscript (British Library, Egerton MS 3028) was made with an illustration of Arthur defeating the governor of Gaul. Curiously, rather than the usual Virgin and Child or three crowns on his shield, Arthur is bearing Edward III's royal blazon, the three English leopards. Likewise, the shield of the governor of Gaul bears the fleur-de-lys associated with the contemporary kings of France. The message of the illustration is clear: by seeking to conquer France, Edward III was doing nothing new. He was simply restoring Britain's former greatness. It should thus be understood that these stories, entertaining as they are, held real political import for medieval readers and, from Diana's prophecy to Brutus, to Arthur's conquest of France, shaped an understanding of what it meant to be British and what gave its rulers the right to claim empire.

19

The King, the Dog and the Boar

There is another miracle in the region called Buellt. There is a heap of stones there, with one stone on top of the heap, bearing the footprint of a dog. When Arthur the soldier hunted the boar Troynt, his dog Cabal left his footprint in the stone, and Arthur later gathered the heap of stones and placed it on top, and called it Carn Cabal. Men come and take up the stone in their hands for a day and a night, and the next day it is to be found again on the top of the cairn.

Nennius (attrib.), History of the Britons
(early ninth century)

Cafall knew something was afoot. He slunk out from his bed and slid his head under the King's arm, nudging his wrist with his snout. Arthur smoothed the dog's muzzle, then rose to speak to Kay. Cafall felt the humans' agitation as if it were his own. There were boots being pulled onto legs and mantles over shoulders. That was good. He whined. He dropped back onto his haunches.

Then suddenly the King called his name – 'Cafall!' – and the names of all his comrades. It was happening again. The hounds ran to the call.

While the riders mounted and prepared outside the stables, the dogs read the sky with their noses. Then the King brought them a bristle of silver. They gathered round, as they had done every day for weeks. Familiar by now, it smelled of a man. No, more than a man. It smelled of a boar. It was both and it was neither. It smelled of no creature that Cafall had ever hunted before: of virile rancour, of piss, of saliva, and of something less tangible, something malevolent. But he felt no fear; he would find the source of that scent. He would track it down. A horn sounded and the hunt took off at once, sprinting into the trees. As Cafall's blood grew hot, the hounds weaved this way and that before the galloping horses. They bayed and raced and flung out their snouts and tongues to catch the scent on the air, and they continued through the day, pursuing the slipstream of the silver bristle, and the horses ran behind them and the riders shouted encouragement.

The hunt did not end that day, or even the next. They inhaled the contrary landscape, bounding through marshy fields, along rivers, over walls and past the inhabitants of farmsteads, until the bristle led them to a hill. Cafall's back was being pelted by an onslaught of hail, unabated by the low, scrubby trees. But he hardly felt it. He was transfixed by an accent on the air: the rancour, the piss, the saliva, the unnatural something that bound them together, had brushed the mossy boulders and was trailing up the slope, out of scent and sight. The chord of decomposition, fungal slime, snail slime and the dark hearts of mosses was thrown, by a jarring aberration, by the astringent reek of the quarry. He sprinted after its call. And though he heard the King shout his name, and felt the other dogs dropping back, instinct drove him on. The creature had come this way.

Up. Up. Up. Closer. Closer. Now breaking out of the band of woodland, Cafall raced for the summit, where the wind would be richest, the trail strongest, where he might find the bearer of that odour. It was hailing harder now – icy pebbles shooting out of the sky as though the clouds were full of slingshots – but Cafall carried on, splashing from stream to boulder to bracken. And then, just as quickly as the hail had come, the clouds began to clear, so that when Cafall at last reached the summit, planting his front paw firmly on the topmost stone, their shade was receding, chased by the sun. And the sun's light was exposing the landscape, and the wind told his nose where to point, seeking the source of the smell.

On a peak across the valley stood a creature, dark at first, then the sun hit. And all at once it was shining like a lightning ball, the coat of silver bristles hoarding the sudden brilliance. On the fleeing storm, Cafall was struck by its aggression, as if its eyes held all the malice in the world.

This was Troynt, who had once been a king in Ireland, but, condemned for a terrible, long-forgotten crime, now wandered in the shape of a boar.

In the evil power of that gaze, Cafall was paralysed. It held the cruelty of a hundred leather boots in the ribs, of sticks broken across the spine, of freezing nights without food or water, of violence, neglect and betrayal. The stone on which the great dog stood was turning to lava beneath his paw. He cowered, till the boar trotted out of sight.

Now that the monster had gone, he found he could not move. He struggled and whimpered, and then he felt a hand on his back. He recognised the large palm, the scrunching fingers, and turned his nose towards them, smelling the warm sweat, the horse dust and the tang of iron. Arthur smoothed his fur and spoke comfort in his ear. Then, as Cafall let out a whine, the man rested his hand where the front paw had burned into the stone: now cool, now solid, and holding the dog like a vice. Arthur felt around each toe, extracting it carefully, and Cafall waited as he did.

After Arthur had released Cafall's foot, the King took the imprinted stone and placed it on a heap of others,

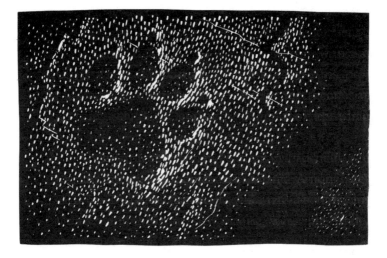

forming a cairn. Cafall bounded his thanks about him, licking his master's face when he could. Then the King and the hound went back down the hill, knuckles brushing fur. That day, the hill earned the name 'Carngafallt', after Cafall. For centuries thereafter, if anyone took the stone away, it would be back on that cairn by morning. Such was the power of the place.

Later in the hunt, the boar-king Troynt would be caught and submerged in the Severn's flood long enough for a pair of scissors and a razor to be taken from between his ears, but Troynt escaped with a comb the king also sought. The hunt would catch up with him in Cornwall, where it would drive him into the sea, never to be sniffed out again.

And when King Arthur was betrayed by his nephew, mortally wounded and carried to the Isle of Avalon, no being in Britain awaited his return with as much faith as Cafall.

❖

I went to Carngafallt during a storm. On my way to the summit, the winds were so strong that the driving rain was funnelled down my back and my hair whipped my face. As the tree cover thinned and I ascended the summit's balding pate, the rain transmuted into hailstones the size of broad beans, stinging my calves and ankles as if they had incurred the wrath of a fairy army. But, with the last scramble of stones, everything changed. The sun broke through, the hail stopped and the clouds' shadows drew back like a curtain. I turned and looked back at the landscape. The view was flexible, wild and breathtaking. I always forget the magnificence of nature when imagining it from my desk.

It was an epic ascent, a reminder of the sheer quantities of weather these parts of Britain can offer in under an hour. And the feeling of elation at the sudden appearance of the sun inspired such grateful awe.

The earliest mention of the Cafall legend comes from the early ninth-century *History of Britain*, attributed to a British historian called Nennius. In fact, we know very little about this Nennius and are not even sure it is his work, but the text speaks for itself. As well as offering an account of Britain's deep history, which was heavily mined by Geoffrey of Monmouth, it contains a catalogue of 'marvels of Britain'. Many of these stray into the realm of the supernatural. For instance, 'Near the River Wye, apples are found on an ash tree'; or:

> The third marvel is a hot pool . . . surrounded by a wall made of bricks and stone. Men go into it to bathe at all times, and the temperature changes for each of them as they wish: if one man wants a cold bath, it will be cold, and another wants a hot bath, it will be hot.

The marvels also include a fountain-side tomb in Archenfield, Herefordshire, which will shrink or grow to the same size as anyone who lies in it, and, what is more, in a region called Buellt, there is a stone bearing the footprint of Arthur's dog, Cafall or Cabal. It was created while hunting a boar called Troynt and left atop a hill that was subsequently named after him.

So here I was, on the summit of Carngafallt, intrigued to know why, of the abundance of such hills in mid-Wales, this one in particular features in the ancient legend. Was it the grandeur of the Elan Valley: a suitable node in the journey of Arthur's hunt? Now, when you go to that cleft in the Radnorshire terrain, the main attraction is a series of Victorian dams, shouldering three expansive lakes. But when the legend of Arthur's pursuit of the boar Troynt was written down, the river still ran fast and free between the hulking hills, themselves an interlude between the towering mountains of the Brecon Beacons to the south and Snowdonia to the north. Perhaps it was not this at all. Perhaps there really was a stone on Carngafallt bearing a mark reminiscent of the paw print of a dog.

Stones that bear such corporeal forms, whether man-made or natural, are a real geographical and anthropological phenomenon, and are called 'petrosomatoglyphs' (*petra* = stone; *soma* = body; *glyph* = symbol). All over Britain, not to mention the world, there are stones with carvings or naturally occurring undulations akin to the form of hands, feet or other body parts. Many have been incorporated into local legend. Take, for instance, Maentwrog, in Gwynedd. The name of the village means 'Twrog's Stone' in Welsh. It is said the early medieval saint, Twrog, threw a stone from the mountain onto a heathen temple and that the very same stone stands outside the current parish church. It is said that the concentrated craters and bumps on the edges of the stone are Twrog's two handprints.

While I don't imagine Arthur's dog actually imprinted a stone with his paw, there is an intriguing correspondence between Nennius' 'marvels' and the story of the hunt of the boar Troynt in the Welsh *Mabinogion*, namely 'How Culhwch Won Olwen'. It tells the tale of a prince called Culhwch who is compelled by a curse and by love to win the hand of

Olwen, the daughter of a giant. The giant claims he will only agree to the union if Culhwch completes a number of difficult tasks. These include fetching the razor, comb and scissors caught between the ears of the legendary boar Troynt, the son of a prince, who has been cursed to roam the land in the form of a boar, so that the giant may have his hair ceremonially trimmed. Culhwch seeks help from King Arthur, who is holding his court at Celliwig, in Cornwall. Arthur agrees, and rallies a company of men, not to mention the hounds, among them Cafall, 'Arthur's own dog'.

The hunt begins in Ireland, then they cross the sea to Britain, docking at the harbour of Porthclais, near the town of St David's, and proceed more or less east across Wales, until they come to the Severn. Carngafallt is not among the many obscure place-names listed in the *Mabinogion* tale. However, those that can be identified – Garth Grugyn at Llanilar, Llwch Tawy and Ceredigion – are in Mid and South Wales. It's easy to imagine that Carngafallt could be added to their number without disrupting the internal logic of the tale. Probably some version of it existed and mutated for centuries, centring on the heroic distance travelled by the Arthurian hunt, and the forbidding, epic magnitude of the terrain it covered. It is the mountainous landscape in this story that demonstrates the superhuman stature of the fabled King.

I had a good hunt around on the summit of Carngafallt and I couldn't find a stone bearing the footprint of a dog.

Perhaps the old magic that made it return to the cairn wore off long ago, or perhaps it's always been too hard to find among all the other stones to ever have been stolen at all. What I did discover was a sense of Arthur's stomping ground that has existed for over a thousand years: in the contrary eye of the storm, in the lichen and moss-mantled rocks, and in the exhausting, rolling land.

20

Lothian's Daughter

The pregnant young woman, as best she could, dragged her-self at once to the place indicated by God, and, in her extreme necessity, with anxious groans, she made a little heap with the wood . . . having lighted the fire, she brought forth a son.

Fragmentary Life of St Kentigern (late medieval)

Arthur had a sister whose name was Anna. She married the pagan King Loth of Lothian. Their sons' names were Gawain and Mordred. They had a daughter too, whose name was Teneu.

As soon as they were old enough, the boys had migrated south to fight for Arthur. Teneu didn't miss Mordred much, but she pined after Gawain. His letters spoke of feasts, quests and castles, and giants dressed all in green. She would have liked to have gone with him, to stand out of sight and see it all for herself. Her brothers were part of something noble, as she wished to be. And in time Arthur had conquered Rome. He might have been crowned Roman Emperor had Mordred not turned out to be a traitor. While Arthur was gone, he seized the throne of Britain and claimed Guinevere. In the wars that followed, Mordred and Gawain were killed and Arthur mortally wounded. They said he was carried away to Avalon, to the place of Joseph of Arimathea's first church. They said that there Arthur was hidden away and no one knew if he was alive or dead. Everyone prayed he would return. Teneu didn't think they would ever lose hope, such a glorious king he had been.

But all that really remained was the solitude. The King was dead, Gawain and Mordred were dead, and, way to the north in Lothian, Teneu was alone with her parents.

As Teneu grew older, her father retreated ever more into grief at the loss of his sons, and she grew to depend on her mother. The two of them would read the same books, sitting together like learned bishops, untangling the threads of the text, debating their meanings. But when Anna became ill and died, Teneu's father, Loth, wasted no time in finding a new wife, who would have no love of the quiet, pensive Teneu.

Sir Owain, one of Arthur's former barons, came to Loth's castle to ask for Teneu's hand. He was famous and well-mannered, and it was clear to Teneu that her father wanted her to accept. He laughed with the suitor as he had with Gawain and Mordred, and loved to hear stories of his exploits with the King. When Teneu met him for dinner,

Owain would pass her gifts across the table. She received caskets of walrus ivory, rings bearing verses of love, and brooches of gold and enamel. Then, after dinner, he would recite poetry to her about knights on quests to win the love of a woman. But the faith she had learned from her mother had taught her a deeper poetry. While she longed one day to have children, she could not bear the thought of life with this man, or, perhaps, with any man at all. At night, in the silence of her room, she swore never to give up her virginity.

Her father was kind at first, teasing her towards acceptance. Only when she openly turned down her suitor did his humour disappear.

'Accept or I shall disown you. I shall send you to live with a swineherd,' he said through gritted teeth.

Teneu would not relent, so she was sent away.

She found life in the swineherd's cottage happy. The lowly man with whom she lived was a secret Christian and had spent time in Culross with a missionary called Serf, whose parents were the King of Canaan and the Princess of Arabia. Teneu had a bed in the corner of the cottage, and learned to work with animals, and to cook and clean alongside the swineherd. In the evenings they prayed together, and, after a few weeks, Teneu began to pray on her own that she would conceive a child despite her chastity, so she could be like the Virgin: so she would never have to sleep with a man.

Every day, Teneu would drive the pigs into the forest to the place where the mist fell thickest. There was a spring, flanked by sedge, beside which she would sit and sing to herself, or recite the readings she had learned with her mother. She was alone but for the pigs, and never expected to meet anyone else. But then one day she saw a girl walking towards her through the trees. The girl had long, flaxen hair and a fine, familiar face, though she was sure they had never met.

The girl said, 'I could listen to your singing all day.'

Teneu blushed and nudged at the ground with her toe. The girl went on.

'I have firewood over there in the trees that I need to strap to my back. Would you help me?'

'Of course,' Teneu replied.

The girl got up and walked ahead, her hips swaying.

They descended deeper into the woods. Holly was growing over them now, and there were many fallen trees. Teneu touched the girl's shoulder, intending to ask where she lived. But, at that moment, the girl spun round and struck Teneu hard across the face. She fell into the wet and jabbing twigs, her eyes full of stars and her head spinning. Then she was pinned to the ground. She felt the girl's hands tearing over her body, lifting her skirt. She could hardly breathe. And suddenly she saw the girl's neck sliding back and forth above her face, the veins standing proud. Ashamed, frightened, hurting, Teneu cried out, but the girl neither heard nor cared. After too long, when she thought her teeth would break from clenching, the weight lifted from her. Teneu rolled over into the leaves.

She wiped away her tears, averting her gaze.

'Don't worry,' the girl said, smoothing down her skirt. 'I'm a girl, so you are still a virgin. I have not done what a man can do.'

Then she crouched, a silhouette in the holly.

'It's up to you whether you cry and make a fuss, or are quiet.'

With that, the girl walked off, disappearing through the trees. That morning she had been Sir Owain, but she had stolen clothes from the servant girls and transformed into one whom Teneu would trust. Now, Owain had punished Loth's daughter for the humiliation she had caused. Unaware of the truth, Teneu waited till the footsteps abated, and then she picked herself up. She hurt all over and wished she had somewhere to wash. The girl should not have hit her, she thought. But where were the pigs? Teneu went to find them. When she had done so, she cleaned herself in the stream, tied back her hair, and picked her way home to the swineherd.

It was easy to keep the attack a secret, as much through bewilderment as piety. After a few weeks, she hardly remembered it at all. A girl had attacked her in the woods. Anything else was too strange to articulate. When her bleeding stopped and sickness began, she wondered if after all she had been granted the virgin birth for which she had been praying.

Winter came, and Teneu and the swineherd went into town to sell the pigs for slaughter. The people saw the swollen belly of the exiled princess and word got back to King Loth. In that province, mothers who conceived children out of wedlock were sentenced to death. He did not ease the rules for his daughter. Like her fellows, she would be taken up Traprain Law in a cart and pushed off the cliff.

Soldiers came to the swineherd's cottage at dawn and seized Teneu. Then they took her to the hill, where the people of Lothian had gathered for the spectacle. It was a solitary mound in the landscape, with one flat side of bare grey-white rock. She was lifted from her horse, her hands were tied behind her back, and they led her up the path to the summit. Teneu did not resist, because it had come to her that, in desiring a virgin birth, she had provoked God's anger, even if he had answered her prayer. Who was she to emulate the Mother of God? If this punishment was divinely ordained, then she would not try to escape. She only hoped He would let her live, for the sake of her unborn child. She could smell the sea from the top of the hill, though the mist was thick as smoke.

Teneu was laid in the cart, and she felt the wheels start to turn beneath her. Then she was being pushed backwards towards the edge of the cliff, gaining speed, catching on stones and tussocks. And suddenly she was in freefall, her hands folded on her smooth, round stomach, the wind pushing her hair over her face. But, by some miracle, the cartwheels caught on the bank of the cliff and carried her down the rocks and onto the clinging grass. When the cart had come to a halt, she realised she was safe and thanked God for her deliverance.

When told of the news of her survival, her father's anger grew. He thought she had done some devilish magic and, having recaptured her, prepared a second death. This time King Loth took his daughter to a place on the Forth river called the Mouth of Stench. It had earned its name from the great hauls of fish that were dragged onto its beaches, with so much wastage that the sand and the blood made a paste. In later days it would come to be known as Aberlady. There Teneu was placed in a round wooden boat, lined with animal skins, and cast adrift as a thick white mist redoubled its grip on the sea. She drifted all the way to the Isle of May, followed, and perhaps sustained, by the fish that shoaled beyond the Mouth of Stench.

Once beside the island, Teneu saw no means of escape. The cliffs spinning past her were bleached with bird muck and too high to compass. Even if she made it onto one of the lower rocks, even if she managed to pull herself to standing, her hands would surely slide on any surface they attempted to grip. Once or twice she saw a seal's slick head break the water and watch her with eyes at once bright and dim. Lines of gannets flew over her like strings of pater-noster beads. Then she felt a wetness break down her legs.

Teneu drifted as the fog-blind moon rose and fell, as waves of agony took her, and did not notice, and could not have known, that fish were teeming in masses beneath her boat, drawn by the power of her plight. Beneath the white cliffs of the Isle of May they swarmed as a current and flowed silver. The one thing she could discern, through the fog of the sea and the fog of her mind, was a certain warmth on the wind. Afterwards she would know that these two powers, the breeze and the fish, were drawing her back to the land.

Hours passed and dawn was breaking when Teneu realised the little boat had stopped rocking, and she was looking at the pebbles of a beach. She crawled out of the surf and, between cries of pain, prayed for the safe delivery of her child.

By now, a rose light was warming the sides of the rocks around her, and she saw a heap of ashes, still smoking from a fire. Teneu groped for driftwood and twigs, laying them on the ashes and blowing with trembling breaths until flames appeared. By that meagre warmth, she abandoned herself to labour.

How she wished she was back in the cottage with her

swineherd, delivering her God-given child onto soft blankets, with herbs for the pain, and someone to hold her hand. But instead, here she was, kneeling on hard stones, sand on her face and in her hair. There was nothing to lessen the agony, and no voices but those of the gulls, until, with a final cry, she pushed her baby onto the beach. She took the quiet grey creature from the sand and brought it to her breast, opening her tunic to expose the meagre warmth of her skin.

'Hello,' she whispered, 'hello.'

Then the child, a boy, seemed to come to life, a cry breaking from his mouth, his face flushing. She kissed his cheeks, curling herself into the sand, drawing her arms about him. Now Teneu was too tired to see that she and her infant were no longer alone. To her, it was as if the voices of the men were merely the cries of more gannets. To her, the hands that cradled her head and back were figments of a dream. Unconsciousness overtook her.

The fire Teneu had rekindled had been made the night before by shepherds. Now it was morning, they had returned to the beach, which is where they had found the girl, clothes tangled, giving birth on her own. Doing what they could to help her, with the skills they knew from their work, they cut the cord and buried the afterbirth. They stoked the dying fire, heated water and gave the mother a drink. When she was warm, one shepherd carried her, and another carried the baby, to a missionary called Serf, whose monastery was in Culcross. He would know what to do.

Serf was once a prince of Canaan and now he was a missionary to the Picts of Albany. He welcomed the shepherds and found a room for the mother and child. When she was well enough to tell him her story, she realised how she had been violated. Teneu named the boy Kentigern, though he came to be known as Mungo to his friends, which meant 'dear one'. Teneu hoped that her child would come to know God, in whom she had always trusted.

And as for Loth, her father, he had tracked down the swineherd and pursued him to a marsh near Traprain Law. Once in that place, the man had heard the hooves of the King's horses approaching, had grasped his sharpened spear and used a leather strap to launch it towards the advancing men. It had pierced King Loth's heart. The swineherd felt no regret.

To mark the place where Loth fell, a great stone was set up. Today it is called Loth's Stone. And where Teneu's cart hit the earth beneath Traprain Law, water bubbled up to form a spring. And where the wheels drove into the stone, they left deep ruts. And the fishermen who worked at the Mouth of Stench had to move out to sea, competing for their catch with the Belgians and even the French, because, after Teneu had passed that place, the fish refused to go there, preferring waters off the Isle of May. And the descendants of Joseph of Arimathea, of Igraine and Arthur, sought not dominion over the world, but souls for the Kingdom of Heaven.

❖

On the day I visited Fife, the fog was thick over the estuary. So disorientating was it, that, for a while, the car became untraceable at the base of the Traprain Law. But, before that, the walk up the hill and to the base of the cliff-face had been all the more ominous for the thick white vapour that marched ahead in vertical bands. At the site of a story about oppression, the weather could not have been more evocative. It weighed on the hill and on the spirit, so that to imagine Teneu's punishment by her father, to imagine being pushed off that high cliff in a cart, without that fog was impossible.

Springs have been found to the north and east, consistent with the legend's claim that one appeared after Teneu's fall. And, at the foot of the rock-face, two giant, diagonal slashes could almost have been made by the wheels of her cart.

If Traprain Law was forbidding enough as the site of an execution, the Isle of May was all the more ominous. The ferry takes you out of the estuary, to the basalt fortress of puffins, gannets and kittiwakes, to the very base of the cliffs under which Teneu's little boat would have drifted. These cliffs soar out of the water in awful magnifi-cence: every small platform or crevice offered by the rock is a long-standing gannets' roost. Everywhere the white stain of their droppings shows like candlewax, dribbling down the cliffs, intensifying the diffuse light of the sun and deepening the shadows of those places that the flow could not reach. There would be no hope of ascending those guano-encrusted walls if you were drifting alone on that side of the island, especially if you were on the very brink of labour. And though the seals would have bobbed like corks about you, watching in their mildly curious way, they would have been no help.

It so happened that, on the ferry's return leg from the Isle of May, just as we left the cliffs, one engine of our boat cut out, and we, like Teneu, were cast adrift. The unpredictable motion of the waves had us spinning and rocking until the skipper managed to restart the engine, but not the steering. It fell to one of the crew to stand on the upper deck and call instructions to his colleague, who in turn was in charge of a manual rudder. It was by these means, or by the hand of St Teneu, that we were guided back to shore.

The story of Teneu resides in the late medieval *Aberdeen Breviary*, as well as a *Life of St Kentigern* (alias St Mungo), which survives alongside a Latin version of the Albina legend, a life of Merlin, and, intriguingly, a remedy for spasms, in a manuscript, also late medieval, kept in the

British Library (Cotton MS Titus A XIX). The fragment names Teneu as the daughter of King Leudonus of Leudonia (the Latin for 'Loth of Lothian'). It does not explicitly say that her own mother is Anna, sister of Arthur, nor that her grandmother was Igraine, but I have added it here because it is Loth of Lothian whom she marries in Geoffrey of Monmouth's *History of the Kings of Britain*.

The Arthurian connection is reinforced by the name of her suitor and rapist, 'Ewen Son of Ulien', who is said to have 'sprung from a most noble stock of the Britons'. And indeed Sir Owain, also known as Ewain, or 'Yvain, son of Urien', is one of Arthur's knights of the Round Table throughout the Arthurian tradition. It is reasonable to imagine that a medieval audience may have conflated these characters, as I have done above.

Teneu would not be the only early saint in Britain to have connections with the Arthurian court. In a poem in the aforementioned manuscript, Teneu's son, Mungo, meets an aged Merlin in the woods, as you will soon read. Likewise, in the legend of St Cadog, held to be a contemporary of King Arthur and his knights, the saint often outdoes Arthur, who is repeatedly abashed by his brilliance and forced to beg for forgiveness. Similarly, Teneu reveals the superficiality of Owain's chivalry in the face of her chastity.

In later life, Teneu's son, Mungo, is said to have founded both Glasgow and Glasgow Cathedral, and he remains the dedicatory saint of the latter. In the Middle Ages, a chapel to St Teneu stood in what is now St Enoch Square (St Enoch may be a corruption of the name St Teneu). And today, on a wall of Glasgow's High Street, a monumental mural painted by the artist Sam Bates (alias Smug) in 2018 shows Teneu in modern dress, breastfeeding her son.

In the Teneu legend, the Britons are occupying lands well into modern-day Scotland. And as well as residing in Glasgow, Mungo is said to have spent time in South Wales with St David. We are now at the start of the sixth century, when the Britons still dominate Britain. But, thanks to Arthur, new ties have been formed with Denmark, whence another wave of settlers will come. And the Saxons are biding their time.

21

Havelok the Dane

The Danes, however, felt great hatred for them [the British] because their relatives had died in the battles that Arthur waged against Mordred, whom he subsequently killed . . . I have found it recorded in the written source that during the reign of Constantine – the same Constantine who was kinsman to Arthur who owned Excalibur – there were already two kings in Britain . . . These two kings became such close acquaintances that they swore to be bosom companions, and so intimate was the friendship between them that Edelsi gave his sister in marriage to Adelbriht, that powerful king of Danish extraction. As far as king Edelsi was concerned, he was a Briton.

Geffrei Gaimar, History of the English (c. 1136–7)

Pushing wet strands of her long dark hair from her eyes, Argentille drew the knot tight, fixing the corpse to the stake. She was well-protected in her thick outdoor clothing, and her legs – they had carried her many miles – were braced against the wind. From a distance, the dead man would seem to be standing. This was it. She shook the water from her nose and checked the ranks of bodies around her. She was the only living soul left on the endless marsh, and her task was complete.

Argentille had been robbed over and over again. Death had robbed her of her father. Her uncle had robbed her of her crown. The Danish knights had robbed her of her dignity. Now that she and Havelok were back in Norfolk, she would be robbed no more.

Before his death, her father had been a lesser king within Britain, ruling Norfolk and part of Denmark under Arthur. His sister was married to Edelsi, who ruled the territory of Lindsey to the north. When King Arthur had died, Constantine had succeeded, and Britain's grip on its domains had weakened. When Argentille's father had died too, Edelsi had married her off to 'the highest man in the land' and quietly taken her throne.

The 'highest man in the land', it transpired, was Cuaran, a servant who was taller than anyone she had ever seen. He was also loved by the whole household. His young limbs were long and strong, and Argentille had often observed him when she had still held her position in the court. She had heard too of his reputation as a skilled wrestler, feared far and wide. Never had she dreamed they would one day share his small, splintered bed, but any pleasure she might have enjoyed from their union was prevented by the strange thing that he did each night.

Every evening, Cuaran would meet her at their bedside, say goodnight, climb in, turn his back to her, and sleep with his face pressed into the pillow. He did this so deliberately that she wondered how he was breathing.

So it continued until one night, when Argentille's desire for her mysterious husband grew too strong for her to hold back. Cuaran got into bed and she cajoled him with gentle kisses and whispered words until the servant and the princess knew joys alien to that splintered single bed. They fell asleep afterwards, and as she slept, Argentille had a dream. She dreamed she was on a beach with Cuaran, the sea on one side, trees on the other. Before them she saw a bear, surrounded by an army of foxes. The bear menaced Cuaran, taking no notice of her. Then suddenly a herd of wild pigs came out of the sea, shaking foam from their bristles. They started attacking the bear and the foxes, which had been about to consume Cuaran, till the pebbles of the beach were bloody. There was nothing Argentille could do.

Then the biggest of the pigs singled out the bear and charged, its tusks bright in the sun. They sank into the bear's shaggy chest, and Argentille knew that its heart had been cut in two. All around, the army of foxes bowed before Cuaran, their tails between their legs. More creatures appeared after that, at first fierce, then reverent, until suddenly Argentille was awake.

Where was she? She was no longer on the beach. She was certainly not in her childhood bed, with its soft pillows and clouds of silk. She was clutching someone's arm. Cuaran. There was light shining beyond her closed eyelids. She opened them.

Her face was close to Cuaran's cheek and she could smell his warm skin. He had rolled, for the first time in their marriage, onto his back. And a light, so bright it forced her to squint, was dancing like a crane-fly in his open mouth. She sat up and stared. Was she imagining it? She rubbed her eyes to be sure she was not still dreaming. But no, there was the flame still, licking the insides of his cheeks and spilling over his lips. Each time he breathed out it grew brighter, and each time he breathed in it drew back. It was as though someone had filled his mouth with hot wine and set it alight. Maybe someone had. She realised she must help him.

'Cuaran!' she hissed. 'You're on fire!'

She took him by his shoulders and shook. He awoke, the flame disappeared and they were both at once in darkness.

'You were on fire,' she repeated. 'Let me get you water.'

She made to leave the bed but his hand closed around her elbow.

'Wait,' he said. His voice was not cracked or damaged. It was embarrassed.

'But there was fire in your mouth. You need water.'

'It happens when I sleep,' he said, 'I don't know why – I tried not to let you see.'

Argentille could not believe what she was hearing. But she put her arms around him anyway and told him not to be ashamed. It felt nice, she thought, to hold him. After a moment she told him of her dream. She felt Cuaran shrug. Maybe, he suggested, it was about the leftovers he would collect after tomorrow's feast, and give to the eager squires. She knew his explanation was wrong and that the dream and the flames were connected. She longed to learn more.

'You know what's really shameful?' she whispered.

'What?'

'Living here as servants in my uncle's castle. Why don't we go and stay with your family? Where do they live?'

'In a town called Grimsby,' Cuaran replied.

'Then we will go there.'

Argentille and Cuaran set off as soon as they had received permission from the King, which he granted happily, doubtful they would last long without his succour. The couple took with them Cuaran's two brothers, also servants at the castle. When they came to the town of Grimsby, Argentille found it to be small but well built, with houses that ran right down to the shores of the Humber. Fishermen and -women were working along the harbour and, as it was midday, the night's catch had been sorted and sold, but the boxes were still stacked where the town met the beach and glittered with the scales of fish.

Cuaran and his brothers led the way to the home of their sister, Kelloc, where she lived with her husband. She welcomed them in, exclaimed at their damp clothes, and, after being introduced to Argentille and told of her history, took both her hands and kissed them. There was no mistaking her cleverness, nor her kindness. From the moment of their arrival, no time was lost in stoking the hearth, so that, before long, they were beside a bright fire, wrapped in blankets, sipping broth. When her husband got home, he greeted Cuaran warmly, and that evening, over ale, Kelloc asked Cuaran a question.

'Do you know who you are, and where your family comes from?'

He answered that he was Cuaran, she was his sister, his father was a fisherman called Grim, and his mother, Seburg, helped him in his trade. But, when he had finished, Kelloc shook her head.

'I am not your true sister, and my mother and father, Grim and Seburg, are not your true parents. And they are not from Grimsby – they are the reason it exists.'

Then Kelloc told them a story. She told of how her

father, Grim, had been a knight in the court of King Gunter of Denmark and his Queen Alvive. She said he had been Queen Alvive's godfather, and she had become Kelloc's godmother in return. She had been good and learned, and sometimes she had let Kelloc hold her baby, whose name was Havelok. When King Arthur had come from Britain and conquered Denmark, King Gunter was killed. All was chaos and terror in the court, and Grim had said they should flee. He invited Queen Alvive to come with them, along with her baby son. They all boarded a ship for Britain.

Argentille saw that Kelloc's sharp eyes were shining more brightly now, but her voice did not falter.

'During the sea passage we were attacked by pirates and Alvive was thrown into the sea, along with many others. When the pirates finally left, we sent ropes into the ocean, but the ship had been blown far off course. I still dream of finding her.'

Argentille could only listen in wonder. It was after this, Kelloc continued, that Grim, his family and the baby Havelok had drifted to a river-mouth, which they came to learn had been called the Humber since the days of the first Kings of Britain. They landed and made camp, using half the timbers from the ship to build a shelter. Later, they used the rest to build a fishing boat. Grim caught fish in the sea – cod, salmon, turbot, mackerel and many other kinds of sea creature – and what they didn't eat themselves, they traded for bread. Over the years, others moved

to Grim's settlement and built their houses. Because of Grim, they called the town Grimsby.

Cuaran bowed his head. 'I am honoured to be at table with the daughters of a knight and a king.'

Kelloc smiled.

'Alvive was your mother, Cuaran, and you are Havelok. You were the baby. And that flame we used to tease you for is a mark of your royalty. You belong on the throne of Denmark and for our sake you must reclaim it. We will pay your passage.'

At this, Kelloc's husband told them that he travelled often to Denmark to trade, and that its British king, the brother of the one who had been installed after Arthur's conquest, was a tyrant whom many people despised. He believed they would have much support on arrival.

When Argentille and Havelok went to bed, she could tell by the darkness that he too was lying awake. But she was not scared. She was eager. With Havelok's strength and her cunning, more than one wrong could be righted.

Over the next few weeks, Kelloc helped Argentille and Havelok find fine clothes to wear for their journey, to show their royal status. When they were ready, they sailed to Denmark, but as soon as they disembarked, the King's knights — little more than thugs — abducted Argentille outside their lodgings. Havelok chased after them, killing one of their number, and together he and Argentille fled to a church tower. Soldiers were sent in pursuit, but as soon as Sigar, the man in charge of the troop, saw Havelok's face, he dispersed the men. Then he invited Havelok and Argentille to his castle, though he did not tell them why.

Later, Argentille learned that Sigar had once been loyal to King Gunter, Havelok's father. He had recognised the boy's features at once as those of his former lord's and, realising who he must be, had sent a servant to spy on Havelok as he slept. The man confirmed that a flame burned brightly in his mouth, so other barons were called who had once supported King Gunter, and Argentille wondered if Havelok was to be condemned when she saw the great crowds assemble. But all Sigar did was offer Havelok a horn that no one could blow but the rightful

King of Denmark. Everyone celebrated at the peal of the horn, and, once the knights had pledged themselves to Havelok, they went back to their domains to raise an army. When they had more than thirty thousand knights, they declared their rebellion and met the British King in battle. Havelok killed many men and, with the help of his barons, he won back the throne of Denmark.

While Havelok was fighting, Argentille was forming a plan of her own. She had to win back the throne stolen from her by her uncle. There was no world in which he would escape, not while she had breath. But, for this, she would need Havelok and the armies now under his command. She spoke to him after his victory and soon they were sailing back across the North Sea, this time at the head of a fleet. Argentille could already see the ranks of clouds, advancing like mounted cavalry, the light flexing over the flatness of the land. Hers was a kingdom of deep skies and slow, shallow waters.

They docked beside the salt marshes, made the long walk across the beach and set up camp. Fires were lit, food was shared and the men were lively. Word was sent to Edelsi, stating their claim and offering peace, but he rejected it at once: the battle would be fought tomorrow. Argentille listened as Havelok and his barons conferred. She could have told them where Edelsi might hide his spies, how to fight from the great ditches that traversed the open marsh, but her presence was not welcome. She waited outside the tent. On the cold evening air, she could hear the cry of a curlew. A pair of ducks flew overhead, silhouetted against the sky. By this time tomorrow, she told herself, she would be queen and that was all that mattered.

The next day, Havelock and Edelsi met on open ground. The slaughter was great, but the same on both sides, and when evening came with no victory, it was agreed they would meet again in the morning. As the survivors returned to the camp, Argentille heard their news. She saw defeat and reproach in their eyes, as if they were blaming her. And there were so many dead and injured for the sake of her claim. In the privacy of her tent, she wept. She had no doubt in her claim, but could not watch more lives being lost, nor live with the suffering of the injured. She had to help.

Argentille seized her cloak and drew it about her, throwing the hood over her long hair. She stepped into the night as a thunderclap shook the sky, and weaved through the tents, braziers and mounds of huddled mantles, searching for Havelok's voice. When she found it, he was conversing with his barons, as usual. They looked up, their faces sheeplike by the light of a guttering lamp.

'I have a plan,' she said.

That night, in the hollow, rain-spattering darkness, she led them and fifity other men. And there, beneath the bellies of the clouds, they undertook the worst task of their lives. They harvested hazel poles and drove them in

lines into the field. Then, following Argentille's instructions, they dragged the bodies of the fallen to the poles
and tied them upright to them. Argentille shouted over
the wind, securing the ropes and checking the lines in the
bright flashes of lightning. The men worked with sober
horror. When they had done as she had asked and returned
shivering to their tents, she surveyed their work, securing
the final knots. Rows of dark corpses were standing as
though alive, their eyes reflecting the storm. Rain running
down her face, she prayed the plan would work.

In the morning, Argentille rose early and stood at
the edge of the battlefield. The rain had ceased and the
sun burned off the morning mist as she watched Havelok
and his soldiers arrange themselves between the ranks

of the dead. It was convincing. Next, she saw her uncle's scouts survey the assembled troops and leave to report to the King. And when she saw them return to concede defeat, she crossed the plain to Havelok, a great triumph in her chest. And she imagined the two of them seated on their thrones either side of a great stretch of sea. And she imagined their hands reaching and clasping across the waters. And she knew they would rule in harmony and their union would be remembered.

❖

The version of the Havelok story used here survives in Geffrei Gaimar's *History of the English*, written in the first part of the twelfth century for a Lincolnshire patron called Constance. It seems to attribute the very real phenomenon of Danish influence in the north-east of Britain to the consequences of Arthur's legendary conquest of Denmark. It reflects how, at the time in which Gaimar was working, just as today, the legacy of what is known as 'Danelaw' in Lincolnshire would have been palpable. In reality, it was established in 886, after years of attacks on England from the Vikings, when Alfred the Great came to a formal agreement with the Danish King Guthrum. The Danes took control of fifteen shires in the east and north of England. Danelaw covered a vast area, running from what is now North London to just shy of Durham and west to the north of Wales.

A later, Middle English version of *Havelok the Dane* is better known and differs from the account in Gaimar in certain key ways. For instance, it is set in tenth-century England; Grim is not a knight but a Danish fisherman, born and bred; Argentille is called Goldborough; and she does not have the ingenious idea of propping up corpses on the morning of battle to fool Edelsi. This last detail is especially compelling; even more so as, when I stood looking out to sea on the salt marshes of the Humber Estuary, eating the finest fish and chips in the land, I happened to witness the RAF practising so-called 'shows of force' with military planes. These flat lands and coastal waters, so rich in seals, samphire and battered fish, are rich too in stories of war.

Grimsby's thirteenth-century town seal (a matrix to be imprinted in wax, rather than a mammal), once used to authorise important civic documents, shows three figures enclosed by the border inscription, 'SIGILLVM : COMUNITATIS : GRIMESBYE' (The Seal of the Community of Grimsby). The centrally placed and largest figure is a man, shield raised, sword aloft, with a divine hand descending from the upper edge of the seal to bless him. To his right, beneath two inscriptions, is a smaller figure with an axe in his right hand and a ring in his left. Floating just above his head is a crown. Opposite him is the veiled figure of a woman, gesturing towards the ring with her right hand and holding a sceptre in her left, a crown also above her head. In illustrations from England in this period, the axe is frequently used to identify Danish characters, while the crown and sceptre are unmistakably royal attributes. The ring, as today, implies marriage, which is consistent with the way in which the female figure is seeming to receive the ring from her male counterpart. Between them, the central figure's size and centrality, not to mention the blessing being bestowed by the hand of God, indicate his high status in the scheme; he is the main character. While the visual clues go a long way to revealing the identity of the trio, it is made explicit by the three inscriptions lying within the image field. They read 'Gryem', 'Habloc' and 'Goldbvrgh' – the last of these the name given to Argentille in the later Middle English version of the Havelok legend. It is intriguing that the medieval Grimsby town seal uses the later name, Goldborough, for Argentille, but depicts Grim with the weapons of a warrior, as in the earlier version. Grimsby, it implies, owes its origins to a man adept as much with the sword as with the net. From its place on the north-east coast, where the nearby Continent has historically represented both a source of potential trade and military aggression, it's little surprise we find such a hero.

From here on in, we will see more Danes in Britain, and indeed more Saxons. The sun is setting on the Golden Age of Arthur – even Merlin is getting old.

22

The Death of Merlin

The same hour was the thing fulfilled upon Nebuchadnezzar: and he was driven from men, and did eat grass like oxen, and his body was wet with the dew of heaven, till his hair had grown like eagles' feathers, and his nails like birds' claws.

Daniel 4: 33

His treasure was the cry of cranes as they flew their staves across the sky, calling in the first glimmer of sunrise. It was as if dawn came for their song, not the other way around. His solace was in the indifference of the hog, doe and hare to matters of the future. They never asked him what would come to pass. And though he still read the heavens, he was not beholden to them. Nothing he read there required him to act. That is, not until last night.

It was not that he did not love her; it was that he was, and always had been, alone. There were times when he remembered with nostalgia Guendoloena's eagerness to be his lover as well as his wife. He wished he could have let her. He wished he had been able to surprise her with gifts and poetry, like the other men of the court. He wished he had been able to fight in her name, as the knights had done. But then he remembered how false he had felt when he had come close to submitting. He belonged alone.

Merlin had married Guendoloena when Arthur was king. But his soul had pined for the mellow incense of the forest, the privacy of its airy halls and the darkness of the chambers beneath them. Since then, Arthur had departed and Merlin had left his wife alone in the court of King Rhydderch. Now that she was to remarry, as he had urged her to do since his madness had come, he would at least offer a gift.

Merlin stepped out of the cave in which he had been sleeping and stretched up to grasp a branch that overhung the entrance. He dangled from the tree as he did every morning, the weight of his legs pulling at his shoulders and spine. It was a tree he knew well, ancient and crooked like himself. He remembered seeing the acorn from which it had germinated fall from the beak of a woodpecker and land on this spot. Merlin remembered when the forest had been a hunting ground and he had ridden through it on a horse. Merlin remembered riding into battle, too, though that was a memory he wished he could forget.

A squirrel was watching from a higher branch, its nostrils deciphering the bark. It was well used to the old man, whose beard was long and whose naked skin was loose, and who often left small fragments of food on the ground at the entrance to his cave. It watched him as he lifted and lowered his legs, for no purpose that it could fathom. It watched him as he dropped from the tree and ran, bow-legged, down to the water and along a fallen tree-trunk. Springing from it, his buttocks real and reflected clapped and disappeared in a scatter of glancing light.

Once he had resurfaced, Merlin swam till his breath was his own again. Then he pulled himself onto the bank, delighting in the heat of his wrinkled, chill-rosy skin. Now, he thought, he was ready. All he had to do was prepare the wedding gift.

Many animals lived in the vast forest in which Merlin lived. There were boar, stags, sows and does, all fat from the abundant vegetation. He had often thought of the lengths to which the kings used to go to obtain such meat, riding out early in the morning with slathering hounds and snorting horses to chase the creatures for hour upon hour. Merlin had little to offer, but the game with which he shared the trees would be a handsome gift even by the standards of the court. He would find his own food as he went, he decided, as he strode off into the trees. The squirrel followed.

Aided by a little of his old magic, which he used rarely these days, the elderly Merlin encouraged the beasts he saw to follow him. There were wild boar with their striped piglets, now getting larger, which trotted together, their dainty feet and bristly bodies jostling through the leaves. Then there were deer, young bucks among them, growing out of the delicacy shared by the fawns and does and towards the pungency of the older stags. Some had lost their antlers; it was that time of the year. Goats came too, which lived wild in the forest. Soon, Merlin was surrounded by a herd of game.

He climbed onto the back of the largest stag, which had a crown of tawny spears as wide as Merlin was tall, and a body so deeply furred that Merlin had no need for reins. His fingers creaked into its warm shoulders as he clutched handfuls of the wiry hair, enflamed by the rays of the sun. Beneath his legs, Merlin could feel the beast's web of muscles. Thus seated, excited by the splendour of his gift, Merlin began to lead the herd on their long journey out of the trees, towards the court of King Rhydderch, towards the wedding of Guendoloena.

When they reached open plains, they ran as fast as the piglets could manage. Sometimes Merlin found himself racing ahead for the thrill of the cold in his hair and beard, and the flow of the muscles beneath his calves. This was his charger, the beautiful stag. Its antlers were finer than any spear or sword. This was his palace: the reddening piers of the autumn forest, the auburn marshes and the open vaults of the sky.

It was late morning before the buildings of Rhydderch's court – a place which would one day be called Glasgow –

came into view, either side of a river and beyond a band of forest. Merlin emerged from the trees with his following in a line either side of him, the fur as bronze as the leaves. He led them to the main gate.

'Guendoloena,' he called from his mount. 'Look! These gifts are for you!'

She heard him from her room and rushed down to the gates. As they were opened for her, she smiled to see the man she still loved. He could see her wondering, as she gazed at the assembled animals, at his powers. Then, from somewhere above her, came the sound of laughter.

From his place on the back of the stag, Merlin could see into one of the upper-storey windows. The bridegroom, dressed in silk, with thick dark hair and taut skin, was pointing at him from the window and laughing. His teeth were white in the darkness, but his laughter was brighter. Merlin had never much liked being laughed at.

And suddenly he saw himself, as if through the eyes of the laughing youth. He was naked, shrivelled, half crippled, his aged genitals flat in the fur of the stag, useless, his hair tangled and silver, his chest a hollow cave, his heart a flapping moth. And the man was still laughing, as if he had never beheld anything so pathetic. And Merlin felt a rage that was red and fire-breathing. And before he knew it, he had seized the base of each of the stag's antlers, and torn them from its head. The beast bellowed, the weight of a year's growth lifted too soon. And the man barely had time

to stop laughing before Merlin had hurled the antlers, tine over tine, through the air and into the open window. They struck the head of the groom.

Merlin thought he saw the mottled red and white of brains and blood hitting the back wall of the chamber, but he did not wait. He did not want to see Guendoloena's face. He kicked the stag, turning away and charging back into the forest with his herd of wild beasts. As he rode, he felt as if a tree had been uprooted in his heart. And with that a fresh madness seized him.

Merlin stayed in the forest for many years, and in that time the child of a princess of Lothian, whose name was

Teneu, rose to the rank of bishop and built a church beside Rhydderch's court. His name was Kentigern, though he was better known as Mungo.

One evening, as Mungo prayed among the trees of the Caledon, he heard the sound of running feet. Looking up, he saw an old man with hair and beard like wild clematis. Mungo knew him at once to be Merlin, the soothsayer of Arthur's court, who had fled to the woods in his dotage and of whom so many stories were told. Abandoning his prayers, Mungo caught up with the old man and took hold of his arm. The frail chest played like bellows.

'Why do you live out here on your own?' Mungo asked.

'I am Vortigern's bard – I have done terrible things.'

Then Merlin began to weep, slipping from Mungo's grasp and running into the trees. The Bishop did not follow him, but returned to his cloister at Molendinar Burn, deep in thought. In his cell overlooking the town, he prayed for Merlin's soul.

Sometime after this, Merlin started to visit Mungo at his monastery. And though the wind was biting, he would sit on a crag near the church, shrieking prophecies into the valley. Within their chapter house, the monks whispered between themselves.

'It is Merlin!'

'He built Stonehenge with magic!'

'He was fathered by a demon!'

What with Merlin's prophecies and the whispering he provoked, Mungo began to wish he had never met the old man in the trees. But he would not desist and continued his visits for weeks, until, one morning, they changed. Now, rather than cries of discord and doom, he spoke quietly of his own impending death and asked to receive the Eucharist. Mungo was much irritated by their guest and said to the monks:

'He has spoken nothing but lies since taking his place on that rock. God sent him to the wild. That is where he belongs.'

But the monks stood around him, their eyes bright with sympathy.

'If you don't believe he is mad,' Mungo continued, 'why don't you go and ask Merlin how he will die?'

So they asked him, and he said, 'Today I shall be stoned and clubbed to death.'

The clerics rushed back to Mungo. He was going to be murdered! What should they do?

'He is lying. Ask him the same question again.'

They did, and Merlin declared, 'Today my body will be pierced by a stake.'

The brothers relayed his reply.

'I do not think we should give him Communion,' said Mungo.

But the monks went to Merlin and asked him of his death once more, eager to save his soul. This time Merlin told them, 'Today I will drown.'

At this, the clerics asked why he insisted on lying if he wanted them to grant his request. But Merlin, with his leather-bellows ribs, just pulled at his clematis hair.

'I have spoken the truth,' he wept.

They went into the church and implored the Bishop to give him the Sacrament. And, at last, seeing the old man weeping on the rock, Mungo felt his heart soften. Stepping outside and approaching him, he heard the prophet say:

'When you prayed for me in the woods, a demon left my body. If I eat the Sacrament, I will be rid of him forever.'

And Mungo knew that he could not deny Merlin a chance at salvation. He helped him wash and dressed him in fresh robes. Then the whole company gathered in the church. And, just as the evening sun entered by the west window, Merlin approached Mungo on the chancel steps and took the bread in his mouth. And, when he had eaten it, he made one last prediction:

'If I die today, the King will follow me within a year.'

From the moment Merlin had entered the church, he had been still and quiet, but as soon as the blessing was finished, he flung off his robes and raced naked back to the woods. He preferred it there, after all.

The next morning there were reports that shepherds from a village called Drumelzier had mistaken a wild-man for a thief and attacked him with clubs and stones, causing him to fall over a precipice. The corpse was found face down in a fish pond, with a sharpened post through its stomach. Mungo realised that Merlin had predicted his death correctly. And just as Merlin had been correct in this, so his last prophecy came true. Within a year, the court of King Rhydderch, a Briton, was sacked by Áedán, King of the Scotti, who had strongholds in northern Britain. This was the same Áedán whom St Columba crowned.

❖

In the twelfth-century *Life of Merlin* attributed to Geoffrey of Monmouth, Merlin goes mad during a battle between the Britons, led by King Rhydderch, and the Scots. In this account, King Rhydderch's queen, Ganeida, is Merlin's sister, and his wife, Guendoloena, lives in the court as well. When she remarries, he takes her game from the forest as a gift. However, in a sudden rage upon hearing the groom's derisive laughter, he hurls antlers ripped from the head of his stag and kills his rival. By the end of the narrative, Merlin has retreated permanently to the forest, joined by two other men: a soldier cured from madness and the bard Taliesin. His sister Ganeida joins them too and begins to prophesy. The poem closes with Merlin's words: 'Has the spirit moved you, sister, to foretell the future, thus closing both my mouth and my book? The task is now yours: take joy in it . . .'

That is one way in which Merlin the Prophet 'dies', by passing the baton of prophecy to the character of his sister. But he dies in other ways too. In French retellings of his legend, he is seduced and consigned to eternal sleep by his student, Vivien, which is also the story told by Malory in his *Morte d'Arthur*. I have given you yet another version, in which Merlin foretells his own death to St Mungo (alias Kentigern). In this form, the character of Merlin remains a trickster, as well as a seer. And the place of his death, the forests of Caledonia, seems both to reflect and absorb his nature in Geoffrey of Monmouth's *History of the Kings of Britain* and, if he was indeed the author, his *Life of Merlin*. Even today these forests are the haunts of wildcats and pine martens, creatures that, while cunning, shy away from human settlement, preferring a life of solitude among the trees.

The inspiration for the Merlin-Mungo episode is the late medieval *Vita Merlini Silvestris*. And, although the wildman is called 'Lailoken' throughout, we are told in his own words (here translated by Alexander Penrose Forbes) to identify him as Merlin: 'I am a Christian, though unworthy of the name, once the Bard of Vortigern, and called Merlin.'

It is typical of Merlin that there is no dominant account of his death. His fading from view, however, marks the end of the Britons' supremacy in Albion and the dawning of a land dominated by the progeny of Scota and invaders from Woden's North. It is to this land that we now migrate, and it is no less short of wonders.

Part Four

The Middle Ages

23

The River Ness Monster

They said they had seen a water beast snatch him and maul him savagely as he was swimming not long before. Although some men had put out in a little boat to rescue him, they were too late, but, reaching out with hooks, they had hauled in his wretched corpse.

Adomnán's *Life of St Columba* (late sixth century)

Lugne Mocumin was Columba's most loyal companion. While still living in Ireland, he had endured a nosebleed for many months and had sought out the saint for aid. Columba had pinched Lugne's nose shut and said a prayer. Not only had his nosebleed stopped that instant, but not one drop of blood had fallen from it since, nor would it for the rest of his life.

He followed Columba from that day forth and the holy man was intent on crossing the Irish Sea to spread the Christian faith among the Picts. Columba knew the Scotti there, who had travelled from Hibernia and made settlements. He had crowned their king, Áedán mac Gabráin, on the holy island of Iona.

Columba took his followers across as far east as they could go, to where the waters once again grew briny. There was a town ahead of them, which straddled a river called the Ness. The river was wide, deep and pebble-bedded, flanked by forests, hemmed by purple mountains, and the air was still and warm, but Lugne was too distracted to admire this beauty, for, as they had been walking, they had found themselves in the company of a swarm of little flies.

Plagued by the hundred malicious motes dancing around his head, Lugne was suffering worse than the others. The cool river water called to him. Lugne scratched his arms and neck, which were growing raw from the scraping of his nails.

But then, from across the hazy waters, Lugne heard talking. Squinting ahead, he could just make out a boat, moored to the opposite bank of the river. On the shore beside it was a group of men, crowded around something on the ground. They drew closer and Lugne saw that a man lay on the bank. He could hear someone retching. And then he understood why.

The man was dead and his corpse was a mess: its stomach had been punctured and the insides had slid out onto the stones, connected to the chest cavity by a blue sinew; the side of the man's face was missing and the skin had been flayed from one of his legs. Around him, and spanning the river, the bloodlust of midges intensified. Lugne felt bile rising in his throat and his tongue itched, as though the flies were crawling into his mouth. One of the people on the opposite bank was waving in warning.

'There is a monster in the water,' he cried.

Columba had stopped walking and Lugne could see that, though his face and neck were covered in midge bites, he had not scratched them at all. Lugne rubbed the unholy scratchings on his own skin.

'Bring me that boat,' said Columba. 'I want to cross the river.'

The boat was on the other side of the water and who-ever fetched it would have to swim, despite the threat of the monster who had killed and savaged the man whose corpse now buzzed on the far bank. Still, Lugne obeyed without hesitation. He dropped his bag, kicked off his shoes, pulled his tunic over his head and took a running jump into the middle of the water; then, gliding beneath the flow, he struck out for the opposite bank.

The cold hit him.

No. The cold *caressed* him.

He was passing through icy ecstasy, each hole and cut on his skin soothed by the water, which not only held him, but held back the tide of biting insects. But when he opened his eyes, he knew the monster had been no fantasy. Something was blocking out the glimmer of the overwater world. He saw the curve of a neck. He saw a face staring

down at his: jaws, bovine eyes, and smooth, glistening skin. Everything was reverberating in the current. Lugne felt his body resign. He shut his eyes and waited for it all to end.

But no deadly bite came. There came a rush in the current, but there was no sinking of teeth into flesh. Chancing a look, Lugne saw through the murk what was happening. In the cool green of the water, the monster was shooting backwards, as though ropes had been strung around its flippers and were dragging it away.

The need to breathe took hold of Lugne's lungs and he kicked his legs, making for the surface glimmer. His head broke the water, and he gasped as he re-entered the hostile, humming world.

Columba was standing on the riverbank with one hand outstretched. Around him his followers were weeping and raising their arms in praise. And Lugne realised he had been witness to yet another miracle. The saint had vanquished a monster. And as Lugne swam to the opposite bank and unmoored the little boat, the insects fell hungrily upon him, reunited with their host.

❖

It was August, and I was standing on a bridge in Inverness. There were no midges here, which are most voracious in the damp, still glens of the west, and there was no monster either. So much for my story.

I had come from Glen Coe via Loch Ness to see the river and to imagine Columba's progress with his missionaries as they traversed the Highlands. The journey had carried me through realms so lofty I swear I felt the clouds brushing the crown of my head, and so majestic the mountains and hills around me seemed a royal council in robes of purple heather. To come to this territory before modern roads, to trust in the friendship of strangers and the kindness of the weather, when both were unpredictable, must have taken great resolve, whether or not there were monsters.

The sixth-century River Ness monster is often cited in relation to the modern legend of its more famous Loch Ness cousin. I like the coincidence, but that's all it is. Water monsters abound in medieval saints' lives, along with dragons and sundry demons of land and sky.

Columba lived from AD 521 to 597 and is traditionally credited with the Christian conversion of the Scots. An account of his life and miracles was written down by Adomnán (died 704), one of his descendants at the Abbey of Iona, which Columba is said to have founded. It was also there he is said to have crowned Áedán mac Gabráin, successor of Fergus Mór and King of the Dál Riata: an Irish-rooted kingdom that stretched from what are now parts of County Antrim, Ireland, into Argyll and Bute, Scotland.

On the one hand, there are no midges in the *Life of St Columba*; I made them up. On the other hand, any summer traveller in Scotland will, at some point or other, encounter this particular species of monster. Stories abound of swarms of midges crowded so densely around their human prey that they climb up noses and into ears, making skin burn, invading socks and trouser legs, and biting, biting, biting. Their tiny bodies, so easily nudged by a breeze, are like ash floating from a bonfire and do not seem capable of the torture they inflict. And yet some people are more vulnerable to them than others, scratching away at the red marks in agony while companions look on in bemusement.

As I stood on the bridge in Inverness, I considered how few medieval saints' lives feature miracles concerned with the more mundane irritations of life in Britain: wasps, for instance, or the tinnitus flight of the mosquito. I imagined Lugne diving into the river to escape a swarm of midges, preferring to risk death by one bite from a monster than to suffer a slow death by a million. And as I leant on the Inverness railings and looked down into wide, deep waters, I saw movement. A flipper shattered the placid surface. A bow-shaped ripple sliced through the stream. I readied myself for the flash of vicious teeth and glowing, demonic eyes. But then, flowing directly beneath me, visible as if through glass, a seal descended in a corkscrew to nose the riverbed.

24

Kenelm of Winchcombe

'You labour,' he said, 'for nothing and you are wasting your time. For I shall die in another place.'

St Kenelm, in *The Early South English Legendary*
(late thirteenth century)

Curly-haired Kenelm was the only son of an English king whose domains stretched from Gloucestershire to Staffordshire, forming a kingdom then known as Mercia. King Kenulf's court was in Winchcombe, among the Cotswold Hills, and from the upper timbers of the palace it was possible to see right the way across the trees of the Severn Valley, beyond the Malverns, which looked like jagged teeth, to the land of the foreigners, the Welsh, guarded beyond by hostile mountains. Kenelm's nurse, Olwen, had been raised behind those mountains and she told wonderful stories.

One story much beloved by Kenelm concerned Augustine, a missionary sent from Rome, who had converted the

King of Kent and brought the faith to his people. In those days, the Saxons, who were made up of Angles and Jutes as well, started calling their territory 'the land of the Angles' or 'Englalond', and called themselves the 'English'. And the Britons whom they had driven west they called 'foreigners' or *wealas*, which is where the word 'Welsh' comes from. Olwen did not like the word. She was a Briton, she said, descended from the Trojans led by Brutus.

One day, she told him, Augustine had visited the town of Dorchester to convert the English population. He had found the people bringing in a catch of fish teeming with skates and rays: winged, pipe-nosed fish that dwell in the seas around Britain. Some rays have a line of spikes running down their backs all the way to the ends of their tails. The English called those tails 'muggles'. It so happened that the fishermen were cutting the muggles from their catch when the pious Augustine arrived with his followers. As soon as the saint was close enough, one of the fishermen threw a spiky muggle, which caught on Augustine's vestments and hung there. Everyone laughed, so another was thrown, then another. Before long, every fishy, thorny morsel – skin, guts and bones – lying in the place was hanging from the missionary's clothes and he looked like a bird, arrayed with silver feathers. With that, he fled with his procession from the town, only shaking off the mob once he was at the summit of a hill five miles away. It is said that, in punishment for their treatment of Augustine, the people of Dorchester grew tails and that they came to be known thereafter as 'mugglings'. Some say that the affliction spread to all their people, and that from that day forth the English had tails.

Olwen was round and warm, with hairs on her chin and stories and prophecies in her blood. She told Kenelm – who did not have a tail – of a time when her people had roamed the whole island, led by giant warlords who built enormous cities, the ruins of which were still standing, and were called to conquest by goddesses. She knew how to interpret the stories too. 'That story is about extinction,' she would say, 'and this one about the call to a higher service.'

At birth, Kenelm had been baptised a Christian, and among the stories he loved most were those of angels, warrior martyrs and the holy explorers who spread the Christian faith. Olwen had filled Kenelm with the desire to be a saint. Not a quiet type, but a survivor, an adventurer and a daredevil. When he played, he would pretend to speak to the birds, pray in tongues or live on the back of a whale. He would banish dragons and vanquish devils. Sometimes he would fast till he was faint with hunger.

When Kenelm's father died, the boy was only seven years old, but despite having an older sister who was eager to be queen, he was placed on the throne. That same sister, Quendryda, felt cheated. She decided she would do whatever it took to rule instead, and began by concocting a poisonous draught. But when her brother drank it down, it did not even make him ill. She was not deterred and resolved to try again.

Each morning after Kenelm had finished his lessons, he would rush out to play. Then his tutor, Askobert, would stay in to plan the young King's learning for the next day. At these times, Quendryda would go into the classroom and ask for the young tutor's help translating her book of Psalms. Of course, struck by her rank and beauty, he would agree.

Quendryda proved a slow but attentive learner. She pressed her shoulder to his as she leant towards the words. She would gasp at his cleverness and laugh at his nervous jokes. And, though her Latin improved little, within a month all she had to do was touch his arm and he would falter as he spoke. When the time was right, she kissed him. Then their lessons were lost to passion. Askobert the tutor forgot all about his calling. Askobert the puppet of Quendryda would have done anything she asked of him.

One night, after Kenelm had said his prayers and fallen asleep, he was visited by a dream. He dreamed that a tree was growing at the foot of his bed and filling the sky. He started to climb, using the giant fissures in the bark as hand and footholds. As he looked up, he saw the canopy was ablaze with lanterns and laden with flowers. They drew quickly nearer as he climbed, though the tree was very tall, so that soon Kenelm had reached the uppermost bough and was crawling along it to find a seat among

the flowers. Never before had he seen anything so grand and perfect as the tree in which he was sitting. And when he looked ahead, he recognised the hills and rivers of his kingdom opening out before him: Gloucestershire, Worcestershire and Warwickshire and beyond, all within his view.

But then he heard footsteps coming from the ground below. Someone with an axe had begun chopping at the tree-trunk, making great chips fly and the whole canopy shake.

'No!' cried Kenelm from his perch on the high bough, but the person did not stop. He struck away at the vast trunk until he was surrounded by a mound of chips and splinters. And then Kenelm felt the tree beneath him begin to fall. And then he was falling with it. And he was in a whirl of lanterns, blooms, fruit and branches.

And, suddenly, Kenelm was flying, rising up through the air as the tree crashed past him. He had wings. He was a dove, free of the crushing branches and the hard forest floor. He left the world behind: the view of the Malverns, the snaking river, the vast palace woods.

When at last, with a jolt, he awoke, he was back in his bed, his face sweaty. Hearing his cries, Olwen had come running, had gathered him in her arms and was whispering words of comfort. Kenelm described the dream to her and she told him what it meant.

The next morning, Askobert came to find Kenelm and offered to take him hunting. Knowing what was to come, the boy smiled and took his tutor's hand.

'I'd like that,' he said.

They could have gone hunting nearby, but Askobert took him much further away, to the very borders of the kingdom, to Clent, where a forest covered two lonely hills. Kenelm chatted happily as they rode, and though the weather was mild and the paths well tended, it still took them a whole day to get there. As the sun began to set, Askobert thought of Quendryda and of all she had promised him.

When he had led Kenelm some way into the woods at Clent, he heard the boy say, 'I would like to sleep, Askobert. Here will do.'

He had already hopped off his horse, laid his cloak on the ground and put down the stick he had been using as a staff. He curled up on the cloak and within a few moments his breathing was deep and slow. Askobert wandered until he found a glade deeper in the woods. Then he set to work.

Tying up the horses, he took a small spade from his satchel. In his life as a cleric and tutor he had done little digging, so his progress was clumsy, but in time he had scooped away at the region's red soil enough to have made a grave for a child. Night was starting to fall when, with a start, he heard the voice of Kenelm. The child was standing beside him.

'You're wasting your time and effort. I will die in another place, where God decides. This staff in my hand will mark the place of my death.'

They walked on, to a clearing in the valley between the hills, where Kenelm pushed the staff into the ground. At once it began to grow. It grew upwards and branched out-wards. Buds formed, leaves unfurled, roots drove into the soil. Finally, an ash tree was standing between the tutor and the boy. Then the child began to chant, in a high young voice, a Psalm praising God, and descended a little further into the valley between the two hills. '*Te Deum laudamus*,' he sang, as he knelt down beneath a hawthorn tree.

Askobert approached the boy until he was so close behind him that he could make out the curls on the nape of his delicate neck, seen so often before when craned over a book. And then he saw Quendryda, and imagined all the rewards she would give him if he just . . .

He reached into his satchel for a knife as the boy kept on singing, invoking the martyrs and the saints. The little voice lilted in the silent forest like that of a nightingale. But then it stopped short. For, in one movement, Askobert had seized Kenelm's curls with his left hand and cut into his neck with his right. Then, and it seemed to take an age, he heard the body fall. And the curly-haired head was dangling from his fist. And as the tutor squeezed his eyes shut with horror, there was a flap of wings. And ascending before him, the cooing of a dove.

Some moments passed before Askobert dared to open his eyes again. He put down Kenelm's head, picked up the shovel and started, once more, to dig. Burying the little body where it lay was easy enough in the soft earth, though the sight of the blood mingling with the rust-coloured soil repulsed him. He consoled himself with the knowledge that had done as he was told.

But the Queen had other plans and forgot all about the tutor. Now that she had the throne of Mercia, she threatened anyone who mentioned her brother with immediate decapitation. And though she garnered a large army, those who served her did so out of fear. And the poor, murdered Kenelm might have been forgotten altogether, had it not been for the cow.

An old woman lived in Clent whose cow had taken to

spending each day in the wooded valley, sitting beneath a hawthorn tree. The villagers began to call that part of the valley 'Cowbach', which today has come to be called 'Clatterbach', and they wondered at how, although she refused to eat, the cow's udders expressed bucketfuls of sweet milk every morning and night.

Meanwhile, in St Peter's in Rome, the Pope was saying Mass. As if out of nowhere, a snow-white dove flew down to the altar and laid a piece of parchment before him. This caused much amazement in the church, but when the Pope tried to read the golden words upon it, inscribed by the Lord's hand, he found them to be in English. Envoys were sent into Rome, until they found natives of that land. They told the Pope the meaning of the note:

'Beneath a thorn tree in Clent, Cowbach, the King's son Kenelm lies with his head severed.' Between the cow and the dove, Quendryda's treachery would be unearthed.

So it was that, some weeks later, Quendryda was sitting in a side-chapel of her father's church in Winchcombe. She was alone, for her promises to Askobert had been empty. Where he was she neither knew nor cared.

As she admired the sleeves of her embroidered gown by the light streaming through the glass, she knew nothing of the note that had caused such a great stir in Rome, nor of the message that had been sent to Wulfred, Archbishop of Canterbury, regarding the body of her brother.

Nor did she know that the residents of Clent had told the search party about the cow, nor that the grave had been found. She did not know that, when the body had been recovered from the dark red soil, still tinged with her brother's blood, a spring had bubbled up on the spot. She was ignorant that, after much arguing, God had shown by a miracle that the monks of Gloucester, rather than Worcestershire, were to have the body and build Kenelm a shrine in Winchcombe. And she was none the wiser of their journey from Clent to the Cotswolds and the second spring that had miraculously surfaced only half a mile from the town. There was so much that Quendryda did not know, as she revelled in her finery, that when she looked out the window and glimpsed on the hills a great procession of women and men, she felt no foreboding.

Quendryda walked to the door of the church, where her attendant stood waiting, and asked what the crowd was about. The girl told her they were bringing the body of her brother, which, praise the Lord, had been found. At this, the Queen was enraged. She rushed back to her seat and snatched up her Psalter, turning to the Psalm which has long served as a curse upon oppressors. She hissed the holy words, her eyes darting to the window after every line, but would have been more cautious if she'd known what would happen next.

No sooner had she uttered the final malediction than her face grew red, then purple, and then the vessels

ruptured under her skin, until, with a horrible sound, her eyeballs burst out of her head and splattered onto the pages.

When the company with Kenelm's body entered the church, they found Quendryda groaning over her open Psalter and her eyeballs lying upon it, wet as rotten fruit. And though she was still uttering little cries of anger, she soon died. At this, the book was displayed beside St Kenelm's miracle-working shrine, where all could see and rejoice in the two round stains left on the parchment by her eyes. And just as gloriously as Kenelm was honoured, that's how little they honoured the Queen. They threw her body into a ditch where people emptied their bowels.

❖

By the time of Kenelm, England, the territory of the Saxons, was formed of kingdoms known as the 'Anglo-Saxon Heptarchy'. In the ninth century, Mercia was one of the mightiest kingdoms, spanning much of the Midlands and the South-West. Winchcombe, on the Welsh Marches, was an important royal and ecclesiastical centre in Mercia, along with Lichfield.

There are some historically verifiable elements of the tale of Kenelm and Quendryda. We know that their father, Kenulf (or Coenwulf) of Mercia really did reign until 821 and had a daughter called Cwoenthryth (therefore Quenthryth, and so Quendryda) and a son called Cynehelm (or Kenelm). We know that Quendryda was something of a law-breaker. For instance, there is evidence that she fraudulently acquired the title of Abbess of Minster-in-Thanet after a long dispute with Archbishop Wulfred. We also know that Kenelm's relics were being venerated at Winchcombe Abbey by the tenth century, when he was seen as a martyr and saint. However, there is no evidence Cwoenthryth had her brother killed. Cynehelm witnessed charters from 803 to 811, and probably died aged around twenty-five, rather than seven.

To all intents and purposes, the story of Kenelm belongs to the realm of legend. But his legend had some longevity. Pilgrims flocked to his shrine in Winchcombe Abbey throughout the Middle Ages – though the bucolic quality of the landscape as well as the power of the story must have been an attraction too. I walked the old way a few years ago when the wheat was golden and the willow leaves silver in the wind. It felt like Normandy, or northern Spain, until I was caught in a sudden rainstorm and took a bus home (I had an elderly dog with me and to do otherwise would have been too cruel).

Pilgrims visited Clent too. Grass-topped and red-earthed, the summits of the lonely Clent and Walton hills now constitute a favourite day-trip destination for residents of nearby Dudley, Kidderminster and Bromsgrove. But it is down in the less crowded valley, in the woods of Clatterbach, along St Kenelm's Pass, and where the spring flows from beside St Kenelm's church, that their medieval counterparts would have remembered the treachery of Askobert and the eventual triumph of his victim.

With its fairy-tale readability and vivid characters, it is little surprise that, after coming into being from the quills of monastic historians, we find Kenelm's story translated to the compendium of Middle English saints' legends known as the *South English Legendary*, dating to the late thirteenth and fourteenth centuries. These verse retellings were suited to domestic consumption; you can just imagine the dramatisation of the villains by an ebullient performer, while an audience of all ages and stages of education – members only needed to be able to understand their own mother tongue – gazed rapt, or listened with eyes absorbed in handiwork. From the *South English Legendary* came images of dragon-slaying, devil-bursting and dream visions, offering listeners not only entertainment but a view of history, universal as well as local, and a Christian moral code. Such stories were copied and recopied, added to and adapted, until at least the eve of the Reformation. As for the tale of Augustine's assault by the people of Dorchester, that is found in Anglo-Norman and Middle English translations of the *Brut*.

At this point in our story, the Britons are no longer the dominant force in Britain. Though King Áedán of the Scotti killed King Rhydderch of the Northern Britons, he has now been defeated by a Saxon King called Athelfryth. So the Saxons hold lands from Kent to Cumbria, and the Scotti must look further north, to where there are Picts to resist them, and Vikings who will prove unrelenting.

25

Mælbrigte Bites Back

These two agreed between themselves to meet, Sigurd and
Melbricta Toothy the Scot-earl, that they should meet and
settle their quarrel at a given place, each with forty men.

Orkneyinga Saga (early thirteenth century)

Somewhere in the region of Argyll, Moray and Ross, Mælbrigte the Bucktoothed was working a toothpick between
his large incisors. These were an advance guard behind
which trooped his face and body, well-fed, well-armed
and hairy. As he dug and twisted the pick, he was thinking
about the Norse raiders.

Tomorrow he would meet Sigurd Eysteinsson in battle,
and Mælbrigte would show him what happened if you
crossed a Pictish warlord. Oh, Sigurd would rue the day!
From his seat at the end the hall, Mælbrigte the Bucktoothed chewed the toothpick flat and narrowed his eyes
at his men.

*

Meanwhile, some distance away, his enemy Sigurd Eysteinsson was showing his own army how two could ride a horse.

'Hold on to his waist, Einar. Exactly. Now, gallop.'

The pair thrusted off into the gathering dusk and the watchers howled with laughter. Thorstein the Red, who really did have red hair, clapped the back of Aud the Intellectual, who blinked and said, 'Why are we doing this?'

Thorstein reminded Aud that Sigurd and Mælbrigte the Bucktoothed had agreed to meet with forty soldiers on each side. Except this was not what Sigurd was planning to do. He did not believe the Picts could be trusted. He would have forty horses, but two men on each horse. That meant two axes and two screaming faces from Sigurd's army for every spear and screaming face in the army of Mælbrigte the Bucktoothed.

'But isn't that cheating?'

Thorstein explained that, yes, it was cheating, but the cheated were no trouble if you killed them. Accepting this logic, Aud mounted his horse. Soon, forty pairs of men were galloping around the outside of the camp, whooping their glee to the stars.

When morning came, Mælbrigte the Bucktoothed glared toothily at his soldiers as they washed and dressed. And when they were finally mounted and ready to advance, he jabbed at them all with choice words of encouragement.

'Stick your spears up their arses.'

The soldiers roared and made for the field of battle. It was wide and flat, and as they approached, they could see Sigurd's men, arrayed on horseback in a long line, with the rising sun behind them. But as the sun ascended, it became clear that there was something wrong. A young Pict voiced their shared realisation.

'Each of the Norsemen has four legs!'

Mælbrigte the Bucktoothed spat, and peered at Sigurd's army to see if this were true. Then he bellowed like a walrus. The cheats! But he would not retreat. He would kill his share of men and die rather than betray a moment's fear.

Maces were whirled overhead, eyes rolled, and the feet of men and horses stamped. Across the plain, Sigurd could see Mælbrigte's front teeth flashing in the morning sun. He wondered if his men would stand up to this wild mob, even with double the fighters. Changing his strategy, he ordered the second riders to dismount, instructing them to appear to retreat, but then to outflank the enemy once fighting had begun.

And that is how it happened. Just when the fight between the Picts and the Norsemen was at its height, and the two sides were well matched, a new storm of Norse troops swept in from both sides, fresh-faced and wild. And they massacred the Picts and put Mælbrigte to death. Tough as a whale, it took him a long time to die.

Finding Mælbrigte's body, Sigurd cut off his head and tied it to the saddle of his horse, along with the heads of many other Picts. Then he galloped back to the camp, jumping streams and walls, singing victory songs. Around his legs, the heads bounced and jostled. This was his fatal error.

Spurring his horse, a sharp pain shot through his ankle. Looking down, he saw Mælbrigte's head glaring at him, lips drawn back in a grimace, his great front teeth smeared with blood. The blood had come from Sigurd's leg; the sharp white incisors had sliced into his skin. For a moment, the Pict's eyes seemed alive, but Sigurd kicked the head away. It nodded back into place.

Later that night, while in bed with a Pictish girl, Sigurd's leg began to ache, but he was too drunk to care. The next day, when his soldiers finally got up, they could not wake their leader. And when they lifted the covers from him, they saw the skin of his ankle was red, his leg swollen and his nails were blue as mussel shells. Within a day, Sigurd Eysteinsson was dead.

Thorstein the Red, Aud the Intellectual and the other Norsemen buried Sigurd beside the River Oykel and sang eulogies of his cunning. His only son ruled for one winter and died without an heir, thus ending Sigurd's line. When a new earl was sent from Norway, the northern settlements of the Vikings grew. But somewhere among the heads of the dead Pictish soldiers, worms picked at the

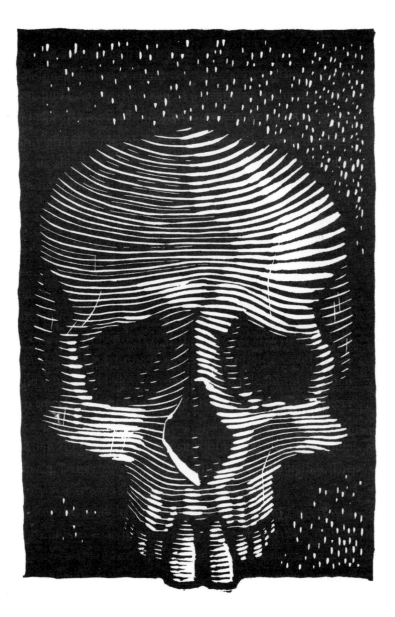

remains of Mælbrigte the Bucktoothed, leaving his teeth perfectly clean.

❖

The story of the toothy nobleman who caused the death of Sigurd Eysteinsson is preserved in the Icelandic *Orkneyinga Saga*, and may be found in the astonishing late fourteenth-century illustrated manuscript of Norse sagas known as *Flateyjarbók* (and by the shelf-mark GKS 1005 fol. at its home, the Árni Magnússon Institute for Icelandic Studies). While its historical accuracy is debatable (not least because it opens with a mythic genealogy starting with Frost, the father of Snow), it distinguishes between the Norwegian ruling classes and the Norwegian earls who governed the Orkney and Shetland Islands from the early Middle Ages.

For our purposes, it shows how, while the English kingdoms vied and coalesced in the south, eventually conceding to Danish pressure in the late ninth century and forming Danelaw, Norwegian influence was growing ever more strong in the north. This is the case in history as much as in legend. By the end of the eleventh century, the islands of Shetland, Orkney, Man and the Hebrides were all under Norse control.

Sigurd's bizarre death is one of the more memorable of any medieval warlord, and that's not for lack of contenders. The moment of the injury is described thus:

And so they met and there was a hard battle, and not long ere Melbricta fell and his followers [did too], and Sigurd caused the heads to be fastened to his horses' cruppers as a glory for himself. And then they rode home, and boasted of their victory. And when they were come on the way, then Sigurd wished to spur the horse with his foot, and he struck his calf against the tooth which stuck out of Melbricta's head and grazed it; and in that wound sprung up pain and swelling, and that led him to his death.

No one knows whether Mælbrigte's teeth inspired the tale of Sigurd's death, whether this flattering epithet was applied retrospectively, or whether both details are an entertaining fabrication. All we can know for certain is that the narrative is a memorable one, offering a warning to all who cheat. Not only is Sigurd personally struck down by the posthumous revenge of the man he cheated, but his son dies childless, and his dynasty comes to an end. This is not a coincidence. This is divine justice.

26

The Angel of the Scots

It was also the two thousand, three hundred and forty-ninth year of their exodus from Egypt under their first king Gaythelos, son of Neolus, king of the Athenians, and under Scota, wife of Gaythelos. Kenneth reigned as sole ruler over these kingdoms of the Picts and Scots for about sixteen years.

Walter Bower, Scotichronicon (1437–49)

It had been the strangest commission the tailor had ever received. Sworn to secrecy, he had erected a model of the King in his lodgings and gathered the materials. The fishes he hand-picked for their large, iridescent scales. In them, the tiniest beam of light would be caught and scattered. Skinning the fish, drying the skins on racks, working them with oils and sewing them into one cloth, he had created the King's strange request.

Kenneth MacAlpin was more than satisfied with the tailor's work. His wardrobe had seen nothing like it, till now the home of soft linens, supple leather and fine wool. The garments he usually wore were colourful, from ivory tones to forest green, from fox-fur red to midnight blue. He had yellow tunics and ermine cloaks, and on special occasions, his servants brought an array of dyed furs and silks that shimmered like the plumes of the peacock. He had ermine lining his hood and there were patterns on every hem and panel of his cloak. And that's not counting the jewels. Kenneth MacAlpin employed gold- and silversmiths on both sides of the Irish Sea. They spun him brooches, pins, buckles, sword-hilts and mace-handles inlaid with enamel and gems. He drank from goblets of gold and his meals were served on silver. But despite all this marvellous wealth, nothing had ever come close to the costume made of fish. Their skins formed a floor-length cape with a hood to cover the face, and the fabric shone like frost under moonlight.

Standing out of sight of the window, Kenneth put on the hood, breathing through his mouth as the skins pressed against his nose. He had to admit, the smell was almost overwhelming.

King Kenneth, son of Alpin, was descended from Fergus Mór, first King of the Scotti in Alba, who had brought Simon Brecc's throne from the Hill of Tara. The prophecy had said that the Scotti would rule wherever that throne stood. And Kenneth's own well-tended head had taken the crown as he sat on its cold marble. But the domains he inherited were small, surrounded by territories claimed by Picts, Danes and Britons.

Of all those peoples, it was the Picts that Kenneth hated most. It had been the Scotti who had sent the Picts to Alba, giving them wives from among their own women. It was agreed that succession to the kingdom would pass through the female line. But, in recent years, the Picts had committed unforgivable crimes. They had stolen a royal hunting dog from the Scotti, allied themselves with the Saxons in battle, and begun electing kings from the male line. Then they had murdered Kenneth's father. In these deeds they had broken treaties that had held for centuries, and there was no doubt in Kenneth's mind that the Picts sought to destroy his people.

But would his barons listen? Try as he might to persuade them, they would not agree to invade the Pictish lands. Each night, for weeks, Kenneth had given them speeches of valour and conquest, of the imperative to dominate or else be oppressed, but nothing moved them to action. The last battle they had fought – the fight in which Kenneth's own father had been killed – had traumatised them with the din of metal on metal and the stench of vomit and blood. The barons were of one obstinate voice: not even divine intervention – not even an angel sent by God, they declared – would make them change their minds. That had given Kenneth his idea.

There was dinner as usual that night. As usual, they avoided talk of conquering the Picts, their eyes sliding to Kenneth if the subject came too close. When the light of the full moon was falling on the floor in great stripes, they took themselves to bed.

Kenneth watched the men leave and waited till the last footsteps had faded to silence. Then he went to his chamber and the wooden chest in which he had hidden the cloak. As he opened the lid, the smell of fish wafted up to greet him. He lifted the garment out and took it to the window. Moonlight splintered in each scale. He put on his disguise, drew the hood over his face and crept out of the room.

Thus disguised, Kenneth tiptoed through the castle, sending triangles of light dancing over the walls whenever he passed a window. The corridors looked strange through the fabric, as if full of smoke, and the smell of fish was pungent. He stole into the first baron's chamber, opened his mouth and, in the voice he had been practising, began to speak.

'In the name of the Living God,' he intoned, somewhat higher than he had meant to, then paused. The baron was still sleeping. Kenneth cleared his throat. The fabric dangled from his outstretched arms like feathers and shone with silver gleams.

'In the name of the Living God,' he repeated, more loudly. The baron did not stir.

Kenneth clapped and the man jerked awake, his eyes widening as they found the apparition. Then the King flung out his arms again, and shards of reflected moonlight raced round the walls.

'IN THE NAME OF THE LIVING GOD,' he sang in the perfect wail, 'I ORDER YOU TO OBEY YOUR KING'S COMMANDS AND AGREE TO DESTROY THE PICTS.'

The baron did not move. His mouth was open, and his eyes were as round as those of a landed roach. Then Kenneth stepped back into the shadows and slipped out of the door. He visited all his barons that night, relaying the same angelic message. If any of them saw through his disguise, or noted a lingering smell of the harbour, they did not make it known.

The next day, they agreed unanimously to make war on the Picts, each of them sharing the vision of an angel that they had received in the night. When the invasion began, Kenneth was merciless. He spared no one in the enemy lands: not women, children or animals. And when raiders from Denmark weakened the Picts in the furthest north, Kenneth crossed the mountains and subdued them altogether. In time, he became king from the Forth to Orkney, and the greatest power in the north. And the loyalty from his men never faltered. He had got them: hook, line and sinker.

❖

Historically speaking, Norse pressure on the Picts is one of the factors that enabled the Gaelic-speaking kingdom of the Dál Riata to take over Pictish domains and establish a Scottish kingdom, or the Kingdom of Alba. Prior to this, the Dál Riata occupied a territory spanning from North-East Ireland to the westerly regions of modern-day Scotland. Afterwards, it occupied territory to the east, and as far south as the River Forth. By the tenth century, the Pictish language had died out and Gaelic was the dominant language outside Norse territories.

Kenneth MacAlpin (Cináed Mac Ailpín), also known as Kenneth I, is held to have died in 858, and is still seen as the founding father of the Scottish royal dynasty. Some chronicles have Kenneth make the first swipe at the Picts by inviting their nobility to Scone for a feast at which the benches had been fitted with removable pegs. When the benches collapsed, the Picts were sent plunging into hidden pits filled with blades, thus meeting a grisly, subterranean end. You will remember that the motif of treason at a feast is also used in relation to the Saxon Hengist, who massacres the British nobles, and the manuscripts in which the earliest versions of these stories survive are roughly contemporaneous.

However, in his fifteenth-century *Scotichronicon*, Walter Bower offers quite another story of trickery, which I have retold above. According to Walter, the first King of Albany (that kingdom later called Scotland) dressed himself as an angel, crept around the castle at Scone and performed a celestial message to his barons, convincing them to attack the Picts. As far as regnal myths go, it doesn't get better than that.

27

Danes, Giants and Pilgrims

Ther com an angel fram heven-light . . .
He seyd, 'King Athelston, slepestow?
Hider me sent thee King Jhesu
To comfort thee to fond.
Tomorwe go to the north gate ful swithe,
A pilgrim thou schalt se com bilive
When thou hast a while stond.
Bid him for Seynt Charité
That he take the batayl for thee
And he it wil nim on hond.'

'The Stanzaic Guy of Warwick' (c. 1220)

The famous Guy of Warwick gripped his lance. He had
been wrong to agree to this. To one side of him, on the
margins of Hyde Mead, stood the people of Winchester,
Ethelstan with them, seated on a warhorse. To the other
side were the Danish soldiers, led by King Anlaf, who had
destroyed every castle in the land and were poised to seize

this final English stronghold. When the crowds discovered who he really was, now on the brink of a great defeat, they would lose not only their freedom but a hero. His true identity was, for now, unknown, but for how long would that last?

After years of travelling to the shrines of saints from here to Jerusalem, he had at last come home. He had not told anyone of his return and he had hoped it would go unnoticed. The divine had other plans; an angel appeared to King Ethelstan as he slept in his golden bed, telling him that a worthy opponent for the Danes' greatest weapon – an African giant by the name of Colebrand – would be found the next morning, passing through the gates of Winchester in the garb of a pilgrim. Guy, dressed thus, had been accosted at the city gates, taken to the palace and begged by the princes and nobles of the Winchester court to stand against the giant. In his spiritual frailty – in his vanity – he had agreed to their request. Mass had been said, oaths had been sworn, relics had been venerated. Now, here he was, waiting for the giant and the fight that would send the Danes packing – or, more likely, hand them the English crown. And if it came to pass as he anticipated, he would be slain, his identity realised, and the myth of his heroism shown for what it was.

Behind the ring of spectators, he could see a towering figure being fitted with armour. The attendants were lifting plates of steel out of a cart, which was full to the brim with weapons. Ethelstan's armourers had done their best. Guy's horse was bedecked with embroidered leather and fine trappings, its mane and tail plaited. He himself had on a hauberk of steel, a heavy helmet encircled in gold inlaid with jewels, and carried the King's sword. In the centre of the circlet, above his forehead, was a shining carbuncle. An ornamental flower made of feathers had been attached to the top of the helmet, and his shield bore an image of the Three Magi. In his youth he would have felt gloriously arrayed, and indeed the crowd gasped and swooned when it saw him, but now, after years in rags and prayer, he felt like a decorated fool.

Relics were brought and the terms of the combat agreed. If Ethelstan's mysterious knight won, the Danes would leave England and never return. By the same token, if he lost, Ethelstan would become King Anlaf's liegeman, submit his land and pay tributes to him.

When all this had been sworn, a horn blast sounded and Colebrand the giant could be seen striding onto the field. He had no horse, and his armour covered his body. The plates of black steel slid over each other silently, like scales. His helmet was ugly and huge, pressed over his basinet, hiding his face. Colebrand was strung all over with weapons. In his great, steel-plated hand, he carried pointed javelins. Strapped to his chest were axes with curved heads and throwing knives. Each keen edge shone against the armour, which devoured light like darkness made matter.

And beyond, in a cart, were yet more weapons, each blade perilously sharp. Images rose, like spectres from Guy's memory, of the mutilated bodies of soldiers on the streets of Arascune. What lay beneath that armour? A monster or a man? Would that flesh bleed if he pierced it? He would have to wait and see.

Colebrand let three javelins fly. The first two missed, but the third drove straight through Guy's shield and sliced past his flank. As he twisted to escape, he felt old scars on his ribcage stretch. Colebrand's spear whistled through the crowd and into the turf of the meadow. And the giant was before him when Guy turned back. The knight charged, his lance striking Colebrand's shield and shattering, just as it had done all those years ago when he had fought the dragon. Scaly, serpentine, the giant reared and the colossal blade came down, cutting through Guy's saddle, cutting his horse in half, and Guy fell in a tangle of reins, kicking his legs and scrambling to his feet. He could hardly remember where he was, but he still had his sword. And then the giant – fire-breathing – was before him again, rising up to strike. Mud, grass, metal. The crushed heads of cornflowers and daisies. Guy raised his own blade and swiped. The hard edge cut beneath the black steel breast-plate and he saw blood on metal.

Colebrand roared and hit back, slicing the colourful flower from Guy's helmet, splitting the circlet, cutting the carbuncle in half, and, with the descent of his axe, cutting

the shield on his arm into two golden moons. And now the renowned Guy stood like a mouse beneath a snake, Colebrand's enormous black-clad legs above him, and his shield blocking out the sun. The knight heaved his sword over his head and struck, sending sparks over the steel like fiery breath across a midnight sky, and though the giant's shield had now split too, Guy's sword was also broken, and he knew that all was lost. He was unhorsed, undefended and unarmed. Now, at the jaws of the fire-fiend, he would at last be killed.

The watching Danes were laughing and jeering. 'England is ours,' they called. And, opposite them, some of the English watchers fled, but the rest were rooted to the spot, their hands over their mouths.

Colebrand laughed. The meadow trembled.

'Now, Sir Knight,' he said in a voice of bedrock, 'you fight well, but you've lost your sword, your shield and your horse. Yield to me and I will take you to my lord. You will be cared for as befits a soldier.'

Guy pictured Felice, and now, as in years gone by, she fortified him. He had to fight for her love.

But, no.

He pictured Christ.

He had to fight for redemption.

When he spoke, his voice was steady.

'Give me an axe,' he said.

The giant growled his dissent. 'By Apollo, you will die a painful death.'

Before Colebrand could act, Guy raced for the edge of the field, to where the stash of gigantic blades stood in its cart. The giant was coming after him, but, weighed down by his armour, his progress was slow. Throwing himself towards the cart, Guy seized an axe with a long handle. Then he spun round to face his enemy.

Colebrand roared, and brought his blade down too fast. He missed, and buried it in the soft tussocks of the meadow. As he heaved to drag it out, Guy, just as he had once severed the tail of a dragon, struck the monster's shoulder, cutting through his arm. The giant roared again, bringing round his remaining hand, crouching low to pull the axe free, and with this Guy swiped at an exposed flash of neck, cutting through the skin and sinew, till Colebrand's head slid down from his shoulders and crashed onto the grass. When the giant's body had fallen too, there was a long, ringing silence.

Then there came a confusion of sounds: angry shouts from the Danes, crying and cheering from the English. The victory was theirs. The pilgrim had won.

After the body had been dragged away, and the crowds had dispersed in celebration, the King approached. Without recognising him, he offered the unknown pilgrim land, property and gold. But he refused it all. Ethelstan pressed him further, asking who he was and why he had not heard of him before, given his great prowess in battle. And finally he confessed his identity, for they had once been friends, but swore him to keep it a secret.

The pilgrim whom the King had found at the gates of Winchester was none other than the famous Guy of Warwick, hailed from Iceland to Antioch as the hero who had fought Duke Otun and slain the Irish dragon. Returning from his adventures, having won the love of the lady Felice, he had married her. But what he did not say was that, no sooner had they been married, he had found himself tormented by his past, and had been unable to stay.

Guy had left Felice on the tower of their castle, where, by starlight, he had told her of his wish to become a pilgrim. The campaigns he had fought for the sake of her love had been no game: he had killed, maimed, burned and desecrated; he had barely escaped with his life; he had seen sights that haunted him still. Only when she had agreed to marry him – because he was at last a worthy knight – had he realised his mistake. She was barely three months pregnant when he had left for the Holy City. She had pressed a gold ring into his hand, to remember her by.

Now, in the aftermath of the defeat of the Danes, though King Ethelstan offered Guy lands and riches, he longed only to see Felice. He travelled to Warwick, to where she was providing food and drink for the poor, and, dressed in rags, he joined their number. It is said she did not recognise him, but that is not true. She had held his face in her mind every day since he had departed, had caught its shadow in the face of her son, and though she bit her tongue when she saw him, her heart leapt to know he was alive. To drink, she gave him wine in a golden cup, and with sadness she watched him leave once more.

After that, Guy retreated to a hermitage in the forest and lived there for nine months. At the end of that time he fell ill. An angel came to him then, assuring him of God's forgiveness. And so, absolved at last, he sent a message to Felice, along with the gold ring he had treasured on his journey.

When Felice came to his hermitage, couched among the mute trees of early winter, he was lying on his narrow bed and felt her kneel beside him. He wished himself back to how he had been when they had married: the firmness of his chest, the muscles beneath his battle-scarred skin. Now his body was wasted, his skin loose. Felice whispered his name, and Guy opened his eyes. Up close, she was just as he remembered her.

Felice watched him as the birds sang and the canopy exhaled its dead-leaf smell. They were young lovers grown weary with time, reunited, until the thinning clouds of his breath had vanished altogether. And his soul seemed to watch from a distance as, when she saw that he was dead, she let out a great cry and kissed his mouth and chin. And until he was buried in the ground beneath the hermitage, the sweet aroma that hung around his holy body healed all the sick who went there.

❖

The legend of Guy of Warwick appears in French manuscripts dating to the early thirteenth century and grows in popularity in the form of verse translations into Middle English. It is a 'romance', which is the name given to poems in French, or 'Roman', on account of its relationship to Latin, the language spoken by the Romans. (That so many romances have love as a central theme gave rise to its modern meaning.) I have not told the whole narrative, preferring to begin when, by and large, Guy's fighting days are over and his death close.

The archetypal villain of this story is Colebrand, the African giant, who, like the white dragon in the days of Lludd and Vortigern, embodies the threat of invasion. Colebrand is not unlike the Old Testament's Goliath, described in 1 Samuel 17: 4-7:

And there went out a champion out of the camp of the Philistines, named Goliath, of Gath, whose height was six cubits and a span:

And he had an helmet of brass upon his head, and he was armed with a coat of mail; and the weight of his coat of mail was five thousand shekels of brass.

And he had greaves of brass on his legs, and a target of brass between his shoulders.

And the staff of his spear was like a weaver's beam; and his spear's head weighed six hundred shekels of iron: and one bearing his armour went before him.

Compare this to the language used in the *c.* 1300 'Stanzaic *Guy of Warwick*':

He was so great and so fierce
That no horse would bear him . . .
Such armour he wore
You have never heard the like
Unless it were that of the devil.
His hauberk was not of mail,
It was of another work,
Which is marvellous to hear,
It was all thick plates of steel . . .
Well-wrought leg-guards he had too,
So he was nothing but steel plates from neck to foot.

The text goes on to describe Colebrand's helmet and weapons, all as black as pitch. As with Goliath, the only characterisation beyond his trappings is the description of his marvellous size and his ethnicity: 'out of Aufrike stout and grim'. Colebrand is a confluence of literary ideas: of the monstrous races described in Chapter One of this book, of the characters found in the biblical tradition – and, of course, the legacy of these ideas lives on in ways that have contributed to modern racist stereotypes. With his dark, reptilian armour, Colebrand is demonic, while his African ethnicity is an indicator of his otherness in relation to Guy.

But Guy is not the simple knight in shining armour, cheered on by the spectating English. In his youth he fought campaigns abroad to compensate for his low birth and win Felice, but when he came home, his guilt forced him back to a life of wandering, this time as a penitent. His compulsion to seek atonement may be seen as a kind of Christian rebuttal to chivalric clichés. But at the heart of his legend there also exists a consciousness of the struggles faced by soldiers who come home from war too affected by trauma to return to life as normal. It highlights the early naivety of Felice, whose lofty standards compelled Guy to prove his valour, but who lost her husband as a result.

When it appears in medieval chronicles of the English, Guy of Warwick's victory over Colebrand is celebrated as a major point in pre-Conquest history. It takes place during the reign of King Æthelstan (died 939), whose status as a model of good kingship rests on his piety. At the turn of the fourteenth century, the *Chronicle of Pierre de Langtoft* describes Æthelstan praying to God for help in defeating the Danish invaders, and God answering his prayer by sending the vision of the angel. This angel tells the King of the arrival of the pilgrim who will deliver England. Æthelstan does not baulk at the absurdity of the message, but has faith. His faith is rewarded when the pilgrim turns out to be none other than the famous Guy of Warwick.

But what it all comes down to is this: the Saxon descendants of Hengist and Horsa, the English, the invaders of old, are now themselves threatened by invasion. All that stands between them and external subjugation is the competence of the monarch. And what guarantee is there of that?

28

Elfrida and Edward the Martyr

[King Edward] had a dwarf, Wulfstanet, who knew how to
dance and perform acrobatics, and how to leap and fall, and
to perform other tricks.

Geffrei Gaimar, History of the English (c. 1136–7)

An acrobat was working the King's table. His chin and
neck were pressed into the damask cloth. His feet were
shuffling together so his cheeks were squeezed between
his ankles. If he got things right this evening, he would
leave here and never come back. He could take his wife to
the countryside, sleep at night and throw his face-paints
in the river. Wulfstanet blew a raspberry and tipped into a
forward roll. The cheering and gasping faces of the diners
rotated past him until he came to a stop before King
Edward's seat. When he stood up, his nose level with that
of the King, Wulfstanet was looking at a laughing young
man with blushing cheeks. They glowed like candlelight
through wine. The King tossed a coin at the acrobat.

'More of the same, tiny man!' he said, laughing at Wulf-stanet.

Wulfstanet folded his arms and did not move.

'I said more,' the King repeated.

Again, Wulfstanet refused. The diners coughed and giggled, and the youthful red flags on Edward's cheeks began to flood his neck and ears. The acrobat turned around and farted onto the King's meal.

'God. Damn. You.'

He had hit his mark. Wulfstanet sprang from the table and ran, and the tempestuous King Edward followed. The diners – the barons and their wives and whores – applauded them out of the door and fell laughing back to their feast.

A tawny owl heard them before she saw them. To her eyes they were shadows, racing over the frozen leaf mould, first one horse, then a pause, then the next. They were charging between the trees, first Wulfstanet, then the King: a hunt unlike any the royal forest had yet seen.

But Wulfstanet saw the lights of another castle glimmering beyond the last tall bank of beech trees. He laughed with relief; the hooves of the King's horse might have been clattering on his skull. And now he was bursting onto an open, diamond-frosted lawn and approaching the porter at the gates. Just in time, they swung open. The pristine flagstones rang an alarm. Wulfstanet just had time to leap from the saddle and hide before the King entered the enclosure. When Edward did so, he found himself quite alone.

The panting of Edward's horse was loud and urgent, fogging the air. There was no sign of the dwarf, but a servant was coming out of a doorway and the King asked her what she knew. She lowered her head and hurried away. Edward barked his frustration at the walls, then called to the upper windows. Deeper in the castle, a child stirred in his sleep.

The next person to enter the courtyard was a woman: Edward's stepmother, Elfrida. His grip tightened on the reins as she glittered across the moonlit space between them, her body swathed in a black cloak that trailed on the floor behind her. He did not know her well, but he knew not to trust her, even if her gaze was gentle and kind. *She is not your friend*, he told himself.

Elfrida had been married to Edward's uncle, Ethelwold, but then, when his father King Edgar's first wife had died, Ethelwold had been attacked and killed in the North. King Edgar had not delayed in taking Elfrida for his own, and they had borne a son, whose name was Ethelred. Some said King Edgar had sought to wed her years before, when she was young, but his brother had told him the rumours of her beauty were lies and secretly secured her for himself. It was true that there was no denying his stepmother's beauty, but Edward had long suspected that she wanted her own Ethelred to have the throne of England.

'My servants say the man you are looking for has not come here,' she soothed, clasping the horse's reins in a jewelled hand. 'Why don't you stay with me tonight? You have ridden far.'

'I can't,' Edward replied.

'But it's so cold.'

'I must get back.'

'Then share a drink with me, before you go?'

He longed to be back at the feast, but it would be discourteous to refuse.

'Only if you drink too,' he said.

Dark-cloaked Elfrida called into the house, and a servant emerged with a horn. She took it in her free hand and drank. The pale horn was ringed with metal bands, which were embossed with twining serpents, snapping and chewing their own tails in the moonlight, soaring higher as the dowager drank. Now she had drained half the wine and was passing the horn up to Edward; the moonlight in her eyes held him as the serpents snapped again. She was beautiful, he thought: as delicate as a kestrel. He'd always known it, even as a child, but tonight it mattered more, somehow. Slowly he took the drink, and she turned up her face for a kiss.

It was customary among the English to kiss when exchanging drinks, and had been since the days of the first Saxons in Britain. Elfrida approached her stepson to mark this custom, just as she had done in earlier days with his father, Edgar. Just as Ronwen had approached Vortigern, who, trapped by Woden's blood, could never have refused. Edward bent to his stepmother's face. And that was all it took, for she was not his friend.

A dagger slid between his ribs. When the blade was drawn out, blood poured onto his saddle like the wine from the horn, now tumbling to the ground. Edward cried, and kicked the horse, which, unloosed, bolted out of the gate. Then the King was thrown out of the saddle and, as he lay, steaming blood flooded the icy flagstones, draining his cheeks, mingling with the hot wine. Elfrida drew her black cloak around her and turned to direct her servants.

Edward's horse bolted north, all the way to Cirencester, where it was caught and identified as the warhorse that Edward had taken from the feast. Meanwhile, Elfrida's servants took the body just as far south, to a marsh near Shaftesbury, and sank it among the reeds. A strange uncertainty settled over the land as the people looked for the King. And when Edward's barons visited Elfrida, she was nowhere to be found. She was not seen until her son, Ethelred, was crowned at Winchester. And then, because she was Queen Regent, she was absolved of all her sins.

Thus, while the glittering halls of Winchester were filled with candlelight and song, Edward's body fed the lampreys. But, one day, a ray of light, which seemed to come from a star, or from somewhere among them, so bright it could not be viewed directly, fell upon its resting place. Those who saw it from the dry paths wondered what

it could mean. The locals of Donhead, close to that part of the marsh, had stories of lights that tempted travellers to their doom, but their superstition was scorned by their priest. He told them the light was a sign from God and that they must go out to meet it.

He set out for the holy site with pilgrims. Some were blind or deaf, others had walking sticks and crutches, and others still were being carried by their friends and family, or bore afflictions that could not be seen. They struggled over the boggy ground till they came to the place where the light was resting. And they found the priest had been right. There, they found the waterlogged remains of a man, dressed in the trappings of a king. And suddenly, from between the hushing reeds, a feeling of peace came over them and they began to speak in excited whispers:

I *can walk.*

I *can see.*

I *can hear.*

I *can speak.*

The gasps of the pilgrims joined the songs of the marsh animals and birds. And as they pulled at the corpse, the sucking bog released it. And they carried the bits of Edward on their shoulders to the church at Shaftesbury, where they built him a golden shrine. And when news of the discovery reached Elfrida, she was unmoved. Edward was dead, and her Ethelred was king.

❖

The boundary between myth and history are blurring as we edge through time. All the characters in this story, with the exception of Wulfstanet, are historical figures, but their actions are the product of an evolving legend regarding the circumstances of Edward's death. In this period of history, the English are about to experience a string of defeats, first by the Danes and then by the Normans. Æthelred will reign twice: from 978 to 1013, and from 1014 to his death in 1016, briefly losing the throne to the Danish King Sweyn Forkbeard. Æthelred's son, Edmund Ironside, will rule after him, then Cnut, also a Dane. After Cnut's sons, Harold Harefoot and Harthacnut, there will be one last hurrah for the English in the person of Edward the Confessor, but a dispute around his successor, Harold Godwinson, will lead to the Norman Conquest of England, with far-reaching consequences for Wales, Scotland and Ireland. Æthelred, which means 'well-counselled' in Old English, will become known as the 'Unready' ('ill-counselled'). His, possibly murdered, half-brother Edward, notwithstanding his reputation for having a fiery temper, will be canonised a saint, and his shrine at Shaftesbury will become a major pilgrimage destination.

King Edward the Martyr is held to have been killed near the residence of Ælfthryth (that's the Old English for Elfrida) and Æthelred in Corfe Castle, Dorset. One early source for this may be found in the *Anglo-Saxon Chronicles*. The entry for the year 978 reads: 'Here King Edward was killed in the evening time on 18 March at Corfe Passage; and they buried him at Wareham, without any royal honours.' Other later sources suggest he was killed by Ælfthryth's henchmen. Geffrei Gaimar, who wrote his French verse *History of the English* in *c.* 1136–7, offered an especially long account of the incident, which forms the basis of the above retelling. And while he does not explicitly reveal who was responsible for Edward's death, Ælfthryth's involvement is strongly implied:

> The butler filled a drinking-horn with good spiced wine, then she took hold of it. She drank a whole half of the horn, then put it into King Edward's hand. As she delivered it she was going to kiss him. Then came I know not which enemy, with a large sharp blade: he struck the king to the heart with it. The king fell down – he let out a cry. The horse bolted, bloody as it was . . .

In the exchange of drinks and kisses, which also appears earlier in the story when Ælfthryth meets King Edgar, her future husband, we see echoes of the story of Ronwen, the Saxon girl who long ago seduced the British King Vortigern into giving up Kent to her father, Hengist, and thus initiated a slow Saxon invasion. Ælfthryth, likewise, through her sexuality and exploitation of an ancient custom, achieves her political aims. Did the fall of England to the Danes and the Normans begin with a woman offering a drink to a man? It might as well have been an apple.

29

The Conquest

She gracefully removed her fur-trimmed dress, but when it came to her shift, she ripped it open, tearing it from top to bottom – much to the puzzlement of the duke.

Benoît de Sainte-Maure,
Chronique des Ducs de Normandie (1180–1200)

Around Herleva, the other girls were dangling their feet in the water and talking. They were reluctant to begin the work they'd been given by their mothers, and no wonder, for on that morning the winter sun was shining and the air was warm. But Herleva's mind was too full for idleness. She was the daughter of a tanner, with no love of the future laid out for her. She felt restless and excited, though she could not say what for. And as she wrung out her shift, she looked up to see the rich man, who had been watching her from his horse, riding out of sight. She'd been pretending not to have noticed, but nevertheless she had let her bare legs catch the sun as she stepped from stream to bank.

When she got home, the laundry washed and mostly dry, she was surprised to see her father sitting at the table, holding her mother's hand, and her uncle, a hermit who visited only at times of great moment, sitting in the corner. Herleva sensed, from their grave expressions, that they had something important to tell her.

Her father told her that men from the court had visited him that day, asking that she spend a night with the Duke of Normandy. At first he had refused, but his brother, the hermit, had counselled otherwise. And so it had been decided, while she was washing the clothes, that she would go to him for a night.

Herleva ran to her room. The Duke of Normandy must have been the man watching her from his horse. He had not been unattractive, she thought. And she imagined how the sun must have danced on her skin as she stepped from water to grass; how beautiful she must have been to impress him. Herleva felt as grand as the castle in which she would, before long, be a guest. She was thrilled by her parents' decision. Her father's first instinct was always to protect her, but she thought of the wealth this could bring. She would have to find a new dress and borrow furs from the tannery.

When the evening came on which she was due to see the Duke, two of his men came to her home. But they did not knock on the front door. Rather, they called out from the back yard. Dressed in her best clothes, Herleva went to them and did not take the cloak they were holding out to her, as if they expected her to put it on.

Lifting her chin, Herleva told them how they would proceed. She knew she must be very beautiful to have attracted the attention of the Duke, and would not therefore be insulted by secrecy. Her parents were good citizens and hard workers, and she had no cause to be ashamed. This would bring honour upon them all.

The two men watched the girl's – the woman's – eyes flash as the darkness fell about them. When she asked them to return with a saddle-horse, it did not occur to them to refuse. They fetched one, just as she had asked.

Shawled heads turned in the cold evening air to see the tanner's daughter riding past in her finery of pale silk and squirrel fur, with her arms and shoulders bare and a silver circlet on her hair. Only she knew that her cheeks bore traces of the tears shed when saying goodbye to her mother: so much did Herleva love her, and so moved was she by her mother's fear on her behalf, that she had almost changed her mind. When she came to the castle gate, the men knocked. People had stopped their drinking and evening games of dice to watch. A few moments passed, then the porter opened the side door, and the Duke's men helped her down from the horse, but when they gestured for her to go inside, she shook her head.

Herleva told them, just as she had done before, that if the Duke wanted her, he must treat her with respect. She would not take a step forward, she said, unless the porter opened the main gate. The men obeyed, seeing the sense in her words. They had the porter open the main gate, and Herleva walked forward, passing under the great arch and feeling her heart leap at her daring. Then she was led up to the Duke's chamber, where he was waiting for her to arrive.

Duke Robert of Normandy was not what she had expected. Despite the luxury of his surroundings, he was as eager to please her as a servant. He told her how captivated he had been by her beauty when he had seen her from his horse, and that he had dreamed of nothing but this night since. He would lavish her with gifts, if she would have him, and she would want for nothing.

Herleva believed the Duke meant what he said, for she saw his hands were shaking. And while she knew he might change his mind in time, she sensed that this would set her on a different course from the one trodden by her parents. And it was not only she who would benefit. Herleva thought of her mother, whose eyes had pleaded with her to stay, but who would grow old in comfort if her daughter won the love of a duke. And so the choice was easy. She knelt down, aware of the eyes of his attendants glittering from the corners of the chamber, and promised to be his lover, mistress and concubine, as he liked it.

Herleva and the Duke spoke for many hours that night. She listened to tales of his travels, and he was enchanted by her anonymous life in the country, away from the politics of state. And as their conversation roamed, their fingertips touched, and when the Duke had the servants clear the room, so they could begin getting ready for bed, Herleva was not too shy to act.

By the light of the many candles, she took off her dress. Once she was just in her shift, she let the Duke look at her. Then she raised her hands, gripped her collar and ripped the linen down to the hem. When she let the shift fall to the floor, he looked at her body. She knew she was everything he had dreamed of, and more, and that he was longing to reach out and touch her. He asked her why she had torn her shift, and she told him it was so that his noble face would not come near cloth that had swept the ground. His expression told her that he thought her wise as well as beautiful.

It was morning before they went to sleep. And the night was spent in breathless exploration. At last, Herleva, tired, warm and satisfied, pulled the covers over herself and pushed her face into the pillow. She listened to the sound of the Duke's sleeping, and beyond that, the movement of people in the castle and the hooting of owls in the grounds, until sleep descended for her too and the dream came that told her everything would now be different.

She dreamed she was lying on her back, groaning with the pangs of labour. Looking at her body, she saw her breasts were large and the skin of her stomach stretched tight, her

navel standing proud at the end of a line of darker skin. She was bathed in sunlight, in a large and empty landscape, and her knees were bent and her legs open. And now there was a strange sensation, just out of sight. When the cause finally appeared, she was frozen with amazement. She discerned two leaves connected by a fragile stem, and felt it sliding from the out-of-sight place between her legs and coiling into the air. And then the seedling was becoming a sapling, and the stem of the sapling was thickening into a bole, and branches were bursting out along its length and growing smaller branches, and from these were growing twigs and buds, which were bursting into leaf. As she moaned and wept on the ground, she found herself staring up at a mighty, spreading tree, growing from her tearing loins, blocking out the sun, casting her and the surrounding plains in shadow. Then that same shadow was sliding across the familiar plains of her homeland, but they had reached a sea and were crossing over white cliffs onto a land beyond. All that vast landscape was covered by the shadow of the tree. And all of this was being forced from her body. She tipped her head back and screamed.

Herleva woke suddenly, disturbing the Duke, and he asked her what was wrong. She whispered the strange vision to him in the dark and he listened in wonder. And in the days and nights that followed, while Herleva won the Duke's heart forever, a change was taking place in her womb. Two small leaves were opening, and a root was twisting into the dark. And when, as a tree, its boughs came to stretch over lands, the people would whisper a name. And that name would be: 'William'.

❖

In the British Library, there is a fragile scroll (c. 1300–1340) showing a genealogy of the Kings of England (Royal MS 14 B VI). Diagrams like this would depict the line of royal succession running down the length of the scroll, dividing to show the progeny of the various kings and queens. Because of the diagrams' shape, which was not unlike the long leg and long toes of a wading bird, they were called the medieval

French for 'crane's foot', *pé de grue*, which is where we get the word 'pedigree'.

This particular pedigree begins with an illustration of the so-called 'Anglo-Saxon Heptarchy': the conglomeration of kingdoms held to have been originally created by the first Germanic settlers. It is then followed by roundels depicting the Kings of England up to Edward the Confessor, who has removed his crown with his right hand and looks at it while waving his left hand in a gesture somewhere between a shrug and a wave.

Beneath him, Harold has no connecting ribbon. Predecessors of William the Conqueror, also known as 'the Bastard', come next, including Robert, William the Conqueror's father, the Duke who falls for Herleva in the legend. The row of roundels depicting Robert's progeny, including an illustration of William, his son with Herleva, is surmounted by two tall and twisting oak trees, complete with lush leaves, acorns and wildlife (even a monkey).

As you have read, a tree features prominently in the Herleva legend, and this is no great anomaly in the stories of the age. You have also read how the child-king Kenelm dreamed of the felling of a magnificent, lamplit tree, prior to his murder. And these could be cited among numerous medieval examples of trees being used as metaphors for the royal line and associated with prophecy. For instance, in the mid-thirteenth-century *History of Saint Edward the*

King, by chronicler Matthew Paris, Edward the Confessor prophesies the future of the English royal line with these words:

> The green tree which springs from the trunk
> When thence it shall be severed,
> And removed to a distance of three acres,
> By no engine or hand
> Shall return to its original trunk,
> And shall join itself to its root,
> Whence it first had origin.

Trees, with all their vigour and growth, are compelling metaphors for royal succession. I have seen one manuscript (Oxford, Bodleian Library, MS Rawl. D. 329) in which the heads of princes and princesses, and then, further up, the heads of kings and queens, sprout like acorns from the branches of an oak vine. Such playful devices derive, at least in part, from the biblical image of the Tree of Jesse. In the Old Testament Book of Isaiah (11: 1), the prophet describes new growth ascending from the severed tree stump of Jesse, who was the father of King David and forefather of the Messiah: 'And there shall come forth a rod out of the stem of Jesse, and a Branch shall grow out of his roots.' In medieval art, this prophecy was represented in the form of a man with a tree growing out of his loins, the busts of Christ's descendants resting in its branches. Often, the Virgin and Child are shown in the canopy.

The story of William the Conqueror's low-born mother, Herleva, first appears in two twelfth-century French histories of the Dukes of Normandy by chroniclers called Wace and Benoît de Sainte-Maure. After sleeping with the Duke, she dreams that a great tree has grown out of her body, to overshadow Normandy. In Wace it stops there; in Benoît it covers England too.

And so, thanks to the ambition of Herleva, we come to the birth of a 'bastard' who will bring the Normans to England. And from this moment on, Britain will be a conglomeration of Trojan Britons and Graeco-Egyptian Scots, as well as Danes, Saxons and Norsemen with mythic roots also in Troy. And thus legend lent its listeners an explanation of Britain's cultural variety, as well as a glorious pedigree.

30

Gogmagog Rises Again

And then an evil spirit entered into the body of Geomagog,
and came into these parts, and long did he defend the country,
so that never Briton dared dwell there.

The History of Fulk Fitz-Warine (late thirteenth century)

At the very start of things, Corineus wrestled Gogmagog
and threw him into the sea. When the Trojans peered over
the cliff-edge, the great body was already out of sight. In
silence, it was descending, coming to rest, moon-eyed, on
the seabed. But the giant was not dead. A thousand and
more tides rose and fell. The corpse grew green and grey.
Particles of skin and sinew swelled and puckered with
water and brine, but some force resisted rot, and the giant's
heart went on flickering in his chest.

While Gogmagog slept, Scota's fleet sailed by, Weland
pined for Hervor, and Bladud broke his back on the
Temple of Apollo, until – perhaps roused by the scream of
the dragon in the days of Lludd – the giant's heart began

beating harder. From deep below the earth, a demon had ascended and possessed the body of the giant, just as the seed of the demon had animated giant offspring in the body of Albina. Now fish darted more quickly over him and deep sand started swirling that had rested for an age. Gogmagog opened his eyes and balled his wrinkled hands.

People on the surface of the water might have noticed a churning in the waves, as though they were being agitated by heat. Then a swell in the current might have appeared, making progress west, along the Cornish coast, round the southernmost part of Britain. That was Gogmagog, walking beneath the flow, his head warmed by the sun.

Who can say where he climbed onto land? Perhaps he ascended at the mouth of the Severn, where the mud would have dragged at his legs and dried on his barnacled shoulders, where seabirds would have spiralled in flocks around him, and been plucked shrieking from the air to feed the starving centuries. Or perhaps he crawled, swollen, up the cliffs of Ceredigion, his skin striating like the rock in bands of brown and ochre. Maybe from there he travelled nightly, sleeping in the guise of a mountain or a cairn by day, till he arrived at the giants' ancestral gold. Gogmagog hid upon that gold and covered his kelp-haired head. And there he was undisturbed until Brennius, son of Conwenna, brother of Belinus, came to that part of the land, restored those ancient ruins, and called them Castell Dinas Bran.

On the night of the disaster, the hall was full, and the songs and ale were flowing. To hear the people within was to hear joy, just as to see the sunrise is to see day. So the sleeping Gogmagog heard. So the waking Gogmagog knew. So the malice within him rose.

He destroyed Castell Dinas Bran, gorging on blood and bone marrow, leaving none of its people alive. Then he occupied the ruins, and many diabolical creatures joined him. They raided the ancient treasury that had been dug beneath the ground in Albina's days, bringing out idols cast in gold: peacocks, horses, swans and oxen finely worked, gigantic gods that glistered and hungered for flesh. But the greatest was a bull, which Beelzebub had once animated to commune with Albion's giants. Around the bull, beside Brennius' castle, the resurrected Gogmagog built a city and encircled it with high walls and deep trenches. In that snare for souls, he held tournaments and fairs, and the demons of that place conjured flags and streamers, the aroma of food and exotic spices, as well as the din of trade and revelry. All these they poured down the hillside, and travellers were lured through the gates. Once they went inside, they would never be seen again.

Time passed and, as it did, much of the land that had belonged to the Trojans fell to Saxon and Scottish kings, and devilry thrived. But soon the saints – Augustine, Mungo, David, Columba and Serf – spread the word of God, and Augustine came to the west of Britain and began baptising people in the name of Christ. All those whom the holy water touched were blind to the demons' fluttering streamers and deaf to their perilous music. The baptised could not smell the tempting food and could not be lost to Gogmagog's city. Then, when Augustine built a church, the demons went into hiding. But still they did not disappear. Their malevolence remained like a miasma on the landscape. And the people avoided the hill and the castle.

There were centuries, then, in which Venus, Apollo and Diana, incubuses and the devil, received secret sacrifices in the secluded valleys and caves of Albion, and all the while hypocrites served them unwittingly, claiming to do God's work. But a greater power was coming, like a shadow advancing across the sea. Like an oak tree that towers over all the trees of the forest.

William was not a giant, but time has made him one. On a field in Hastings, an arrow fell from the sky, entering his rival's head, blinding him. Harold could not pull the arrow from his eye, however hard he tried, before he was cut down and killed. He was cut down like a thorn-bush, so William's oaken limbs could take root in Albion.

William the Bastard took the throne of England, wresting it from the hands of the English, from the lank-haired rebels of the fens led by Hereward. And, after that, William's armies marched on Wales. As they entered the wild domain, they met an old Briton, dark as his Trojan forebears, who spoke of the monsters that guarded Castell Dinas Bran. He said they remained there, bringing sin upon the land.

At this, William's young cousin, Payn, addressed the King.

'Let me go to the hill,' he said, seizing his cross-embla-zoned shield, his face shining. 'Let me take on the giant.'

Payn was a good knight. As soon as he had reached the age of understanding, he had sought out stories of war and adventure that would help him become a warrior. As a child, in Normandy, he had practised jousting with hobby-horses and sacks of hay. He learned the deeds of Roland, Alexander and Charlemagne. He held tourneys with the other boys and saved the girls from imaginary

monsters. When he started becoming a man, he exercised every day: fencing, riding, lifting. He had done this so that one day he would prove his nobility. Now, his moment had come.

With the King's agreement, the handsome Payn Peverill gathered fifteen knights and an army of soldiers. They made for Castell Dinas Bran in the wind and growing darkness, for winter was on the land. The hill on which it rested was smooth and steep, the valleys beyond it perilous. Freezing water ran in rivulets down livestock-trodden paths, exposing stone beneath the skin of turf, saturating the moss. Up the troop went, tripping on mud and tussocks, wiping rain from eyebrows, the light of the invisible sun dimming and night falling fast around them.

No fires could be lit for the rain, and, beneath their mail, their sodden tunics chilled them to the bone. They crouched among the ruins, where the wind was least strong, though everywhere it was strengthening. Suddenly there was a flash of lightning and, following it in a heartbeat, a violent clap of thunder. The wind roared and a storm lit up the sky for as far as the eye could see. Once more the clouds erupted and the men dived to the ground, covering their heads. And Payn tried to shout over the noise. But it was no use. His army could not hear him. And if they could, they would not listen. This was more than a storm, he realised. The devil was in their minds, and there he had them fettered.

Payn gripped the handle of his great shield more tightly, and sheltered beneath its gilding. Gusting out of the darkness was more than ice and wind; the storm held all the sickness of war, death, murder, greed, rape and plague; all the injustice in the world was raining on them from the sky, infecting their very blood, clutching at their hearts. What use were his weapons against those? What use was his strength and training? And, in the privacy of the darkness, despite his great muscles and all his years of training in the art of war, Payn Peverill began to cry.

But, in some dugout in his mind, in some place not yet paralysed, he knew what his weapon must be. Underneath his shield, where he could hear his own small voice, he remembered the Virgin's love for her Son; and her Son's love for humanity. Then he remembered his mother, and felt his love for her like a blade in his hand. Then he remembered his dear comrades, and the blade became a lance. It was a flutter of words that he prayed, the last being drowned by a roar even louder than the thunder. Then Payn Peverill stood up and raised his eyes to the sky. He had never seen anything so terrible, nor would he ever again.

The devil, in Gogmagog's altered form, towered over him. In his hand he held a club: an oak tree, ripped up by the roots. His chest swelled and contracted like the heaving sea, smoke billowed from his nostrils, and fire belched from his mouth. The bright glare of those flames bleached the ruined walls, and the shadows they cast bent and scattered, revealing and concealing the cowering groups of soldiers, so not one of them could hide.

Payn crossed himself, trembling, as the giant raised the club. The knight's was an instinctive gesture, mirroring the symbol on his shield. But as the cross was formed, that symbol of self-sacrifice, he saw Gogmagog straining to bring the club down, roaring and trying again, but it was as if the oak tree were held in ice.

'Who are you?' shouted Payn over the wind.

The demon bellowed through the ancient mouth of the giant. He had visited himself upon humans before; he would do so again. And, his club frozen aloft, he spoke in a voice that was like the suck of the ocean on rocks.

'I have come from hell. I have found the giants' treasure and I have occupied their land.'

And the devil told the same story that Payn had heard from the Briton, and, when he was finished, the young knight asked him, because he couldn't help it:

'Where is the treasure?'

'It is not destined for you.'

The voice was fading with these last words and the wind seemed to be lessening. And then a stench met Payn's nostrils, so terrible as to make the soldiers vomit onto the grass. And he saw that Gogmagog's face was slackening and his eyes were becoming dim. The club he held slipped from his hand and men fled to escape it as it crashed onto the ground. Then the body swayed and fell, smashing against the ruins, scattering more soldiers, their cries now audible over the storm, and finally the giant lay still on the hillside. And as the wind dropped, and the ruins sparkled in the first rays of dawn, the stench and the clouds faded away. And Payn could not believe that he was still alive or that the men around him were safe, though their weapons lay bloodless on the ground.

Together, the soldiers lifted Gogmagog's body and bore it back to King William. He had a great pit dug in the town of Llangollen, into which they folded the ancient, swollen corpse and covered it with soil. In reward for his bravery, Payn received lands thereabouts, while the huge club was kept by the King as a trophy of his conquest, though the treasure never could be found.

After that, the Normans ruled, and in time they called themselves 'English' and began to speak the English tongue. In Wales, Brutus' people took the red dragon as their flag and kept the language of Brutus, Cordelia and Lludd. In Scotland, the descendants of Scota defended their freedom, as Gaythelos had done. More peoples came and went than Merlin could ever have foreseen. And the earth consumed Gogmagog, and the water absorbed the earth, till every leaf and sinew in Albion held the memory of his flesh.

❖

Towering over the Northern Welsh town of Llangollen, Castell Dinas Bran is a cone-shaped, grassy hill topped with the ruins of a castle. On my most recent visit, late in the summer, the weather was as duplicitous as the trickster giants. At first, the clouds were low and ominous, but in the time it took to ascend the hill, they had cleared to reveal pale blue skies, though a fine mist of rain still fell. I could not believe the way the air around me shimmered. It was like walking through powdered light. And when I looked over my shoulder, down into the wide green valley, I saw a great rainbow stretching from the bank of Dinas Bran to the slope of the opposite hill. So green was the grass, so intense the light, so colourful the sky and hills, that I could well imagine this to be a place of enchantment. Who knows what became of the giants' ancestral gold, the location of which the demon in Gogmagog's form was so reluctant to share. Perhaps it lies somewhere near Llangollen, along with the body of the giant, and, when the conditions are right, gilds the air with magic.

The tale of Gogmagog's resurrection opens the late thirteenth-century *History of Fulk Fitz-Warine*. Historically speaking, the Fitzwarin family were Norman nobles who lived on the edge of Wales and frequently clashed with its magnates. Supporting their claims to a rich and noble pedigree, the 'history' traces the acquisition of the Fitzwarin estates in Shropshire to the marriage of the family's founding father to the niece of Payn Peverill's nephew (Payn Peverill is not a historical figure).

By bringing Gogmagog into the legend, the writers of this story were able to present Payn Peverill as a second Corineus, and William, by extension, as a second Brutus. It implies that Corineus did not actually succeed in killing Gogmagog first time round. Scholars before me have noted the text's implication that, as a pagan, he could only achieve so much. The advantage Payn and William have over their ancient counterparts is their Christianity. William, like Brutus, is destined to rule over the whole of Britain, but unlike Brutus he will do so by the will of God.

Brutus offered an origin myth with a single patriarch, whose imperial right, steeped in Classical authority and conveyed in a prophecy, was transferred to his descendants. By 1094, after centuries trying to wrest land from the English, Wales was largely under Norman control, falling finally to the English crown with the killing of the last sovereign Prince of Wales, Llywelyn ap Gruffyd, in 1282. In his *Journey through Wales*, Gerald of Wales describes how fiercely the Welsh guarded their territory during the English incursions and quotes the words of an old Welshman to King Henry II of England (reigned 1154–89), during an English campaign in the south of the country. When asked what he thought of the royal army and whether it could withstand that of the Welsh rebels, the old man replies, 'This nation may now be harassed, weakened and decimated by your soldiery . . . but it will never be totally destroyed by the wrath of man.'

Over the same period, the relationship between the English and Scottish crowns was just as tempestuous. In 1072, King Malcolm III of Scotland signed the Treaty of Abernethy, acknowledging William, King of England, as his overlord. But, to abridge a long and fascinating story of political dispute, Scotland broke away from England in 1189 and remained independent until the late thirteenth century, when King Edward I of England reinstated the English claim. What is especially fascinating is his activation, even weaponisation, of myth. Edward had his abbots mine their libraries for historical evidence to support his designs on Scotland. They came back with the example of Brutus' eldest son, Locrin, whom they said had received what would become the territory of England and was the rightful overlord of their kingdoms, along with all his successors (including Edward I). And, while numerous islands to the north and north-west of Britain were under Norwegian control, there was a time when Edward I's wishes for much of the North looked set to be satisfied.

However, the use of myth to support claims to supremacy by the English was rejected by the Scots in favour of their origin myth of Scota, wherein their descendants travelled from the East (Scythia or Greece, depending on the version you read), stopping in Spain, then Ireland, then arriving in the north of Albion. In 1320, the Declaration of Arbroath was signed by Scottish barons, asserting Scotland's right to self-government and favouring their own regnal history. Here is part of the Declaration, translated by Alan Borthwick:

> Most Holy Father, we know and from the chronicles and books of the ancients we find that among other famous nations our own, the Scots, has been graced with widespread renown. It journeyed from Greater Scythia by way of the Tyrrhenian Sea and the Pillars of Hercules, and dwelt for a long course of time in Spain among the most savage peoples, but nowhere could it be subdued by any people, however barbarous. Thence it came, twelve hundred years after the people of Israel crossed the Red Sea, to its home in the west . . .

Referring to the Scots' later migration from Ireland to northern Britain, it continues:

> The Britons it first drove out, the Picts it utterly destroyed, and, even though very often assailed by the Norwegians, the Danes and the English, it took possession of that home with many victories and untold efforts; and, as the histories of old time bear witness, they have held it free of all servitude ever since. In their kingdom there have reigned one hundred and thirteen kings of their own royal stock, the line unbroken by a single foreigner.

As tools and as sources of collective identity, these myths are as heroic and durable as sea and rock. They are invisible roots: sources of enmity and pride. And, once you know where to look, you realise that they are imprinted onto the landscape. From at least the fifteenth century, there was a huge carving of a man wrestling a giant in the chalky turf of Plymouth Hoe, on the Devonshire coast. The image was destroyed in the 1600s, but the locals called it 'Gogmagog'. For those who made it, it must have been as close as they could get to branding Albion's turf with Brutus' claim to empire.

Today we live in an age in which ash trees do not spring up from our walking sticks, threats to our existence cannot be buried in mountains, and we cannot escape on wings. But perhaps there is still a place for prophecy. Learning, debating and growing, we will tell each other stories into the night. Our lives will encircle the sun, setting and rising, setting and rising. Stonehenge will endure; the red and the white dragons will sleep on Dinas Emrys; and a happy Merlin will inhabit Caledonia while, to the south, children dance on the shoulders of giants. And thanks to our labours and our vision, those children will know peace for many years to come. To them, our tales of plagues, tyrants and floods will be as strange and unlikely as myth.

Epilogue

The hope that King Arthur would return and lead the Britons to their former supremacy was extinguished in 1191 when two skeletons were discovered and ceremonially exhumed from the grounds of Glastonbury Abbey. According to a contemporary chronicler, Gerald of Wales, none other than King Henry II of England had told the monks where to look for the bodies. They were identified as Arthur and Guinevere. Gerald, writing his *On the Instruction of Princes* in around 1193, had this to say on the topic:

> In our own lifetime, Arthur's body was discovered at Glastonbury, although the legends had always encouraged us to believe that there was something other-worldly about his ending . . . the body was hidden deep in the earth in a hollowed-out oak-bole and between two stone pyramids which had been set up long ago in the churchyard there. They carried it into the church with every mark of honour and buried it decently there in a marble tomb.

In his *Mirror of the Church*, written *c.* 1220, Gerald develops the episode by describing in detail the discovery in the grave of a lock of golden hair:

> In the same grave was found a tress of woman's hair, blonde and lovely to look at, plaited and coiled with consummate skill, and belonging no doubt to Arthur's wife, who was buried there with her husband . . . [Then] a silly, rash and impudent fellow, who had come to gawp at what was going on, dropped down into the hole . . . He was determined to seize hold of this tress . . . This was a fair indication of his wanton thoughts, for female hair is a snare for the feeble-minded . . . but as he held it in his hand after picking it up . . . it immediately disintegrated into fine powder.

The identity of the bodies was said to have been made clear by a lead plaque also found in the grave. It read:

HERE IN THE ISLE OF AVALON LIES BURIED
THE RENOWNED KING ARTHUR,
WITH GUINEVERE, HIS SECOND WIFE

No explanation is given as to why Guinevere is called Arthur's 'second wife', nor is there reference to an earlier marriage in the legendary record. But, whatever mysteries remain, Gerald of Wales was satisfied. He triumphantly concludes:

> Many tales are told and many legends have been invented about King Arthur and his mysterious

ending. In their stupidity the British people maintain that he is still alive . . . The fairy-tales have been snuffed out, and the true and indubitable facts are made known, so that what really happened must be made crystal clear to all and separated from the myths which have accumulated on the subject.

In 1278, Edward I had the couple's bones translated into a black marble tomb. The reburial suited Edward I's political designs on Wales, given, as noted by Antonia Gransden, how it undermined the British legend that Arthur would return and lead the Britons against the English. The tomb survived in the east end of the Abbey until the sixteenth-century English Reformation. If you go to the grounds of Glastonbury Abbey today, you will find a modern marker on the site of the tomb bearing the inscription, *Site of the Ancient Graveyard where in 1191 the Monks dug to find the Tombs of Arthur and Guinevere.*

It is a fallacy of every age to think it has buried the myths of its forebears and has at last achieved enlightenment. Do we not also laugh at those things once held to be 'historical'? We know better now, don't we?

And yet the stories in this book reflect the desires of those by whom they were first written and shared. They justify political ambitions, and help define communities and hierarchies. If history is about self-knowledge, then let us be wise to the myths we are still creating.

Acknowledgements

If anyone is to blame for *Storyland*, it is Chris Pig: the artist printmaker who gave me tools, tuition and encouragement just when I needed them. Among the guilty stand also Professor Alixe Bovey and Dr John Goodall, of the Courtauld Institute of Art and *Country Life* magazine respectively; their expertise, humour and instinct for storytelling helped inspire this project. Dr Mary Wellesley and Dan Jones helped shape my ideas and introduced me to Georgina Capel's literary agency. For this and more, I am very grateful.

Irene Baldoni, Rachel Conway and Georgina Capel brought me to Jon Riley, publishing director of riverrun, at Quercus, and Jasmine Palmer, who edited this book. I owe much to their gentle criticism and encouragement. Ana Sampson and Elizabeth Masters, both in charge of the book's publicity, not only spread news of *Storyland* far and wide, but by their manner kept at bay the threat of isolation posed by a pandemic. I must also thank the wider team at Quercus, for all the ways in which they have supported the publication of this book.

Acknowledgements

Much research for *Storyland* was unwittingly undertaken while I worked on my thesis at Corpus Christi College, Cambridge, between 2015 and 2019. I owe my supervisor, Professor Paul Binski, much thanks, especially for likening a thesis to a 'breeding sow', the piglets of which do not all need to be reared in the PhD, but which will become the books and articles of the future. *Storyland* has been a chance to play with the piglets and watch one or two of them grow.

Some research 'paths' were just that. They traced hills, marshes and seas, not to mention several motorways. My travel companions included Will Rumney, Chris Jeffs, Dana Weaver and Professor Julian Luxford, who not only compounded the fun, but whose observations brought countless new perspectives and ideas. When travel was prohibited, I was privileged to speak with Georgina Massouraki, Chris Armistead, Richard Tildesley and Cat Crossley, whose personal experiences of the places featured in *Storyland* helped flesh out the bare stone of the landscape with bog myrtle, bracken and trees.

Many of those listed above fall into one of two communities that have proved vital to this book. The first is that of the academy. Dr Seán Hewitt guided me on the Irish material; and among those to help with the Anglo-Norman sources were Dr Heather Pagan, Professor Ian Short and Dr J. D. Sargan. Dr Christina Faraday, Jess Morley, Dr Jordan Pullicino, Dr Anya Burgon, Dr George Younge and Dr Lloyd de Beer have been wellsprings of wisdom and criticism.

Acknowledgements

Another community that warrants thanks is the one belonging to Frome, in Somerset. Its artists and small business owners – Chris Pig and Stella at the Black Pig Printmaking Studio, Simon Keyte of Mount Art Services, Andrew Ziminski of Minerva Conservation, Pete Hempshall at Frama, Laura Holden at the Why Gallery, and Katie Fraser and Nick Fraser at Kobi and Teal – have provided venues to display and discuss the project as it developed. I must thank the team at Postscript, especially Bridie Fry for digitising all my illustrations with such efficiency. And beyond the shops and studios, I have been uplifted and inspired by so many individuals. You know who you are.

Last but not least I owe much to my family. It is a melting pot of many loves – of argument, history, nature, craft, stories and words – and has come to shape me and my work. As part of this, the support provided by my husband, Will, cannot be understated, nor that of 'Mungo', the promise of whose arrival sustains me as the ocean sustained Teneu.

Amy Jeffs
St David's Day, 2021

Further Reading

Primary Sources (Editions and Translations)

1. The Giants' Dance
Geoffrey of Monmouth, *The History of the Kings of Britain,* trans.
    Lewis Thorpe (Penguin, 1966), p. 196.

2. The Naming of Albion
Des Grantz Geanz, in *An Anglo-Norman Reader*, trans. Jane Bliss
    (Open Reader, 2018), pp. 60–75.
Georgine E. Brereton, ed., *Des Grantz Geanz: An Anglo-Norman
    Poem* (Society for the Study of Mediæval Languages and
    Literature, 1937).
Richard Barber, ed., *Myths and Legends of the British Isles* (Boydell,
    1999), pp. 3–8.

3. Brutus founds Britain
Geoffrey of Monmouth, *The History of the Kings of Britain*,
    pp. 64–74.
Nennius, *History of the Britons (Historia Brittonum)*, trans. J. A.
    Giles (1847), pp. 12–13.

4. Scota, first Queen of the Scots
William Skene, ed., *John of Fordun's Chronicle of the Scottish Nation*,
    trans. Felix Skene (Edinburgh, 1872), pp. 6–15.
Barber, ed. *Myths and Legends of the British Isles*, pp. 9–11.
Walter Bower, *A History Book for Scots: Selections from
    'Scotichronicon'*, D. E. R. Watt, ed. (Mercat Press, 1998), pp. 5–7.

Further Reading

5. Woden and the Peopling of the North
Snorri Sturluson, *Edda,* translated and edited by Anthony Faulkes
 (Everyman, 1987).
Bede, *The Ecclesiastical History of the English People*, edited with
 introduction and notes by Judith McClure and Roger Collins
 (Oxford University Press, 1994), p. 27.
Roger of Wendover's Flowers of History, trans. J. A. Giles, Vol 2
 (London, 1849), p. 241.

6. The Naming of the Humber and the Severn
Geoffrey of Monmouth, *The History of the Kings of Britain*,
 pp. 75–8.

7. Weland the Smith
The Poetic Edda, trans. Carolyne Larrington (Oxford University
 Press, 1996), pp. 102–8.

8. Bath and Bladud's Fall
Geoffrey of Monmouth, *The History of the Kings of Britain*, pp. 80–1.
*Anglo-Saxon Poetry: An Anthology of Old English Poems in Prose
 Translation*, ed. and trans. S. A. J. Bradley (Dent, 1982), p. 364.

9. Cordelia and the Soar
Geoffrey of Monmouth, *The History of the Kings of Britain*, pp. 81–7.

10. Conwenna saves Britain
Geoffrey of Monmouth, *The History of the Kings of Britain*, p. 97.
The Owl and the Nightingale, Cleanness, and St Erkenwald, trans.
 Brian Stone (Penguin, 1971), pp. 28–43.

11. The Throne of Scone
John of Fordun's Chronicle of the Scottish Nation, trans. Skene,
 pp. 23–4.
Walter Bower, *A History Book for Scots*, Watt, ed., pp. 8–9.

12. Dragons under Oxford
The Mabinogion, trans. Sioned Davies (Oxford University Press,
 2007), pp. 111–15.
Trioedd Ynys Prydein: The Triads of the Island of Britain, ed. and
 trans. Rachel Bromwich (University of Wales Press, 1961), p. 94.

13. Deirdre flees to Albany

The Taín, trans. Thomas Kinsella (Irish University Press, 1969),
pp. 8–20.

Walter Bower, *A History Book for Scots*, Watt, ed., pp. 10–11.

14. Joseph of Arimathea

*Merlin and the Grail: Joseph of Arimathea, Merlin, Perceval: The
Trilogy of Arthurian Prose Romances attributed to Robert de
Boron* , trans. Nigel Bryant (D. S. Brewer, 2008), pp. 15–44.

James P. Carley, ed., *The Chronicle of Glastonbury Abbey: An Edition,
Translation and Study of John of Glastonbury's CRONICA SIVE
ANTIQUITATES GLASTIONIENSIS ECCLESIE*, trans. David
Townsend (Boydell Press, 1985), given in Barber, ed. *Myths and
Legends of the British Isles*, pp. 380–5.

15. The Red and White Dragons

Nennius, *The History of the Britons*, trans. Giles (1847), pp. 26–9.

Geoffrey of Monmouth, *The History of the Kings of Britain*,
pp. 149–90.

16. Stonehenge

Geoffrey of Monmouth, *The History of the Kings of Britain*,
pp. 194–200.

17. The Deception at Tintagel

Geoffrey of Monmouth, *The History of the Kings of Britain*,
pp. 205–8.

Merlin and the Grail, trans. Bryant, pp. 94–105.

18. The Sword and the Anvil

Merlin and the Grail, trans. Bryant, pp. 105–12.

19. The King, the Dog and the Boar

'On the Marvels of Britain' (ascribed to Nennius), in Barber, ed.,
Myths and Legends of the British Isles, p. 87.

20. Lothian's Daughter

Aelred of Rievaulx and Joceline of Furness, *Lives of S. Ninian and
S. Kentigern: Compiled in the Twelfth Century*, Alexander Penrose
Forbes, ed. (Edinburgh, 1874), pp. 123–33.

Further Reading

21. Havelok the Dane
Geffrei Gaimar, *Estoire des Engleis: History of the English*, ed. and
   trans. Ian Short (Oxford University Press, 2009), pp. 5–47.

22. The Death of Merlin
Geoffrey of Monmouth, *Vita Merlini*, trans. Neil Wright (1998), in
   Barber, ed., *Myths and Legends of the British Isles*, pp. 118–45.
Winifred MacQueen and John MacQueen, 'Vita Merlini Silvestris',
   Scottish Studies 29 (1989), pp. 77–93.

23:. The River Ness Monster
Adomnán of Iona, *Life of St Columba,* trans. Richard Sharpe
   (Penguin, 1995), pp. 175–6.

24. Kenelm of Winchcombe
Charlotte d'Evelyn and Anna J. Mill, eds., *The South English
   Legendary*, Vol. 1 (Early English Text Society, 1967), pp. 279–90.

25. Mælbrigte Bites Back
Orkneyinga Saga: The History of the Earls of Orkney, trans. Hermann
   Pálsson and Paul Edwards (Penguin, 1981), pp. 27–8.

26. The Angel of the Scots
Walter Bower, *A History Book for Scots*, Watt, ed., pp. 34–7.

27. Danes, Giants and Pilgrims
'The Stanzaic *Guy of Warwick*', in David Burnley and Alison
   Wiggins, eds., *The Auchinleck Manuscript* (National Library of
   Scotland, 2003), <http://auchinleck.nls.uk/>.

28. Elfrida and Edward the Martyr
Geffrei Gaimar, *Estoire des Engleis*, trans. John Spence, in Laura
   Ashe, ed., *Early Fiction in England: From Geoffrey of Monmouth
   to Chaucer* (Penguin, 2015), pp. 34–43.

29. The Conquest
Benoît de Sainte-Maure, *Three Anglo-Norman Kings: The Lives of
   William the Conqueror and Sons*, trans. Ian Short (Toronto, 2018),
   pp. 29–36.
'Edwardian Hexametric Genealogy', partially translated by Maria
   Ramandi, in Amy Jeffs, 'Picture-books, Politics and Pedagogy:

Illustrating Histories for a Young Reader, 1338–40 (British Library Egerton MS 3028)', unpublished PhD thesis (University of Cambridge, 2019), pp. 167–8.

30. Gogmagog Rises Again

The History of Fulk Fitz-Warine, trans. Alice Kemp-Welch, with introduction by Louis Brandin (Cambridge, Ontario, 2001), pp. 9–13.

James Fergusson, *The Declaration of Arbroath 1320* (Edinburgh, 1970), pp. 4–10, available online via the website of the National Records of Scotland, <https://www.nrscotland.gov.uk/files//research/NRS_DoA_English_booklet_700_Spreads_WEB.pdf>.

Epilogue

Gerald of Wales, *On the Instruction of Princes* and *Mirror of the Church*, in *The Journey through Wales/The Description of Wales*, trans. Lewis Thorpe (Penguin, 1978), pp. 280–7.

Additional Sources

Thomas Wright, ed., *The Chronicle of Pierre de Langtoft, in French Verse, from the Earliest Period to the Death of King Edward I*, 2 vols (Longmans, 1868).

Gildas, *Gildae de Excidio Britanniae; Gildas: The Ruin of Britain*, ed. and trans. Hugh Williams (Cymmrodorion Record Series, 1899).

Layamon, *Brut* (Early English Text Society, 1963–1978).

H. R. Luard, ed., *Lives of Edward the Confessor* (Longman, 1858).

Judith Weiss, ed., *Wace's Roman de Brut: A History of the British: Text and Translation* (University of Exeter Press, 2002).

Secondary and Other Useful Literature

Ashe, Laura, *Fiction and History in England, 1066–1200* (Cambridge University Press, 2007).

Bovey, Alixe, 'Articulate Giants', in Mark Leckey, Erik Davis, and Alixe Bovey, *The Universal Addressability of Dumb Things* (Hayward Publishing, 2013), pp. 93–7.

Further Reading

Broun, Dauvit, *Scottish Independence and the Idea of Britain: From the Picts to Alexander III* (Edinburgh University Press, 2013).

Clark, John, 'Trojans at Totnes and Giants on the Hoe: Geoffrey of Monmouth, Historical Fiction and Geographical Reality', in *Report and Transactions: The Devonshire Association for the Advancement of Science, Literature and Art* 148 (2016), pp. 89–130.

Cleaver, Laura, *Illuminated History Books in the Anglo-Norman World, 1066–1272* (Oxford University Press, 2018).

Field, Rosalind, and Wiggins, Alison, eds., *Guy of Warwick: Icon and Ancestor* (Studies in Medieval Romance, D. S. Brewer, 2007).

Flood, Victoria, *Prophecy, Politics and Place in Medieval England: From Geoffrey of Monmouth to Thomas of Erceldoune* (D. S. Brewer, 2016).

Given-Wilson, Christopher, *Chronicles: The Writing of History in Medieval England* (Hambledon, 2004).

Gransden, Antonia, 'The Growth of the Glastonbury Traditions and Legends in the Twelfth Century', in *Journal of Ecclesiastical History* 27 (1976), pp. 337–58.

———, *Historical Writing in England I: c.550–c.1307* (Routledge, 1996).

———, *Historical Writing in England II: c.1307 to the Early Sixteenth Century* (Routledge, 2020).

Huot, Sylvia, *Outsiders: The Humanity and Inhumanity of Giants in Medieval French Prose Romance* (Conway Lectures in Medieval Studies, University of Notre Dame Press, 2016).

Hutton, Ronald, *Blood and Mistletoe: The History of the Druids in Britain* (Yale University Press, 2009).

Jones, Timothy, 'Geoffrey of Monmouth, *Fouke le Fitz Waryn*, and National Mythology', in *Studies in Philology* 91 (1994), pp. 233–49.

Lewis, Suzanne, *The Art of Matthew Paris in the 'Chronica Majora'* (University of California Press, 1987).

MacKillop, James, *A Dictionary of Celtic Mythology* (Oxford University Press, 1998).

Further Reading

Macquarrie, Alan, ed., *Legends of the Scottish Saints: Readings, Hymns and Prayers for the Commemorations of Scottish Saints in the Aberdeen Breviary* (Four Courts Press, 2012).

Slater, Laura, *Art and Political Thought in Medieval England, c.1150–1350* (Boydell Press, 2018).

Spence, John, *Reimagining History in Anglo-Norman Prose Chronicles* (York Medieval Press, 2013).

Strickland, Deborah, *Saracens, Demons, & Jews: Making Monsters in Medieval Art* (Princeton University Press, 2003).

Taylor, Rupert, *The Political Prophecy in England* (Columbia University Press, 1911).

Tolhurst, Fiona, *Geoffrey of Monmouth and the Translation of Female Kingship* (Palgrave Macmillan, 2013).

Index

Index

Index

Index

Index

Index

Index

Index

Index

To find out where to purchase original and
giclée prints of the linocut illustrations
in *Storyland*, please visit

www.amyjeffshistoria.com